The Blood Mark

a novel by

Anthony Uzzo

AquarianBooks.com

Published by: Anthony Uzzo

Publisher: AquarianBooks

Print - ISBN- 978-1-7334339-0-7

Library of Congress Control Number: 2019914076

Writers Guild of America West Registry: 1790165

Printed in the United States of America

AquarianBooks.com

DEDICATION

I dedicate this book to my family. To my parents Louis and Pauline Uzzo, that had little during their lives nonetheless, gave incredible love and support to their children. To my beautiful sister Ann who died so very young and to my caring older brother Louis, that was always there for support. And to my loving wife Victoria that was there offering honest feedback, nurturing reassurance and most of all love. Their enduring examples of perseverance and selfless support gave me the confidence to start and determination to ultimately complete this book.

Prologue

The Blood Mark is a compelling story, of an Army veteran's family that must overcome incredible danger and personal tragedies, in order to survive. Our story takes place and in the turbulent tornado ally of central Oklahoma. John Cloud is a decorated Army veteran who is debilitated by PTSD from his experiences in Iraq. His extended absences have alienated him from his wife and two daughters.

ISIS has taken control of a large swath of Iraq and Syria. Mohammad Rafta a ruthless ISIS commander, is emboldened to exact revenge for the death of his family. To do so, he and his merciless group travel to America leaving death in their wake. His mission killing the entire Cloud family.

Carmella Ramirez and her young teenage daughter Angelina are leaving their impoverished farm in Southern Mexico. They must endure a grueling trek north to Oklahoma, to try to reunite with their family. These women must confront horrific dangers, in their search of a better life.

Joy Cloud, John Cloud's youngest daughter, is the interim director of a women's clinic in Oklahoma City. Her own traumatic experiences, distrust of men and broken relationship with her father, add to the worsening situation.

Jason Moore and his mother Barbara Moore recently relocated to Oklahoma City. His job as a Police Detective has thrust him into unexpected situations and an improbable relationship.

All must address their personal issues before they can confront their mortal threat. Unfortunately, a large toll will be taken.

This fast-moving story, extracted from today's headlines, intertwines all these characters, forcing each to make powerful choices to survive. Ultimately, it is a story of incredible suffering and the resilience of the human spirit.

AquarianBooks.com

Note to the Reader

In a few pages of The Blood Mark I have taken the opportunity to identify a few songs being listened to by the characters. I included those songs specifically to help enrich the scene.

It is suggested that when you see the musical note sign: "♪" you take a moment and listen to those songs on YouTube or other music site then continue to read on.

- Charlie Rich - Behind Closed Doors
- Garth Brooks - The Dance
- Dolly Parton - I will always love you
- Garth Brooks - If tomorrow never comes
- Bread - Everything I Own
- Israel Kamakawiwo'ole - 'Over the Rainbow' & 'What A Wonderful World'

AquarianBooks.com

Contents

AquarianBooks.com

CHAPTER 1
July 4, 2017 – Reflections

July 4th, a national holiday, is usually relaxed and festive. The slight breeze and crystal-clear blue sky offer great weather for outdoor activities. With the mid-day heat building in central Oklahoma, it is common for severe thunderstorms to erupt around sunset. However, this morning, for the crowd of attendees, it will not be a festive venue; because for the past few days, the residents of Oklahoma City have been stunned by a series of terrible events. All the mourners anxiously await the arrival of Col. John Cloud. In the only limousine of the funeral procession, he sits stunned, shaking uncontrollably. Overcome by grief, he cannot bear to glance out the window. As he touches the door handle, he flinches instinctively, delaying the inevitable.

As the decorated officer leaves the limousine, he mindlessly comes to attention, then straightens his impeccable Army dress uniform. He is a compelling figure from the square of his hat, crease of his trousers, and expanse of ribbons on his chest. The first step is tentative, then he mechanically regains his gate and marches to the gravesite. He refuses to make eye contact with the mourners about him, for today he must marshal all his strength and focus on his demoralizing mission. Upon reaching the grave site, he performs an instinctive military square turn and sits. He must conjure countless years of training to endure this, his most challenging assignment, to maintain his composure.

Have you ever noticed the unnatural silence around an

open gravesite? So many people are hushed. Cars are parked as far as the eye can see. One would hope there would be some sound, any sound. But not today, there is just a pervasive eerie stillness. All attendees are numb and can only offer contorted remorseful expressions. Late arrivers continue to appear, weaving uneasily past the tapestry of tombstones. Not a sob can be heard above the deafening reverberation of the treetop locusts. They are considered by some to be harbingers of the approaching storms. The final mourners reluctantly converge, cowering around the grave site. The totality of the experience is overpowering. At the road, the gravediggers stand astride, apathetic. With head bent, his blackened eyes are masked by his mirrored sunglasses; Col. John Cloud sits immobile, fighting to contain his emotions.

Though it feels like hours, the ceremony only lasts about 30 minutes. Onlookers stand in place as the priest completes his eulogy. Finally, you hear the honor guard echo; "Present arms; ready, aim, fire!" The crack of seven rifles fired in unison is demoralizing. Though Col. Cloud has heard the sound of gunfire many times before, this time is entirely different. The shocking sequence is repeated three times. With each volley Col. Cloud visibly flinches. From a distance, he is obscured; only the bowed heads of mourners and the arm of the priest, as he casts holy water, are seen.

None have connected the sequence of events predating the funeral or diagnose Col. Cloud's debilitating condition. His hypersensitivity to the rifle volley only plunges him deeper into his private hell. With the distant sound of taps and scent of spent gun powder pulsating past, a dazed Col. John Cloud drifts back to his horrific visions, the haunting experiences in Iraq years earlier; *"How could I have imagined this could happen? What could I have done differently?"*

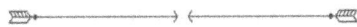

The invasive flashbacks transport Col. Cloud to the darkness of a small village on the outskirts of Baiji, Iraq. On this day he is accompanying a squad of US Special Forces as they cautiously navigate down a steep hillside. During his 30 years in the US Army, Col. Cloud has seen his share of conflict in both Iraq and Afghanistan. However, in the past several weeks, Col. Cloud rarely leaves the security of the base. Cloud, as he is known by his fellow officers, is well-liked by all. The base commander, on the recommendations for a medical referral, believed it advisable to preclude him from unnecessary conflict.

Nonetheless, Col. Cloud insisted on this, his last mission in Iraq, days before leaving for his new posting in Afghanistan. The mission today was a capture or kill. Col. Cloud's pretext for volunteering was to prepare an after-action report and recommend changes to an Army weapon training manual.

The squad slowly traverses the steep rocky slopes to the outskirts of the village. In the shadowy alleys, an eerie green glow reflects from their night vision goggles. The stench of decay from the collapsed buildings gags them. With darting hand gestures, the squad leader signals his men to move right then forward. Not a footstep can be heard. As a technical observer, Col. Cloud is accompanied by four additional soldiers, a requisite for this assignment. They follow in the rear of the six-man Special Forces sniper squad. To ensure that no others will notice his shaking hands, Col. Cloud tightly squeezes his fingers into fists.

In March 2003, at the onset of the Iraq war, Col. Cloud had already served for 16 years, mostly in non-combatant logistical assignments. However, as the Iraqi war morphed into insurgency, Col. Cloud's duties evolved. Based outside Fallujah, he is responsible for documenting the scourge upon US troop convoys from Improvised Exploding Devices (IED). Early in the war, Army vehicles were not designed to protect the troops from these destructive weapons. IEDs took an incredible physical and emotional toll on the US military. As an engineer, Col. Cloud volunteered to examine the bomb-damaged vehicles and design shielding countermeasures. Hundreds of mangled vehicles were towed back to base where Col. Cloud would meticulously study each. In an isolated corner of the base was the vehicle boneyard. Provided with a camera, pencil, and 5x8 bound notebook, Cloud would methodically examine each mangled wreck. With forensic precision, he probed each vehicle identifying structural weaknesses and points of projectile penetration, all the while hoping to expose clues of the insidious bomb maker. Meticulously drawn sketches would detail the damage. The tattered notebook bared sooty fingerprints taken from every charred vehicle. His dogged immersion into the blackened, blood-caked vehicles eventually took its toll. Fellow officers would often observe Col. Cloud and worry about his well-being, listening to him shouting; "God dammit where are you, where are you? Come on, show yourself."

Donning protective medical garments and gloves, at first glance one might think he was a wayward operating room surgeon; not because of the cloths, but from the extent of the blood stains. He would crawl through each wreck attempting to find bomb fragments. Col. Cloud would repeatedly visualize the bomb damage and theorize countermeasures. While the smell of spent explosives would invariably trigger nausea, Col. Cloud steadfastly completed each ghastly inspection. Each examination became more meticulous and demanding for him to complete.

While several of his shielding recommendations were very helpful, the insurgents would routinely alter their tactics, bypassing the countermeasures. After several agonizing months, the Army deployed enhanced, bomb-resistant vehicles. However, for the hundreds of dead and maimed and for Col. Cloud it all came too late. The Army finally acknowledged his contribution for the lives and limbs he did help to save; but it came as a tremendous price to Col. Cloud. The horrific images would never fade, nor would his suppressed guilt for not identifying the IED mastermind sooner. After months of collecting evidence, and with the assistance of Army intelligence, the IED mastermind was finally identified.

Unfortunately, this was not before the accumulated psychological trauma ultimately led to his Post Traumatic Stress Disorder (PTSD.) He would often wake from nightmares wailing, clothes drenched in sweat, imagining the charred faces of the men that were killed. Though he was not initially diagnosed with any disorder, fellow officers observed distinct changes in his demeanor and suggested that the Army halt his work. Nonetheless, Col. Cloud could not quell his anger or desire to eliminate the IED designer. His duty to his men and his country strained his sanity, and ultimately his familial relationships, to the breaking point. When he called home to his wife and family, there would often be one-sided conversations.

Col. Cloud would offer just one-word answers. His reticence due to the war was being projected onto his family. Though he was losing so much personally, he could not divert from his obsession. He knew he had reached his Army career limits; nonetheless, he volunteered to reenlist in a misguided attempt to exorcise his demons.

In his final months in Iraq, just before his reassignment to Afghanistan, Col. Cloud is tasked to evaluate the effectiveness of new weapons. It is the fall of 2011, prior to the US withdrawal from Iraq, and Col. Cloud volunteers to accompany a US Special Forces sniper team that are supporting their Iraqi Army counterparts. Their mission is to seek out remnants of an elite Iraqi Republican Guard unit. Like a silent marauding pack of wolves, this small unit is highly elusive. Despite their numbers, they are highly trained and motivated, though insurgents are still incredibly dangerous.

Col. Cloud's personal mission today is to help to capture Mohamad Rafta, the IED mastermind. Rafta has been the insidious manufacturer of most of the IEDs throughout central Iraq. In 2003, after the fall of Saddam Hussein, coalition forces eased their grip, believing the war was over, and in doing so, they left unguarded dozens of Iraqi munitions depots with tons of explosives. In 2004 when an insurgency arose, fighters utilized any munitions available. They would bury three to four artillery shells under a main road with improvised detonators; a simple no-cost recipe for incredible destruction. The IED was born. At that time there was no means to detect or counter the IEDs. Eventually, the Pentagon destroyed all the ammunition stockpiles they could find. That was not until the insurgents had taken thousands of rounds and hid them throughout Iraq.

Rafta is a highly intelligent, English educated Iraqi officer; fluent in several languages. As a master of evasion, the Americans have no recent photo of Rafta. He frustrates all capture efforts. Early in the war, Rafta was not worthy of the famous Iraq Most-Wanted playing cards, used by the Americans to identify key Iraq Army officers. Nonetheless, as a surviving intelligence officer of Saddam's Republican Guard, he is respected for his tenacity.

After eight years of war, Rafta is growing weary of hiding and wishes the Americans would leave so that he might live with his family in seclusion. Americans have tried everything to stop the IED mastermind. Rafta would be a prized kill or capture for any US soldier. However, for Col. Cloud it has become his own personal mission. Col. Cloud prays that neutralizing Rafta will bring his invasive nightmares to an end.

The Special Forces sniper team nimbly sets up at a strategic position in an abandoned building about a half a mile from the target compound. They are very well camouflaged in an isolated abandoned building and can observe all vehicle traffic entering or leaving the area. Though Col. Cloud is assigned to evaluate the new ammunition for the Barrett 50 caliber sniper rifle, he is really focused on Rafta. The incredibly powerful long-range rifle being evaluated by Cloud has been used for years in Iraq to stop moving cars or trucks. New antipersonnel ammunition being tested has been designed to kill human targets from a thousand yards out.

In a low raspy voice, the squad leader says: "Set up the weapon on that table back from the open window. Stabilize it, quickly, quietly." Two Special Forces soldiers lift a large dining table ten feet from the open window and lay down carpets and pillows to support the weapon. Another soldier sets up a large spotter scope at an adjacent window. You can distinguish the Special Forces unit from their distinctive radio headgear and unusually overgrown beards. None of the US troops can be seen from the street or from adjacent buildings. Referencing his map, a sniper squad leader points; "Range to the two-story building in the center of that distant compound."

In the secluded dark room, Col. Cloud leans his lanky frame against a back wall. He methodically thumbs through his notebook to a selected page. While a subject outline has been made, he scribbles vague notes of every observation. He focuses on the sniper team's placement, sketching the table with placement of men and equipment.

Col. Cloud's is also outfitted with the standard desert uniform with his unique face paint design. Only the distinctive red OU on the side of his helmet distinguished him from the others. The lettering is a reminder to a few fellow officers of his Alma Mater, Oklahoma University (OU). Col. Cloud has learned to cloak his nervousness with rhythmic breathing techniques, as well as controlling his facial expressions. He carefully applies his multicolored camo face paint with a distinctive Native American pattern, understood only by him. Like an alarming Halloween mask, the unique covert design hides his anxiety.

To keep him occupied during the monotony of camp life, he enjoys the spontaneity of freehand sketching. Unused pages and margins incorporate freehand doodles, each distinctive with a theme of its own. However, with his worsening symptoms, recent doodles have taken on an unnatural macabre style.

Leaning back, he closes his eyes for a few minutes and recalls his carefree days, walking through the dense trees of central Oklahoma where John Cloud enjoyed turkey hunting with his father and son. Whether rifle or bow, it made no difference. The quiet solitude among the swirling trees and the faint scent of golden wheat are what he missed most. But the stench of death brings him back to reality; *"Will this ever end?"*

It is a bit early to see any street traffic, just a few goats grazing on a nearby hill. A few chimneys wisp grey smoke, obstructing the rising red sun. As the room becomes silent, a rusty grey van silently glides into the small village. Masked by the pervasive dust, it comes to rest in front of the target compound. After a few seconds, five men cautiously exit, focusing on the windows, rooftops and surrounding hills. As they walk to the compound, they tap off the dust from their shirts and jackets. No military uniforms, just inconspicuous civilian clothes. As Col. Cloud leans against the back wall, he nervously adjusts his field glasses to the obscured compound. Col. Cloud knows that the compound is the right place, not just from their body language, but the fact that they are carrying AK47s. All are focused on the distant compound, except for Col. Cloud who is trying to conceal his shaking hands. The squad leader on the ground whispers into his mic, "Not yet, wait for my command; I want everyone inside the compound... and I want Rafta alive."

The insurgents cautiously enter through the archway of the compound. Dozens of Iraqi Special Forces have accompanied the US Special Forces unit. They are wearing dark blue uniforms to distinguish them from the insurgents. They are strategically positioned around the compound, awaiting the signal to attack. Again, he asks; "Did anyone see a man that matches Rafta's description?" Col. Cloud closes his eyes again leans his head back; "*I can only pray for this to be over. I'm so tired of this shit.*"

It was recommended that when Col. Cloud becomes anxious that he should relax and visualize pleasant thoughts; "*The rustling trees and his time at the lake. Lying across the bronzed thighs of a beautiful college brunette as she gently strokes his neck.*" He shakes his head incredulously, startled back into reality; "*Wow, where the hell did that come from?*"

After about 3 hours of patient monitoring, several insurgents exit the building into the courtyard and line up in front of outstretched rugs for their call to morning prayers. Once they are done, they dust off and fold their prayer rugs. A few pick up their weapons to begin walking back to the van. One man stops, scans the nearby rooftop and pauses for a moment. He leans forward, squints and sees the tip of a rifle barrel moving. He immediately shouts the alarm and begins spraying that roof with his automatic weapon.

The coalition team leader gives the order: "Fire, fire at will." Shots ring out from everywhere. Within seconds three insurgents fall to the dusty ground bleeding out. The van's tires and engine are shot out. As small dust eruptions hop around the compound, two insurgents run back behind and inside the building. On an adjacent rooftop, an Iraqi soldier fires his automatic weapons peppering several compound windows.

Col. Cloud and the sniper team patiently observe, not wanting to reveal their position. Insurgents within the compound are picked off one by one. Realizing their precarious situation and with no easy exit, they abruptly open a rear building door and fire an RPG blowing a large hole in a back wall. Under deafening gunfire, several of the insurgents frantically attempt to flee through the hole. Three disheveled men sprint through the dusty portal and are mowed down by the Iraqi soldiers.

From a darkened second-floor window in the compound, you could hear the loud crack of a single rifle shot. One of the Iraqi squad leaders hits the ground, screaming in anguish that he was hit, then another. The US sniper team is listening on their radio and sees the distant muzzle flash. Through his spotter scope, the US team identifies a shadowy figure darting past a second-floor window; "I have a target, second floor, front center window.... Distance... 750 yards." The team leader barks; "Sargent check and range your weapon. Clearly identify your target and fire when ready."

The American sniper carefully adjusts his powerful scope and focuses in on a shadowy distance target. The insurgent darts quickly from window to window in and out of the sniper's crosshairs. The early morning sun glares into his scope partially obscuring the target, while smoke from the burning van complicates the silhouette. The spotter can only clearly see the gun barrel flash from deep inside the darkened room. The team leader looks over to Col. Cloud; "He's an elusive bastard, too good a shot to be a novice, it could be Rafta." The team leader leans forward and taps the shoulder of the sniper; "Take your shot."

The sniper pulls the gigantic rifle tight to his shoulder, presses his chin against the buttstock, exhales, then in a heartbeat a single cannon-like blast shakes the room. The deafening explosion reverberates; then echoes throughout the village. The shock disorients and blinds everyone as it billows dust from everywhere.

Col. Cloud has come prepared with ear protection and sunglasses. Nonetheless, the blast stuns him, and he reflexively recoils against the back wall. He now begins to shake uncontrollably. None notice as their eyes are riveted to the compound searching for additional targets. Biting his lip; "Fuck..." then slams his notebook closed and adjusts his sunglasses. The team leader barks; "Shit, I forgot to insert earplugs... reload, reload. Spotter, give me a SITREP."

Only the sound of the startled barking dogs can be heard. After the shot, the sniper automatically rotates and slides back the rifle bolt and watches a 50 caliber casing eject out. He effortlessly captures it in midair in his gloved hand. While still blistering hot he looks back to Col. Cloud and playfully flips it; "Here you go Colonel, for your collection." Cloud instinctively catches and hurriedly inserts the scorching cartridge into a vest pouch of his body armor. Through the swirling dust and smoke, the spotter can see an American advisor's hand gestures directing the Iraqis troops to move into the compound.

Bloody bodies pattern the sandy courtyard now obscured by the black smoke from the burning van. Iraqi soldiers carefully check the bodies for weapons, explosive vests and signs of life. Finally, they hear over the crackle of their radio; "Clear, clear, set up a defensive perimeter."

Col. Cloud leans in and points to the sniper team leader; "I'm going to take my men down to the compound Sargent and assess things for myself. You're secure here. Right." While he said he wishes to report on the new bullet, he really hopes to count Mohammed Rafta among the dead. With an unsteady hand, Cloud nervously withdraws his pistol and checks to ensure a round is in the chamber. He gestures for his men to join him.

The neighborhood is dusty and deserted. They cautiously traverse the narrow debris laden allies for trip wires, continually scanning the rooftops and windows for possible shooters. This town has been the focus of several attacks on both US and Iraqi forces in recent weeks. Numerous streets are blocked by collapsed buildings and debris. It seems impossible that anyone can still be living there. While Army intelligence has indicated little chance of finding other insurgents in the town, Col. Cloud and his men are still on high alert. As they line up at a small intersection, Cloud checks his compass and map, then looks cautiously around the building to the next street. They soon come upon an open doorway where a young red-haired girl is curiously peeking down the street. She is not at all upset by the armed men passing by her door. "Go ahead little one, get back inside," as he gestures with his hand.

After ten minutes of scurrying past abandoned buildings, they finally reach the compound entrance. A few village elders emerge from nearby homes, quivering hands extended. One of the elders notes the unusual and distinctive red OU lettering on the side of Cloud's helmet. As Cloud walks past a guard through the archway as he points his pistol down, fully aware that anything could be booby-trapped and that it is never completely safe. As if on cats' paws they must take every step cautiously.

A US advisor points; "Upstairs sir." Pistol shaking at his side, Cloud pulls off his sunglasses and warily walks up the unsteady narrow staircase.   He peeks into the second-floor doorway where the insurgent sniper was firing.   There he sees a man splayed out on the floor; his body blown open, blood-drenched clothes in disarray. The room has a few makeshift beds interspersed among several dusty Persian rugs.   In disturbing contrast, bright red blood is spattered across the earthen stucco wall.

Iraqi soldiers toss the room searching for any intelligence information. Scanning the room, he sees a young woman in a dark hijab, propped up against a wall, chest heaving, bleeding profusely. Her unveiled face is in obvious distress as she mouths faint words. An Army corpsman is hastily attempting to stop her severe bleeding, applying coagulant powder and a large bandage. Cloud leans over and softly asks; "Rafta, Rafta?"

With her bloodied hands beckoning she leans to one side to touch the motionless infant, just outside her reach. Obscured by the soldier Col. Cloud did not see the infant laying there, white swaddling saturated with blood. As the young woman gasps to breathe, she looks up into Cloud's grieving eyes, mouthing words beseeching for her child. Col. Cloud kneels down next to her and drops his pistol. The medic looks at Cloud and fatefully shakes his head. He turns his head and snarls at the soldier at the door, "***God dammit***! ...Who shot this woman?"

"None of us Colonel, none of us, we never fired a shot into this room." The attending medic; "From the size of that guys wound it looks like a 50-cal hit. It must have passed through him, through the baby, through her, then out that wall. Sorry Major, she has no chance."

Col. Cloud has struggled to control his composure since his tremors were triggered by the thunderous rifle blast. He has no place to run or hide and is unable to avoid the ghastly images before him. As disbelief shrouds his face, no combat training can prepare him for this. He unfastens and drops his helmet between his knees; "***Goddammit***!"

With trembling hands, he gently lifts the child to his face to find signs of life. The child's angelic face and half opened light brown eyes are hauntingly unresponsive. Unseen, the infant's drenched swaddling drains blood into his open helmet. Still shaking, he gently places the baby's lifeless body in his mother's beckoning arms, affording her one final embrace before her last breath.

His remorseful eyes scan the room for possible answers. As he sits back on his heels, Cloud pauses, arms hanging limp, unable to disengage from the dreadful sight before him. With bloodstained hands, he wipes the tears tracing down his camouflaged face and teeters backward.

One of the soldiers; "It couldn't be helped, Colonel. She could not be seen in this dark room. None of us knew she was there. She must have been standing directly behind him holding the baby. With that dark hijab, there was no way of knowing."

Cloud erupts; "Is Mohammad Rafta among the dead? **Rafta!**"

The soldier replies; "No Colonel. No one fitting his descriptions is in the compound. We checked them all. The only one close is this guy, but he is way too young. We did, however, find an IED factory downstairs."

The Iraqi translator at the door is still rifling through bloodstained papers; "Dis guy is a senior soldier... maybe Rafta's lieutenant."

Cloud stumbles to pick up his pistol and looks inside his helmet. He is shocked to see the child's glistening blood has coated the inside liner. *"What the fuck is happening to me?* Incensed and disoriented he angrily kicks the helmet. It hits the wall, spins and comes to rest beside the mother and child. As he staggers down the stairs into the glaring sunlight; *"What is this all for? What have I accomplished?"*

In this hyper-agitated state Cloud's face is sweating profusely. Oddly, it is camouflage for the torrent of tears gushing from his eyes. As he walks into the brilliant morning light, this makes his glistening buzz-cut head visible from a distance.

Cloud stumbles into the courtyard and clumsily adjusts his sunglasses. Squinting, he sees the Iraqi village elders cowering at the gate, heads bent. Before Cloud are a dozen insurgents laying on the ground, belongings were strewn out for the intelligence examination.

The squad leader comes up the Cloud; "Sir we just want to let you know that we found about two dozen artillery shells with detonators. We are going to take them out into that open field and dispose of them."

Cloud standing there dazed, looks around and just nods. He motions to the soldiers examining the bodies; "Rafta... Is Rafta among the dead?"

Another soldier; "No sir."

The elders observe the helmetless Col. Cloud as he slowly walks out of the compound, weapons at the ready. As he exits, he looks back and ponders; "*After 24 years will I ever see an end to this shit.*" After a few minutes, Cloud and his squad rejoin the sniper team at their distant location. The sniper team is packing, awaiting Col. Clouds return. Minutes later a convoy of US Humvees arrived outside their house.

As they continue stowing their gear, Cloud sits at the table and pulls out his weathered notebook to make additional notes. The heat of an Iraqi morning is building, and his profuse sweating has not abated. As Cloud wipes the sweat from his head with his hand, he opens his notebook to the 50 Cal Ammo Evaluation page. To his dismay a clean white page has become stained red with blood from his hand; the child's blood. Generally, most in the military are not alarmed by the sight of blood, but in this instance, Cloud is about to lose his sanity; "*I don't think I can ever escape this hell hole.*" Feeling ashamed and not wishing to draw attention, he just pours water on his hands and washes off as much of the blood as possible. At that very moment in the distance, an enormous explosion reverberates across the town and shakes the room. Everyone is startled. The sniper team leader; "What the fuck was that?"

Without raising his head, trying to demonstrate detachment; "Those are the guys in the ordinance disposal unit, detonating insurgent artillery munitions." Nonetheless, that concussive shock and the blood stains on his hands only reinforce his graphic nightmares.

The coalition troops had departed the smoldering compound several hours earlier. With only the sound of the swirling wind, the remaining village elders have reentered the compound to prepare the dead for burial. As the wind whips up sand, it gently coats the clean white burial shrouds.

From a distance, a tall solitary man moves cautiously through the abandoned streets, his head and nose covered by the traditional keffiyeh. All notice, as he warily peers through the gates, his piercing black eyes meticulously studying every detail. Saying nothing, he walks in, leans down, and pulls back each of the head shrouds. Only the faces are showing through the bloodstained shrouds. He hesitantly moves to the last three. Beside the last man lie the bodies of a young woman and infant boy. He carefully kneels down between the woman and the child, reaches out steel-eyed to touch the face of the infant boy.

One of the elders whispers to another; "That was his trusted lieutenant, his young wife, and son. The lieutenant was guarding the family's house."

As the dust swirls wildly through the compound, all onlookers stand shaking in place. It is as if the earth was eager to capture and cover more bodies. After a few minutes, an elder warily walks up behind Rafta and gingerly places Col. Cloud's helmet beside him; "Mohamad, this is the helmet of the American that we believe is responsible for the death of your wife and son. I saw this soldier come into the compound right after the ambush, questioning everyone. The helmet was found in the room beside their bodies."

Rafta's head is bent as if praying, his face covering slowly falls away. With a shaking hand, he points angrily to the elder to step back. His unbearable grief has twisted his face to a contorted mask. Hand still on the face of his son Rafta turns his head askew; **"Are you sure**?"

Without hesitation; "Yes, I heard him call out your name. He was the only soldier wearing a helmet with the strange red letters."

Rafta strokes the face of his young wife for one last time. Trying not to display any human weakness, he gently covers their faces and stands to walk away. He hesitates for a moment then bends down and carefully picks up the helmet. Staring again into the helmet; "Is this the American's blood?"

Voice shaking; "No!...No Mohammed, he was not harmed, not a scratch on his body. The helmet was found next to the baby's body."

Black eyes glaring, he carefully conceals his face with the keffiyeh. Without a word turns and walks out of the compound, Cloud's helmet dangling from his hand; *"I will get my revenge in this life... or the next."*

Despite Col. Cloud's pointless attempts to mask his anxiety, it is eventually noticed by his superiors. After tens of thousands of patients, the military doctors are now able to document the myriad of PTSD symptoms. Over twenty percent of all US military that served in Iraq and Afghanistan were diagnosed with PTSD. When Col. Cloud finally agreed to a thorough psychiatric examination, they could finally diagnose his PTSD. He was highly respected by the men he led and the officers he served. It was felt that the best thing would be to for him to continue to serve with those that understood and empathized with his condition.

After a much-needed leave back home, Col. Cloud is now stationed in Bagram Air Base, Afghanistan. While the threat of IED's is just emerging there, Cloud has become the Army's expert for IED vehicle damage mitigation. Col. Cloud was at the forefront for developing a methodology for evaluating the reliability of systems and equipment. All the latest gizmos or gadgets would pass across his desk on the way to the battlefield. While he never killed a single person, he harbors undeserved guilt for those he could not save. The flashbacks of the dead infant's face are indelibly etched into his psyche.

One afternoon while packing his gear and body armor vest, he finds the 50-caliber cartridge. He inquisitively examines it for a few moments, then slips it into his pants pocket; *"I don't want to think about this now, I need time to sort things out..."*

Col. Cloud, through his 30 years of military service, projects a reserved bearing, stiff around those he loves. As a consequence of his PTS symptoms, it became difficult to warmly embrace his family or passionately love his wife. He wanted to love and to be loved; however, he could no longer grasp that elusive empathetic trigger.

It wasn't that he didn't love his family, but his inability to project that warmth has made him estranged. The dad they knew years earlier, now seems to be an empty shell. Though he interrupted multiple deployments to be home on extended leave, he felt that a piece of his spirit had been lost, possibly forever. He could diagnose the most complicated equipment problems; however, Cloud is still stymied entirely that he could not find the key to unlock his heart. He knew something in his life was missing but could not explain what it was or how to find it.

Over the past several months, though he could communicate daily by phone, the emotional detachment further estranged him from his family. He would often be on the phone and not find the suitable words to express himself. This alienation was complicated by his wife, Crystal, purchasing and relocating to an extravagant new home in a different part of Oklahoma City. All the familiar sights, sounds, and the few friendly neighbors he once had, are now gone. He was finally going home, but this was not his home.

After what seemed to be an agonizingly long trip from Germany, Col. Cloud is unusually anxious when arriving home to Will Rogers Airport, in Oklahoma City. He stands and waits alone at the arrival gate for several minutes. He is a striking figure even in his travel uniform, adorned with multiple ribbons. As he stands watching, several young people are also disembarking at an adjoining gate. They are amused, pointing disrespectfully, seeing such an imposing figure standing among them. How disheartening that he served so many years to come home, only to be mocked by those that he had sworn to defend.

One of the airline gate attendants, recognizing his discomfort, walks up to him and gently places her hand on his arm; "Is there something I can help you with Colonel?"

Usually stoic, he is able to produce a smile; "No, that is quite all right ma'am but thank you for asking. I'm just waiting for my family."

"Honey if there is anything I can get yeah, Y'all let me know, okay."

Cloud decides not to make a fuss or call, but instead takes a taxi to his new home. He had called several hours earlier from Germany, leaving a message that he would be arriving at 3 PM the next day. He had expected his family or at least a few of them to be waiting. He had observed warm homecomings on TV so many times before; but for Col. John Cloud today, this was not to be.

The ride from the airport to his new home takes only about 15 minutes, and during that time he stares out the window to a city he no longer recognizes. It has been many years since he has spent any meaningful time in the town, where now only a few of the familiar landmarks remain. As he exits the cab and reaches in his pocket for cash to pay the fare, the driver looks up at his new house in astonishment; "Man you live in dis palace? I didn't think the Army paid dat good."

Glaring; "They don't... keep the change." He walks slowly up the long flower edged driveway, with a bright white Mercedes SUV next to the house. As he gets to the front door, he gently knocks. After several seconds, Cloud rings the bell a few times; *"Where the hell are these people."*

His wife, Crystal Cloud, finally opens the door, eyes squinting from the bright sun; "Wow you are here, I didn't expect you until tomorrow or somethin." From her speech and unsteady bare-footed gait, it appears she has been drinking heavily, again. Crystal is the daughter of a retired Army Major General. One might imagine that she grew up as an arrogant and demanding woman and you would be right. Though she was well educated, she never pursued any professional career. Instead, she built her world and notoriety around the social life of her father. The house is spanking new with very spacious rooms appointed with top of the line bright white, leather furniture. Every wall has a unique piece of artwork, every table a thought-provoking sculpture. It is evident that Crystal has spent all her free time surrounding herself with expensive unnecessary comforts.

Cloud walks through the high double oak doors, lays his luggage on the floor, stands erect and looks around. This is a stark contrast to plywood enclosures he has been living with for the past several months in Afghanistan. Hoping for a kiss or embrace, Cloud watches as Crystal quickly turns and walks back into the living room. No hug, no sign of affection. Glaring at her with disappointment; "I left a message yesterday morning about hopping a plane from Ramstein to OKC. I was specific about when I would be arriving. Didn't you get it?"

With her back turned part way to him and speaking with her sharp Okie twang; "I may have but... I've been busy...you know buzzy." Crystal is an incredibly attractive woman that has retained her schoolgirl figure. Her skin is flawless to match her short-cropped, light blond hair. Crystal is precariously carrying a large tumbler with ice and what appears to be her favorite, Vodka and lemonade. She turns her head part way and beckons with her hand; "Well, come on in... and close that door. You're bringing in that awful heat." She looks back to the wide-screen TV.

Cloud walks in slowly and looks around the house. In an attempt to placate and commiserate; "Wow, you did a lot, a great job decorating. I saw some of the photos you posted on Facebook, but they don't do this justice. So where is everyone, Danny, Dawn, and Joy?"

Still not looking at Cloud; "Probably out somewhere, ya know... somewhere."

Cloud realizes that he has a lot to make up for years of coldness. He slowly walks into the spacious room and in a soft but deliberate tone; "I was really looking forward to seeing everyone. It has been several months."

Still not facing him; "Well, I guess you'll have to wait a bit longer but you're used to that by now... Aren't you?"

Discouragingly shaking his head; "Didn't you even tell

them I was coming?"

With her back turned, Crystal slips her bare feet beneath her into a large leather armchair and grabs the TV remote. The View TV show is on as she sets the volume louder. She just sits there rolling her head side to side looking up at the TV in a classless attempt to ignore Cloud.

As part of Col. Cloud's PTSD treatment to contain his emotions, they have reinforced the need for him to control all undesirable emotions. It works most of the time. But Cloud gets uncharacteristically agitated and raises his voice; "**Crystal**... What is going on, what the hell is going on here? I have been away for eleven months, and I would hope to get some sort of greeting from my wife and kids."

Bitterly; "Well, I guess you will have to wait longer for that, aren't you." This is Crystal's default confrontation mode with Cloud; sitting sideways and speaking loudly into the abyss and, it's usually very effective. It has been several months since the two have spent any time together, alone.

In recent months, with meditation and medication, Cloud's PTSD symptoms are dormant. He is rarely hypersensitive or anxious. With preparation, he is usually under control. But Crystal is getting from him exactly what she wants; "Crystal, look at me ***dammit***."

Jerking her head around, with an indignant stare; "John, what the hell do you want, a big welcoming party or somethin? Well, that ain't gonna happen. Not for you, not here, not ***evvver***."

"I don't expect anything at all except to be greeted by my wife and kids."

Turning to face the TV; "Well that ain't gonna happen either."

Rarely a confrontational man; "What? Why? What the hell did I do to deserve this?"

Finally, Crystal musters the courage to stand and face him. It takes few seconds to steady herself against the chair then wobbles toward him. "What did you do? It's what you didn't do. You haven't been here with me, or the kids for ten years. **Ten fucking years!** I have been here alone bringing up your kids. **Alone..!** Do you have any idea what that is like? **Do you...?**"

Cloud is shocked by her screaming; "I had a job, an important job. You knew that when you married me; you wanted me in this uniform. You said so, your daddy said so. You knew that when you met me in this uniform. You were born into this life and wanted this life."

Crystal now pacing and waving her arms wildly, sprays her drink around the room; "Yes, I wanted you in uniform but not away from me, for the past ten years, all over the world in some godforsaken combat zone. You were supposed to be stationed stateside, with me. On those rare occasions when you were home you were never truly close to me; you never gave me what *I* needed. Your heart was always someplace else."

Cloud feels those dormant emotions begin to rise. Flustered, he finds difficulty in expressing himself, pauses and points to the ceiling; "Yes, I know that was your plan, but that wasn't the Army's plan. I had no choice... where or for how long they would station me. **No choice.**"

Crystal continues stumbling around the room; "You had choices. You could have taken a desk job in the Pentagon after you got your commission. With my daddy in the Pentagon, he could have moved you up through the ranks quickly, any assignment, any posting. **But nooo**... you had to prove something to yourself, that macho warrior bullshit. Now, where are you? After over 30 years of service, a washed-up Colonel, only a shitty bird-Colonel. You could have been a Brigadier General by now. He had a promising military life laid out for us. Good postings; overseas, DC or Hawaii. Instead, I'm stuck here in sweltering Oklahoma City, whoppy shit. I married you to get the hell out of here. I hate this pathetic town and these self-righteous assholes. Thanks...for nothing."

Cloud walks towards her, arms beckoning to calm her down; "Crystal, what do you want from me? I did the best I could for you and the kids."

Crystal walks toward Cloud's outstretched arms and angrily pushes him aside, then wobbles to the front door; "You know what I want?... You know what I want?... I want you to get the hell out of my house and never come back, that's what the hell I want. Let me know where you will be staying, I'll mail you the divorce papers. And, don't even try to contact the kids either, because they feel the same way. None of them want to see you, none of them... **Hear me!**"

Cloud shaking his head, realizes he can't talk to Crystal in her drunken irrational condition. Flummoxed he cannot find the right words. He has seen her like this before. Powerless, not wanting to prolong the confrontation, he turns around picks up his bags and walks out the door. Crystal angrily slams the door behind him. She had no way of knowing that the man she once loved has concealed his PTSD for years. He does not wish to share that diagnosis with her. Not now, not in this state.

Days later Crystal is still drinking heavily and seldom leaves her expansive home. She only travels for prepared meals and ingredients for her vodka-lemonade handles. She patiently awaits her favorite visitors, her daughters Dawn and Joy and her granddaughter Samantha. She loves spoiling Samantha with every new outfit and toy she can find. That has become her daily focus. This makes it a lot easier for her to erase the memory of the man she once loved.

Being away from the city for several years several things have changed, and Cloud has no close friends or buddies to call, they are all 8,000 miles away. As he walks down the shimmering 98° streets carrying his military duffel, he pulls out his cell phone and gives Grandpa Cloud a call. The unexpected, stressful altercation with Crystal has triggered excessive sweating from Cloud's face and head. Fortunately, with the heat it is not unusual to see someone profusely sweating, especially in Oklahoma City.

About two hours later Grandpa Cloud rolls up to his son at a local convenience store. Cloud decided to get a refreshing Coke and cool off under a shade tree. From a distance, you could hear Grandpa's pickup coming. The squeaks and loud exhaust are distinctive. As Grandpa's old Chevy pickup pulls up, Cloud leans into the open passenger side window; "You look good pop, great to see ya. I see that you got that old Chevy pickup finally running. How old is this bucket of rust?"

Grandpa just grins and nods his head; "Come-on get in." Joseph Cloud (Grandpa) is an original Okie, or at least he is trying to be one. The midsized lanky, 70-year-old is never shy about giving you his opinion, on any subject...whether you need it or not. His sparkling brown eyes and a disheveled full head of light graying hair always bring a smile to his son's face.

Head cocked; "Don't ya make fun of my personalized Chevy pickup. It's a collector's item. I had to drive around to three salvage yards for original parts. But she keeps me busy. Remember Proverbs 16 son? Idle hands are the devil's workshop.... Or somethin like that..."

Tapping on the door and tugging on the side mirror, Cloud grins; "That explains the multi-colored fenders."

Nodding; "So, what happened this time?"

Cloud flings his luggage into the back of the pickup and slides into the front seat. As he wipes perspiration from his face; "Pop, I may need to stay with you for a while, till Crystal cools down. She is really pissed off this time. Is the cabin in any condition for me to stay for a few days? I need a long quiet vacation."

Tapping his son's knee; "Don't worry son your kids still

love you. Well, I know Daniel still loves ya; but, those girls are a tad like their mom." Grandpa rummages under the seat and pulls out a shiny mason jar and pushes him; "Son you really need some of this right now. Go ahead, have a sip. It's a fresh batch, probably my best batch ever."

As they ramble along in the noisy old truck; "Don't worry about Daniel, I saw him just last week at the cabin, and he can't wait for us to get up there and do some huntin. Lots-a turkey out there... plump ones, good eaten too. Crystal has been a hand-full since ya got married. Seems like only yesterday but it's been quite a while and...people do change."

Cloud unscrews the Mason jar lid, lifts it to his nose, sniffs, then takes a quick sip. Head jutting back, grimacing; "Pop, she just wanted stuff I couldn't give her, a stay at home kinda guy. I could never have been that."

With a broad smile; "Son there is only one man that could give Crystal what she wanted, and that was her General bad daddy. He spoiled her rotten, and now that he is gone, she wants someone else to assume that role."

Cloud takes another sip, and exhales; "Spoil her rotten, well that's not me."

"Some things just can't be changed. It's a shame, but it will make things a lot easier for you in the future."

As Cloud takes another sip; "Jesus Pop, what is the proof of this batch? You could heat the cabin for a month with this stuff. **Woo!**" He continues sipping; then leans his head back as the pickup rocks and tries to recall when life was a lot simpler.

Gently tapping his son's knee: "Stay with me son, you need some quiet time, and it's the perfect place to forget the past and rediscover your future."

About an hour later Cloud is awakened as they drive down a dusty back road. He recognizes a familiar old farmhouse and a small bridge over the running creek about a mile from their family cabin. He smiles as he recognizes some of the tall swaying cottonwoods surrounding the secluded property.

They pull into an obscure, overgrown access road known only to a few close friends and family. It meanders several hundred feet before reaching the cabin, a simple old wooden structure built upon a four-foot tall riprap stone foundation. The foundation's large stones were collected from old mine tailings, when they were plentiful. The cabin actually sits on top of the old mine shaft that was abandoned 100 years earlier. A rickety, unusual looking, old stone chimney juts out at the end of the building. The old cabin is well-positioned among the tall cottonwood trees, so it stays cool during the oppressively hot, Oklahoma summers.

The cabin sits on a secluded section of Grandpa's 500-acre farm. Grandpa and his wife, June Cloud, once lived at the farm for several years. John Cloud grew up there, and spent several hot summer days fishing and swimming in the 15-acre farm pond. He and his friends would often just lay out blankets and soak up the good life. But like many good things, that too had to end.

Unfortunately, June Cloud died about 12 years earlier from internal injuries sustained after a head-on collision on a nearby dusty farm road. She was driving home late one night after attending an old friend recovering from surgery. Both drivers were unconscious in their wreckages. It took county sheriffs several minutes to find, then to call for paramedics. It was too late for June.

It further reinforced Grandpa's belief that;" No good deed shall go unpunished."

Grandpa couldn't accept the loss of the love of his life and the life they shared at the farmhouse. He just closed the door and left. He allows Carlos Ramirez, the attendant, to live there rent free as part of his deal to oversee the cattle, the wheat and the land.

With Grandpa, John Cloud goes into semi-seclusion and lives in their spacious, rustic cabin. While Cloud is on a heavy dose of psychotropic meds to calm him, he still has difficulty sleeping through the night, often waking startled, drenched in sweat. The meds are helpful during the day for anxiety triggers; however, they are ineffective for his nightmares.

With little to do, Cloud struggles, for he has no purpose in life. Sitting around getting shit faced on iced moonshine was never his thing; "So pop you never told me; where do you get this moonshine?"

Grandpa throws his head back and chuckles; "The stuff you're sippin...I make it myself."

"Really!"

"Yup, right here, right below the floor in the cabin. Me and Carlos, we have been making up some small batches over the past few years. It's easy...real easy. An incredible setup man....incredible."

Looking over his shoulder into the room; "So where the hell do you do this?"

Hopping up from his chair he walks over to the far corner of the room and pointing down; "That old basement beneath the main floor. The room is perfect man... perfect.

As he pulls back a flimsy area rug, a large trapdoor is exposed. Arms gesturing wildly; "You know man you use to play hide and seek down there when you was a kid. We use to store all kinds of junk down there then one day some guy told me about making moonshine, and I said sheit.... dang I can do that. Carlos and I went around all the scrap yards looking for copper sheet and tubing. With my work doing car radiator repairs, that welding it was child's play. I found a few plans on the internet, at the library and wha-la that was it. I store all the supplies, copper kettles, tubing, grain, and everything. Perfect man... just perfect."

Cloud is amused by his father's animated arms flailing wildly, moonshine from his mason jar splashing everywhere; "Can't they find out what you doing, isn't it illegal?"

"Yes, it's illegal... but who gives a shit. We don't make enough for anybody to really notice. Plus, when we have a fire cooking beneath the still, the hood vents the smoke through the house chimney. We have the fire under the kettle downstairs and start a small fire in the fireplace upstairs. We use a shit-load of wood man. We have all the electricity we need, and we pump the cold water up from the creek, down below. A perfect set up man... perfect. The batch you're drinkin...we brewed it up last week. A small batch just about 25 gallons worth. And at 150 bucks a gallon that sure helps to pay for the bacon."

Sipping on his jar, he watches as Grandpa scurries about. This produces an unfamiliar broad smile. He hasn't seen Grandpa this happy for years; "So if it such a good business why don't you produce more?"

Grandpa is on a roll; "There's an old adage son; pigs get fat hogs get slaughtered. We keep distribution to just a few people, people we trust. Plus, Carlos and me use our walkie-talkies...when we make late nighttime deliveries. When I drive to deliver the product, Carlos piggybacks me in his truck from a quarter mile behind. If anybody's following my truck, he just lets me know, and we just keep driving past the drop off point. We usually do very fast exchanges, all cash business. All small bills, if you know what I mean. This latest batch you're drinkin is our Peach Specialty. I get crates of cull peaches from an Arkansas farmer friend, in exchange for a few quarts. The peaches are overripe and bruised, but they work great in the mash. The Oklahoma City ladies go crazy for it. They can't get enough of this stuff."

"Pop, just remember, if you get in trouble, it's the federal government that's going to come after you. Even though you have a great set up down the basement, the Feds are pretty good at finding that stuff."

"Son, I got it all under control...all under control."

"Pop, just remember what you always told me... You don't get in trouble when other people believe your bullshit, you get in trouble when you begin believing your own bullshit."

"Ya, I hear ya..."

Grandpa just nods his head as the two sit back down in the shade and continue sipping and rocking. After a few minutes Cloud looks over to Grandpa; "Pop, I gotta make my way into Oklahoma City next week to make an appointment at the VA."

"Is everything okay son?"

"I'm Okay...it's nothing urgent. I just have to follow up on some stuff. I have to go get my prescription filled. You know what I mean?"

"Not a problem son you can always take the other truck, runs fine. Wanna share what's going on?"

"It's kind of personal Pop. I really can't talk about."

Grandpa Cloud had a pretty good idea what is happening. He's been listening to his son moaning in his sleep and even cries out on a few occasions.

The moonshine is loosening Cloud up; "Pop tell me about the town library. Have they updated it with technology? You know... internet."

"Hell, yeah man, they got everything you need there, and if they don't have it, you can find it on the Internet."

Over time, Cloud becomes a frequent visitor to the small-town library where internet access is free. This enables him to communicate with old Army buddies and to try to find any information about Mohammed Rafta.

With the hundred-foot-high stone outcropping behind the cabin, wireless service is nonexistent. The next day, Cloud drives to town to make a call to the VA in Oklahoma City to make an appointment. They told him that he must come in and register before he can make appointments. So, on the following Monday morning, Cloud drives to Oklahoma City, VA hospital.

It takes him about an hour to fill out all the paperwork and hands it to the attendant. Several other veterans of all ages are sitting around and waiting. After about four hours patiently waiting, reading tattered magazines, he gets up to speak to the attendant again; "How long will I have to wait before I see anybody?"

"I'm sorry sir you just have to wait your turn, we have a huge backlog."

"Can't you give me some sort of idea how long I'm gonna to have to sit here?"

"Sorry sir, I have no idea, everybody has different issues with different doctors, and I have no way of knowing. You'll just have to take a seat, sir. If you like, you can give us your cell number, and we can call to let you know for sure when you can be seen. "

"You don't understand I don't have cell service out where I live."

"Sorry, sir that's the best I can do."

He sits for another hour in the waiting room. He watches as one by one the men that were there ahead of him slowly get up and go through double door exit, never to return. He is living firsthand the problems that all veterans are having with VA hospital system. Unfortunately, now it is he that is suffering the consequences.

As he sits back in his chair, he recognizes an officer he served with, in Baghdad years earlier. He jumps up; "Chuck, Chuck Johnson is that you?"

The two men approach each other, look into each other's eyes and smile; "Cloud is that you... you sorry sonofabitch? You finally got out huh?"

"Yeah I guess after 30 years I had enough if you know what I mean."

"How long you been waiting? "

"I got here first thing this morning and waited almost half a day, but nobody will tell me anything."

"Wait here a second." As Colonel Johnson walks up to the desk leans and leans in to whisper. He walks back to Cloud;

"They will take care of you now. If you have any problems you just ask for me, I'll take care of it for ya. Okay?"

"Chuck, do you have a few minutes?"

"Sure, let's go get a cup of coffee."

As the two sat at a secluded cafeteria table, they reminisce of their time in Anbar province. Though it was a shit hole, it was their shit hole, and they made the best of it. A lot of memories, some are good, some not so good. Cloud does not discuss that last mission at the Baiji compound, those images are too difficult to willfully resurrect. He does, however, have one question; "Did you ever hear what happened to that IED master, Mohammed Rafta?"

"Mohammed Rafta... Mohammed Rafta? Oh yes, I remember him now. His name never did come up again. It ends up after the Republican Guard units were finally neutralized; they melted back into the population. If I do find out anything on him, I will give you a call. Let me have your cell phone number."

"Even better, I'll give you my web address."

The two men firmly shake hands and separate; "Cloud you take care and let me know the next time you're in town, we'll go get a beer."

Minutes later Cloud was able to make an appointment with an attending psychiatrist for the following week. If it were not for the thoughtful intercession of a fellow officer, Cloud would have been waiting for months.

During his sessions with the psychiatrist, Dr. Maryanne Fellows, Cloud would say little about his emotional state. He just gave background information about his time in service his duties and what he had seen. Dr. Fellows empathizes with the personal trauma that so many veterans suffer and does not press him for more information. However, after a few sessions, he can discuss his overseas experiences and perceived failures at home. However, he does not divulge the habitual referencing of his field notebook. Dr. Fellows renews his antidepressants and antianxiety prescriptions, but Cloud understands that he will need to be weaned off eventually.

She gives him some mental exercises, cues he could use when he experiences symptoms coming on; like closing your eyes and thinking of a friendly, familiar place; also, rhythmic deep breathing or tapping an object on the table. Any controlled sequence could help to suppress the horrific images. He will try anything that might work.

But as Dr. Fellows revealed; "Unfortunately there is no drug regimen or treatment program effective for everyone. Each patient is unique, and each patient's symptoms must be dealt with individually, through trial and error. The only long term, effective treatment must be found from within."

Cloud listens attentively, looking head askew at an abstract painting of the Grand Canyon; *I'm going to have to find a way to exorcise these demons, myself.*" Cloud would continue to see Dr. Fellows every week for several months. With treatment, the flashbacks and hypersensitivity have diminished and he has learned to avoid episode triggers, like the sound of gunfire or the sight of blood. Also, other activities become triggers to memory intrusions. He must avoid violent TV with excessive blood and overt violence, as some programs include very loud gunfire. He can do little to nullify that. Some images are instant episode triggers, indelibly etched and never to be dissolved.

Sitting with hands clasped in his lap he sheepishly indicates to Dr. Fellows; "Doc, I really appreciate what you have done for me. When I first came in, I had no expectations, but you have shown me a path, not an easy path but a path forward."

"John what I can tell you is that from your file and what you've told me you are an innately strong man. You have seen much death and destruction yet continued to move forward. You never quit. That says a lot. Think of yourself as a piece of forged steel, forged in the fire of conflict, many times. You are stronger than you can imagine, but you have to find new strength from within."

Looking deep into his eyes; "John I want you to think of this quote when you sense your symptoms coming on." Slowly and say; "Today is the first day of the rest of my life."

Looking at her emotionally; "Okay."

"Only you have the power to change yourself."

While his nightmares have lessened in frequency and intensity, he continues to harbor deep guilt for the death of his fellow servicemen and the death of the innocent child. The vivid images of the child's lifeless face are but a dream away. Only

Grandpa's tried and true bedtime ritual offers some respite, a few good swigs of his prized moonshine before bed. That seems to work some of the time.

Weeks later John Cloud gets a message from an old friend in the Oklahoma Highway Patrol Academy. They need an instructor with rifle and combat experience to help train their officers in marksmanship and urban SWAT tactics. While not a full-time position and only a few days a week, it's exactly what he needs to begin his integration. The meager stipend helps supplement his retirement pay and his now Spartan lifestyle.

As the heat of the summer persists, Cloud needs more comfortable lodgings, so a few days a week, he moves into the air-conditioned condo with his son Daniel. Cloud understands that the loud crack of sporadic gunfire will require heavy ear protection, so he doubles up with earbuds and acoustical headphones. Nonetheless, he always carries around the 50 cal casing that he routinely taps while he is watching and giving instruction.

Daniel Cloud is a lot like his dad, not only in physical stature and mannerisms, but temperament as well. An amiable and calm young man, he is always controlled and respectful. Grandpa made sure of that. The tall, light-haired young man always sports a broad smile. He is a terrific catch for any young lady willing to live the demanding Army lifestyle. Shoulders back with a confident gate are a hint that this man is going places. Like his father and grandfather before him, he also attended Oklahoma University and received a commission from the Army through their ROTC program. He is also an engineering school graduate with honors and now plans a military career. He held off on entering active duty until he completed his master's degree. Daniel wasn't sure what direction he would take in the Army. Often when Col. Cloud was able to see his son, he gave him cautionary advice that military life is not an easy path. Despite that advice, Daniel was determined to make his mark and serve his country. Like his father and grandfather before him, he is a natural marksman and excels at sharing his skills with others. For now, he enjoys the notoriety and fascination of his commission and the traditions of the Army.

He has seen his father's shortcomings in not balancing military life with family life and does not intend to make the same mistakes. Once he has a good posting, he plans to marry his college sweetheart, settle in and have children. This would fulfill the dreams of Grandpa Cloud to continue the family name. Grandpa's persistent fixation on the perpetuation of the family name will burden them all.

CHAPTER 2
August 2011 – The Fateful Mission

Joy Cloud is the youngest child of John and Crystal Cloud. She has witnessed the verbal jousts between her mother and father and can't wait to leave for the freedom of college. Like her parents and siblings, she is attending the omnipresent Oklahoma University. The stubborn young girl is eager to emerge from the control of her mother and the shadow of her siblings. With her wild strawberry blond hair, this tiny freshman stands out. While she attempts to project a mature poised 19 year old, it is contrary to her adolescent 15-year-old frame and face. To overcome this paradox, Joy has developed a distinctive language style; what her brother called "propensity for prolific profanity." Her selective use of profanity was refined at a very young age while listening attentively to her mother and other Army brats. Her lack of stature was made up for by adult sized profanity.

The first recollection for her signature language was May 3, 1999. That afternoon the Cloud family lived in Oklahoma City, with John Cloud home on leave. The family had just finished dinner with the kids watching cartoons when their program was interrupted by a severe thunderstorm alert. Joy, wanting to watch her "toons," abruptly started changing channels, grumbling; "I don't want to watch this shit." That misbehavior had her marched to her bedroom by her mother for punishment; "If you keep cussing like that, God is going to punish you."

The young girl sat on her bed pouting, knees tucked under her chin, looking at the window, while still composing elegant combinations of profanity. As the forecast had predicted, the sky grew incredibly dark. Soon golf ball size hail began pounding the roofs, even shattering some nearby car windshields. Hail that size in OKC is not unusual.

Joy sat alone sulking in her bedroom unfazed when the first lightning bolt exploded above the house, scaring the hell out of everyone. Joy began screaming in terror; *"Oh God... I am so sorry. I am so sorry. I'll never cuss again."* She had never been so terrified in her life. John ran upstairs and held Joy tightly in his arms. With the two other children screaming downstairs, the rather drunk Crystal Cloud exclaimed; "Don't worry if it's got your name on it, it's got your name on it."

During the prolonged storm event, John held on to the shivering daughter, providing security and comfort. He would whisper in her ear; "I will protect you my little Joy, I will protect you." The gigantic tornado rumbled through the area. With each thunderclap, the tiny girl would grumble; "**Fuck.**" Hoping God would not hear. It soon became a routine part of her vocabulary.

The F5 tornado that struck was one of the worst in recorded history, producing 300 mph winds utterly destroying hundreds of homes, killing dozens. The Cloud home suffered some physical damage, but nothing to match the devastation in other parts of Oklahoma City. Joy sat trembling in her father's arms through the entire storm, finding all the security she needed.

That was the first, and last time John Cloud would offer comfort to his loving daughter. With his overseas deployments, she became resentful of his extended absences, while growing more terrified with every tornado warning. Any rumble of thunder would immediately send her scurrying to the deepest corner, exclaiming; "**_Fuck._**"

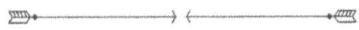

The five-foot one freshman is anxious to display herself as a polished collegian. To that end, she is shadowing her older sister Dawn, attending her first Chi Omega sorority, pledge party. While she projects a confident air, she has no clue what to expect or how to act. She thought about attending the more relaxed Oklahoma State University, then realized that she was no bleeping cowboy. This new unsupervised experience is a departure from her protective Catholic high school dances. Nervous and uncertain Joy weaves her way unnoticed through the raucous crowd. She tries to observe every detail; "What a bunch of phonies. Look at those boobs, I know those are padded."

Dawn Cloud, Joy's older sister, is president of the sorority house. She stands calmly and authoritatively, chin up with impeccable poised decorum. Dawn learned about the qualities of a proper woman from her grandmother Audrey Hopkins, wife of Gen. Gregory Hopkins. Grandma Hopkins would use every opportunity to remind Dawn of her roots and what was expected of her.

On tiptoes Joy strains to project a refined image. With neck craned Joy tries to note her sisters every gesture. In a few hours, it all becomes tedious; she grows tired and takes a seat against the wall. It was not her intent to be a portrait hung on the wall, instead be the elegant, vibrant centerpiece for all to admire; *"Well that's not happening tonight."*

Joy graduated an "A" student from Archbishop McGuire High School. Although outspoken, she has rarely broken any rule, none that she would admit to anyway. Tonight's party is a departure from her protective childhood. She had intended to; *"Throw off her shackles and venture foolhardy into the unknown."*

Apart from the noisy crowd Joy rests next to the table where there sits a frequented punch bowl. She curiously watches the visitors while gazing at the punch bowl. Looking around and since no one is supervising; *"Why not?"* Watching everyone, she repeatedly tests the tasty pink liquid. Tonight, without anyone's knowledge, the punch was spiked by the visiting fraternity members with Everclear 151, an easily masked highly potent alcohol. It sits inconspicuous, awaiting its first quarry; not to kill, but to inebriate.

Though Joy is not a flashy person, she can become quite animated when agitated. Not this evening, for tonight she must master this new social setting and do so discretely. As a student of the digital age, Joy never sees the face of her texting counterpart. So, face-to-face communication is a skill she must ultimately master. With feet rhythmically undulating over the floor, she sits comfortably and thumbs her iPhone at record speed.

With iPhone affixed to her face a striking young lady stops and stares down at her; "And who might you be? I don't believe I've seen you here before."

Face scrunched, barely squinting up; "I'm Joy... Joy Cloud

a pledge… I'm Dawn's sister,"

The sorority house visitor; "So you're Dawn's baby sister…Isn't that interesting."

Head jutting up; "And your name is…?"

With a distinct whiff of arrogance; "I'm Elouise Lion. I'm from the sorority house a few doors down…honey."

Walking up behind Elouise, an impetuous handsome young man bumps her elbow and thrusts a cup of punch at her. Annoyed, she points; "Just put it there on the table I'll get to it. Oh yes… where was I? I'm here tonight just visitin, checkin out the new crop of pledges and to just to say hi y'all."

Joy is not amused by her snobbery; nonetheless, Elouise relents; "You know darlin, if you want to make it in the world you have to get your face out of the phone and move your little ass off the chair and, show it around out there. Just sayin honey…just sayin."

Elouise Lion strolls away wine glass held high, to mingle with the next unworthy group, waves; "Y'all have a nice day… honey."

Neither woman realized that the rejected cup of punch was one of many laced with the potent date rape drug GHB. Elouise, a seasoned partygoer, learned the hard way to never accept an open beverage, especially from a stranger.

Joy uncomfortable with Elouise's brash suggestion

wiggles in her seat then puts her iPhone back into her face.

As the party evolves into a raucous party mode, another young fraternity partygoer strolls up to Joy: "And, what might your name be beautiful."

Annoyed; "My name is Joy."

"Why, yes it is."

Not looking up, Joy tries to stay cool to his overtures.

The young dark-haired man kneels down in front of her, gently clasps her hands and lowers them from her face; "Why don't I try to enhance tonight's memories. Why don't we find a quiet room somewhere where we both can have some privacy and fun?"

Shaking her head and squinting; "What?"

"Come-on honey, let's go someplace and let me rock your world."

Joy searching for the appropriate response, squints and whispers; "Let's don't.. and say we did."

"Huh...?"

With a wide-eyed smile she leans in; "Yah...that's right.. you know, let's don't and just tell everyone that we did... How's that?"

Stunned by her contrived rejection, he jerks back

abruptly. Not wanting to be embarrassed, stands slowly, turns and walks away, not looking back.

Joy, quite pleased with her encounter, whistles an unknown tune and continues to thumb he iPhone. This goes on for a bit longer until her cup of punch is empty. Without being obvious, she leans over and picks up the full cup left on the table and starts sipping. Not realizing the impact, she continues to sip until it is empty; "*Damn, this stuff tastes good..!*"

Now being somewhat sloshed, Joy delights in the partygoers' animations; like slapstick mimes trying to make striking statements. After an hour of not seeing her sister, Joy seeks out a restroom on the first floor, however, it's perpetually occupied. She wriggles uncomfortably in her chair for a few minutes then having to pee really badly, remembers an upstairs restroom. Scampering quickly up the stairs she has a minor accident and dampens her underwear; "*Dammit I got to pee really bad.*" She scurries to find the second floor, guest bedroom. The door to the darkened room door was cracked open as she peeks cautiously; "*Nobody in their good.*" She quickly uses the restroom then begins humming as she rinses her dampened underwear. She looks for a hair-dryer to dry her underwear, but none is found and instead hangs them over the shower rod; "*No one will care I'll get'em later.*" Not wanting to embarrass her older sister about her minor accident she stops and listens at the door for any noise; "*Good there's nobody out there.*"

Since she usually only drinks Dr. Pepper, the effect of the GHB spiked punch is very unfamiliar. As she becomes increasingly drowsy, she fumbles to turn off the bathroom light.

With outstretched beckoning hands, Joy wobbles in the dark to the inviting bed; *"Wow this feels comfortable."* She sits for a moment and listens to muffled music below and playfully flips off her shoes. She pulls back then slides under the alluring quilt. Whispering softly; "No one will miss me," then comfortably assumes the fetal position to sleep.

However, unknown to Joy she is sharing the huge king size bed with another person on the other side; a young man also passed out from the effects of his GHB laced drink.

In the early morning hours, the party finally winds down. As Dawn escorts the last male guests out of the house, she locks the door and realizes she has not seen Joy for hours and attempts find her; *"Where the hell did that girl go."* Dawn checks all the upstairs bedrooms; *"Did she go for an early morning run or is she still in the house?"* Checking with all her sorority sisters, Dawn turns on the light to the guest bedroom, finally seeing her tucked under the covers.

Joy is still in a deep sleep; "Come on baby sister; let's move you to my room." As Dawn gently pulls back the covers and attempts to wake her Dawn notices that Joy's bright yellow party dress is disheveled and pulled up. Curiously she lifts the dress to discover her underwear is missing; *"What the hell is going on here."* She also notices bright red blood stains on the sheets; *"Wait a minute, I know she had her period early last week..."* Believing Joy is still a virgin, this could be an indication that Joy may have had sex last night.

Knowing Joy's strict upbringing and her mom's tight-assed rules, Dawn surmised something happened; "Joy, honey wake up... wake up. What the **hell** happened here?"

Sitting up confused, still half asleep; "Stop yelling sis! I have no idea what you're yelling about."

Dawn finally gets Joy's attention. She looks under the covers for her underwear and can find none; "Never mind!" She sits her up in bed, legs dangling and puts her shoes on as if she were a three-year-old. Joy still disoriented requires support to walk downstairs and to Dawn's car. Dawn immediately drives her to the University student's clinic. No other students are there at that early hour. They walk up to the front desk, and Dawn whispers to the female attendant. Moments later all three walk back to one of the examination rooms. They both help Joy onto the examination table.

Joy, still half asleep, yawns; "Why am I here? I feel okay, I'm not sick."

Dawn still concerned whispers gently in her ear; "Don't worry sis, I'll take care of you, I'll take care of everything."

A few minutes later a young female doctor enters the room, reaches over to an open box of exam gloves, slowly puts them on, and walks over to Joy. Dawn, in a reserved manner, asks; "Joy do you remember what happened to you last night. Do ya honey? "

Joy just shrugs her shoulders; "Nothing really, I just had a few too many drinks last night, I guess. I feel just a bit dizzy. I'm okay."

The doctor gently places her hand on Joy's back; "Please lie back and scoot off your underwear."

Joy looks at her inquisitively; "What... why..?"

She softly responds; "We need to do an exam, just as a precaution."

Dawn leans across the table and whispers; "Doctor I looked around the bed this morning, and I couldn't find her underwear."

The doctor looks at Joy, Dawn stands beside her, rubbing her shoulder; "Don't worry sis I'll take care of everything for ya. This is just a precaution."

Joy wriggles away from the doctor's hands; "Precaution for what?"

Again, the doctor gently taps her on the shoulder; "Please just lie back and place your legs in the stirrups. This will just take a second; I promise I will not hurt you."

Joy still half asleep and annoyed looks at her sister and complies. The doctor slides the lab stool close to the table opens a nearby drawer and takes out a small vile with a swab.

Dawn nudges up to her and gives her a kiss on the head; "Go ahead, do as the doctor asks."

As the doctor lifts Joy's bright yellow dress part way up her slender thighs, Joy recoils and thrusts her hands-down covering her privates; *"What the hell."* The doctor, tapping her foot again, lifts the dress to perform the examination; "Honey it's okay I promise." As the doctor leans to the side to look at Joy in the face; "Just take a deep breath and relax. I'll be done in a second. Promise it won't hurt." She leans over and takes the swab, gently inserts it into Joy, rotates it for a second, withdraws it and places it back into the sampling tube. The doctor takes the vile containing swab and places it on the counter, snaps off her gloves; "Okay honey we are done here. You take your legs out of the stirrups and sit up now. Come on darlin' sit up, pull down your dress and fix yourself up."

As the doctor writes her first name; "Joy - September 4, 2011" on the vile she points at the door; "I'll have the female officer outside come in and take your statement. Also, I have ordered the morning after prescription in your name at the pharmacy for you to pick it up on your way out. You take care now; you'll be just fine."

As Joy yawns and rubs her eyes, she begins to recognize her surroundings and comprehending her situation; "Statement for what, prescription, for what? Sis what the hell just happened and why am I here?"

Dawn walks around the exam table and stands in front of Joy puts her arm on her shoulder; "Honey, I hope I'm wrong, but last night I think you were drugged or something. I found you this morning in the guest bedroom really passed out." Very soft and apologetically; "I think you were raped."

Joy stunned, abruptly jumps from the table. She lands on the hard floor in a thud and turns furiously to Dawn; "**Raped...!**

What the **hell** you talkin about?"

Without hesitation and in rapid succession; "Baby sister I hope I'm wrong about what happened I really do. I'm sorry I didn't keep track of you last night or where you went. Do you remember anything? Don't worry honey, it's okay you won't get pregnant, I have a pill you can take, it will take care of that. Do you remember anything? Who was the guy that did this to you baby?"

Joy finally gets oriented and steps away from her sister; "What? No, I thought I was having a dream, a very **vivid** dream."

Dawn; "So what did this **asshole** look like? When I catch that shithead, I am going to make him **pay**. Sorry for the profanity."

Joy looking bewildered and animated; "I don't know, the room was dark when I went to bed. I thought it was all a dream... But I can say in my dream... he was very gentle when we kissed. I thought I was dreaming, I thought I had a really vivid dream. Don't **you** have dreams like that? He was a so sweet and gentle not at all like those groping assholes I dated in high school. All they did was grope at me and try to force me to do stuff. That's the reason I stayed a virgin, I don't like being forced. I am still a virgin right..?"

As Dawn stands there gently stroking her sister's arm; "No baby sister, not anymore."

Joy bends over pulls up her dress; "Not anymore. What? Are you sure I'm not just spotting?"

Gently stroking her arm; "You're not a virgin any more baby sister the doctor confirmed it."

Shaking her head Joy slowly wobbles out of the examining room; "This is total horseshit."

Dawn walks quickly behind her, sample vile in hand. She walks up to the admitting desk, placing the sample vial on the counter and says; "Don't worry I will find out the name of the asshole that did this to my baby sister. I'll make sure that **he** pays."

Joy aggressively grabs the vile, turns and throws it angrily into the trash; "**No**! You will not use that sample, and I'm not giving a statement to an officer. I don't know for sure that I was raped and do not want my name in any police report." She angrily walks up to her sister; "Do you understand what I'm saying? Are **we** understood here?" She also turns and looks at the female officer; "Do you understand me officer, no record... Do we understand each other?"

The officer amused by this pint-size female trying to intimidate her puts her hands up smiles and leans back; "I understand."

As Joy defiantly stomps barefoot through the sliding double doors, Dawn slyly retrieves the vial from the trash, looks at the officer places her finger over the lips, puts it in her pocket and nonchalantly leaves. Later when Dawn gets to her room, she sets the vial her small freezer, just in case it is needed for future identification. Neither sister ever mentioned the situation again, it was their secret. Later that school year, Dawn graduated with honors and accepted a position as assistant director of media relations at a local oil company.

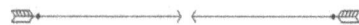

Growing up as an Army brat, Joy never thought of herself as a woman's rights proponent; but after deep reflection of events in her youth, she decided to major in Women's Studies at OU. After pledging her sister's sorority, she stayed in that house for her remaining college years, ultimately following in her sister's footsteps as sorority house president. Despite her diminutive frame, her determination and resilient character made her well-known on campus. She became the face for women's rights issues on the conservative campus. Her skepticism of men, from the sexual encounter's years earlier, provided motivation to offer assistance other women in need and upon graduation accepted a position as a Deputy Director of the Oklahoma City Women's Clinic. Joy's grit and willpower emboldened her and gave her the resiliency needed for her trials to come.

CHAPTER 3
June 2014 – Rafta's Rage

Several months after the death of his wife and child and, not long after the US withdrew from Iraq, Mohamad Rafta has changed his name and altered his appearance to gain a teaching position at Iraq's University at Mosul.   In an attempt to westernize, the University incorporated more international studies. Like many Iraqi veterans, Rafta struggles with the loss of his family, the horrors of war. Nonetheless, he attempts to plant the seeds for his future. He lives a modest solitary life in a sparsely decorated apartment. None of the faculty knows that he is a former senior officer in the Iraqi Republican Guard. In only a few months of teaching, he gains the immediate respect of his students. With a glance from his dark solemn eyes, his students are attentive to his every word. Through his poised, very well prepared lectures, he gained an impressive academic reputation.

Late one afternoon after most of the classes have been dismissed, he sits in an empty classroom. Many of the students have heard of the armed insurgents in the region and have vacated the campus. They know that ISIS is disdainful of any formal education not centered on Islam. Through the open window, you can hear the sound of heavy weapons being fired into the air, the typical ISIS intimidation tactic.

The young man sprinting by the doorway yells terrifyingly: "***ISIS is coming...get out.***"

Within seconds the building is totally empty except for

Rafta. He sits calmly at his desk looking down, grading papers. He has never retreated from the battlefield, and he's not about to start now.   He is familiar with the sounds of automatic weapons and while interested, is not alarmed. He just gazes at his watch then continues with students' papers. He knows there is no place else to go.

Hours later Rafta sits stoic behind his desk reading a newspaper. The campus is empty, with the streets void of life. From a distance he can hear the rumbling of heavy military equipment, moving through the university. Bearded men are yelling chants to non-existent listeners. After a few minutes, one of the vehicles comes to an abruptly stop in front Rafta's building. A half dozen heavily armed men scan the area and jump off.   He is unfazed as he hears echoed shouts and the kicking open of locked doors. The classroom door slowly opens, and four heavily armed men warily enter the classroom. They walk slowly to the front desk, AK-47's pointing at Rafta. Rafta sits hands clasped over his newspaper cool and resolute; *"I am not certain of their motives. Do not make any abrupt moves."*

One of the heavily bearded fighters' barks; "Are you Mohamad Rafta."

Rafta, peering through his reading glasses wryly; "Yes, who is asking for me?"

The men realize by his calm voice and erect posture that this is definitely not a civilian.

One of the guard's stands next to Rafta, coaxing him to rise with his rifle barrel; "Come with us. Come with us quietly, and you will not be harmed."

As the man touches Rafta's arm, he looks at him sternly then removes his hand. Not until that moment did Rafta realize that he was a much sought-after person. His former Republican Guard colleagues recalled his fluency in several languages, and the ISIS leadership now requires him to interpret the information they hear on BBC, CNN, and the web. Most of the leaders of ISIS spread from Syria into Iraq and are an aggregate of former Bath party members, Iraqi Republican Guard remnants, Sunni insurgents and even some remaining Al Qaeda.

Thousands of the ISIS recruits from around the world converge on the area. They are young, unemployed men unable to get work. With the recent import of low-cost clothing, shoes, and dry goods from China, local paying jobs are scarce for the growing Iraqi Sunni male population. If a family does not have a friend in the Shia dominated government the chances of any meaningful job are remote. So, an alternative, though not necessarily the ideal choice, is to join the ranks of ISIS. They are advertising a good salary, disciplined military training, uniforms and food. With initiative, there are evil enhancements: riches from stolen artifacts and the possibility of copious sex with female captives. ISIS has proclaimed the socio-religious justifications for their mission: the restoration of the Caliphate. This combination of factors is drawing tens of thousands of young Sunni Muslims to Iraq and Syria to join their ranks.

Though Rafta was never a front-line combat officer, he was highly successful in coordinating local operations during the final days of the Iraqi insurgency. Today ISIS does not need Rafta to fight. They have an abundance of aggressive volunteers.

They are however in dire need for Rafta to translate and manage their new Internet multi-lingual webpages. They have seen the ubiquitous clandestine power of social media and intend to utilize it not only to motivate recruits, but as a means to garner regional support for the Caliphate.

Rafta calmly walks out of the building, slides into a captured American Humvee, and is driven to the ISIS Provisional Headquarters. He immediately recognizes his precarious situation, especially since ISIS just chained the doors of the University. Nonetheless, over the next several months Rafta becomes an invaluable contributor and is quickly promoted through their growing intelligence organization.

Over several months ISIS has advanced across vast swaths of Iraq and Syria. It has now spread into other Muslim nations in the Middle East, Africa, and Asia. They have amassed enormous sums of money; stealing several hundred million dollars in cash from the Federal Bank in Mosul; selling Iraqi oil to anyone wishing to make a quick profit and pirated artifacts; along with the sale of thousands of captured young women as sex slaves. This newfound notoriety finally attracts considerable attention from the international community.

By early 2016 the caliphate attempts to stabilize its geographical base. They focus on pacifying the populace by terrorizing potential adversaries, committing grotesque mass executions. The strategy is a double-edged sword, as half the populace acquiesced to the terror, while the rest fled in all directions. They fled to Turkey and Jordan, with ultimately hundreds of thousands migrating into central Europe. After only a few years, their effective worldwide publicity campaign raised the anxiety of the international community.

Ultimately with the tepid support from the United States, Europe, and Turkey, precision bombings were undertaken in Raqqa, the headquarters of ISIS in Syria. In early 2017 with the tightening of the borders between Turkey, Iraq, and Syria, a stranglehold around the ISIS capital of Raqqa caused their central organization to implode. Much of their logistical infrastructure lies in ruins, with several senior leaders killed. However, with the active Internet marketing managed by Rafta, ISIS continues to spread around the world, accumulating manpower and territory.

In retaliation for the destruction of Raqqa, ISIS now seeks volunteers to be sent abroad to spill infidel blood on the infidel's home soil. In Iraq, after several months of intense fighting, ISIS' influence is shrinking. The Kurdish militias supported by US advisors and airpower made considerable advances into ISIS' Mosul enclave. Slowly, the noose is tightening around the city with few opportunities to retreat. More and more of the city is in ruin, smoke constantly billowing from almost all directions. ISIS fighters have been forced to construct a labyrinth of deep tunnels throughout the old city to survive the US shelling. This offers some shelter from the overhead bombardment. The coalition forces are utilizing small drones to identify targets of opportunity. Explosions are getting closer to Mohamad Rafta's position and can be heard constantly. In the few buildings that are still standing, door to door fighting by the hardened fighters is mandatory. The stench of the rotting corpses in the collapsed rubble is pervasive. As the noose tightens around the ISIS stronghold, beleaguered civilians must escape the once vibrant city. The coalition forces are so close, they can even smell the cooking of the ISIS fighters.

Late one evening after the shelling has subsided, Rafta is called to his Commander's underground headquarters. They sit in the center of a tiny bunker, with only one lantern to illuminate their dejection. Except for muffled artillery, the room is eerily silent. Rafta sits patiently awaiting his commander's orders. As the commander meditates, his eyes slowly open to Rafta; "Rafta my loyal captain I need you for a special mission. I know you can take many more of their lives for us and continue to fight for our cause. Our fighting days here in Mosul are numbered. I have been thinking on this for some time and watching the sacrifice of our martyrs in Europe and America. I believe if we shed considerably more blood in the infidel's homeland, they will heed our message and leave us to our affairs. I think it is time for *you* my brother, to leave and take the fight to the infidels."

Rafta is perplexed, he was not expecting a new mission; *"What does he wish of me?"*

His Commander whispers; "I wish for you to go and take some time to prepare and think of where you feel you would be the most value to our mission. It could be Europe or Africa or even America. You have been a loyal soldier. I give you this opportunity to select the where, the when and how you may wish to martyr yourself for the cause. Can you do this for me brother? Go now and think on this and return with your answer."

Rafta plods hunched over through the darkened chiseled

tunnels beneath the old city. Turning left, then right, he finally comes to his small squalid dugout, just large enough for him to sleep. He places his lantern down on the floor and sits among the muddy carpets. Despite their best attempts to abate the pervasive dust, nothing works. The constant overhead shelling by Americans artillery perpetuates dust clouds in the underground rooms. Inhabitants can barely breathe. Rafta has changed his appearance again, wearing a black pakul, a traditional Afghan hat. One of his favorite interests is to change his appearance, so few around him can keep track of his whereabouts. Rafta grows the profuse traditional unkempt black beard, but must keep it covered when in the caves. His only personal keepsakes are a weathered photo of his family, his rifle, and the American helmet recovered Baiji. He saves it as a painful reminder. The earthen walls shake and dust billows up around him as a massive bomb explodes only a few blocks away. Except for his eyes he is entirely covered in the pervasive tan dust. He gently fingers through the dust to unearth the family photo, then gently blows it clean.

Another shell explodes this time closer than the last, the concussive force so powerful it bounces the Army helmet, hitting his foot; *"Those miserable infidel bastards."* As the kerosene lamp flickers and dims, a frustrated Rafta picks up the helmet, grunts and flings it furiously. It recoils off the wall, spins and comes back to rest face up between his feet. However, this time something appears different. Not noticed before, beneath the incrusted blood, he sees a white paper. Picking it close to the lantern he scratches furiously at the caked blood, to see some papers; *"I've not seen this before."* He feverishly tears away at the lining to recover the papers. Finally, Rafta jerks out an envelope postmarked June 7, 2011, addressed to a Col. John Cloud, US Army, 1st ID, Iraq. Without hesitation, he opens the envelope containing a letter and… some photos. He finally pulls out the entire liner and beneath are more addressed letters, papers, and additional photos, glued together with blood. In that oppressively dusty tunnel, Rafta moistens his thumb and repeatedly rubs the letter to dissolve the encrusted blood, exposing the return address.

For the first time in many years, a wry smile crosses his weathered face. Hunched over the flickering lantern, a vengeful toothy sneer emerges: *"I have you, I finally have you now."* Rafta now has something to fight for, worthy of his martyrdom. Not the ISIS ideology, but a visceral mission for personal revenge. He looks through the other and letters and photos; *"I will finally avenge you, my wife and son."*

He scurries quickly back, churning up dust along the labyrinth. Breathing heavily, he presents the plan to his commander; "I wish to undertake a vicious retaliatory strike on the American heartland." With blood tinged fingers he withdraws letters and photos from Cloud's helmet; "This is the man who killed my family years ago in Baiji. He brought his killing to my family, and now I will deliver that hell to him."

The commander squints looks deep into Rafta's eyes and sees the anguish on his face. Cagily nods; "I will not deny you this brother, you have waited very long. This is a unique opportunity for our cause. You have the perfect target and are uniquely suited to accomplish the mission. Brother, I want *you* to select the men for this mission. Take a few choice men from Mosul. They are of no use to me here."

Rafta, a stealthy mastermind who has long envisioned retaliation on the American homeland; "I could use some men that speak Spanish."

His commander pausing for a moment; "I know of two fighters here that speak Spanish. I am also aware of many other brothers in Morocco, wishing to rejoin the fight. I believe they speak Spanish. Can you make that work?"

Rafta, with fists, pumping; "Yes, I will make that work. I will collect them on the way to America and train them as we go."

"Excellent brother, we still have considerable US currency in the bank, it will be of no use to us in the coming days, take what you need to accomplish your mission. You should leave immediately while you can. Keep me informed brother, the usual way through your well-disguised internet postings. I will pray for the success of your mission and your martyred soul Mohamad."

After a few days of interviewing men and counting cash, Mohamad Rafta has again transformed his appearance. He now emerges as a clean-shaven well-groomed engineer with passport papers detailing his new identity as a Kurdish oil refinery engineer. The Kurdish Peshmerga fighters are the arch enemies of ISIS in Mosul. The Peshmerga were tenacious in their pursuit of ISIS. In Mosul, they fought street by street, house by house, and room by room to ferret out the ISIS insurgents. For Rafta, the irony is not lost and will use it to disguise their identity. He spent several days cleaning up his accomplices for their trip, not an easy task.

Once they were prepared, they traverse the isolated hills into Turkey. Rafta did not have any trouble renting a Mercedes and drives cautiously to the Turkish port of Ceyhan. Awaiting him is an oil tanker, transporting crude oil from the Kurdish region of Iraq. Within a few days, the grungy oil tanker chugs through the Mediterranean to the seacoast Moroccan port of Mohammedia. Rafta and his men will hold up there for a few days, awaiting the remaining eight ISIS recruits. The Moroccan ISIS recruits can speak fluent Spanish which will be sufficient once they get to their next stop Venezuela.

Rafta has secured passage for all on a much larger oil tanker, destined for Venezuela. Venezuela was chosen as their next destination because of their lax entry visa requirements. Also, Venezuela frequently purchases cheap blended light crude from Morocco, since their refinery exploded several months earlier. While $100,000 is sufficient to procure the 12 berths, the knowledge that his family would be butchered guarantees the captain's silence.

The men are left alone below decks and are only allowed on deck at night. Rafta does not reveal key details of their mission. He only discusses how they must speak and how they must conduct themselves. After twelve days at sea, they arrive in the Venezuelan port city of Maracaibo. This is an ideal transfer point to Mexico, their next stop.

Rafta and his men hide out at a remote fishing village, an hour drive from Maracaibo. There they pay villagers to house, clothe and feed them. Rafta trained the men for several days on accepted Central American, cultural habits. They are to blend in with migrants, seeking farm work in the US. This will be sufficient until they reach their ultimate destination, Oklahoma City, Oklahoma. But for now, only Rafta knows that destination. That evening, as the sun sets, he sits alone on the chair overlooking an open field. He withdraws the photos and letters from his pocket, gently trying to separate the papers in the glued blood. He sees the photos of Cloud and his family; *"Soon, soon you will feel my anger."*

AquarianBooks.com

CHAPTER 4
March 2017 – Almost Too Easy

Mary and Phil Johnson of Greenwich, Connecticut have been married for just a few days. They plan to spend their honeymoon at a remote beachfront resort on the Yucatan of Mexico. Their nights are filled with Cancun hotspots and the days are spent lounging near their new beachside retreat. It is an idyllic hideaway where the two young lovers may begin their lives. Their honeymoon hut is at the end of a quiet sparkling cove surrounded by palm trees.

On their third day at the beach, Mary and Phil are laying out on bright white towels, hiding from the sun, next to a large dropping palm tree. She playfully hops on top of Phil, straddling his chest, kissing his face. "I want to get my book. Can I bring you something?" Her beautiful unkempt amber color hair, brushes across his tanned face. She sits up and stretches, then pulls back her hair behind her head. Then, springs up onto the hot sand.

Phil leans his head looking at her, squinting into the sunlight; "Sure, fill that bucket with some ice and a few more Dos Equis. And, bring a few cut limes too. Thanks, babe."

As Mary walks back in the wet ebbing sand back to the hut, Phil watches her flaunt her bikini butt. Phil lies back on his towel and ponders their bountiful future. They could not have had a more perfect day at the beach; *"Man, this place is really perfect."*

About 300 yards offshore, a Venezuelan fishing boat cuts

its engine and glides quietly to a stop. The sound muffled by the crashing waves. Four men emerge from the fishing boat and throw a small inflatable raft overboard. With wobbling legs, the men nervously enter the unsteady inflatable dinghy.

A tall stubble-faced man with unruly hair sits at the stern and points to the shore. It is Mohammad Rafta along with three select ISIS recruits. In Venezuela, they began their training with light weapons, knives, and learning Central American Spanish. They have studied maps of North America, along with alternative travel routes. They understand that no matter how detailed a plan, once their feet hit shore, they must be prepared for anything.

Rafta's plans are to travel first to the US, then send instructions to the other eight men on the best routes and methods to proceed. All men have drastically changed their appearance to blend into the Central American Latin culture. Being the intelligence officer, Rafta has studied the internet for photos of the indigenous peoples. He has also seen news photos of the migrants traveling across the US border. All have spent considerable time shirtless to gain an almost full-bodied tan. They also purchased tattered western clothes and sneakers to make them appear as credible Central American migrants. No detail will be overlooked. During their training, each has added several pounds. For the past several days they had to accept a new diet, eating very different, rich Venezuelan meals. Everything is okay to eat except pork. The ISIS intelligence network was able to obtain false Honduran passports good enough to travel anywhere.

The four men are frantically paddling their tiny raft to

shore to what was believed to be an isolated Yucatán beach. Almost comical to watch as they never practiced paddling a raft in Venezuela. Rafta never thought to train them as part of this clandestine operation. All the men carry are a few extra clothes in a shoulder bag and their razor-sharp knives. They do not want to be caught with any illegal weapons, for that would surely raise suspicion. After a few tenuous minutes in the rough surf, they finally get the knack of paddling in unison and move carefully to shore. They are headed for that tranquil cove, just ahead, being uninhabited. Rafta checked that on the Internet in Venezuela. However, only in the past few months has this beach been developed as a honeymoon hideaway and it is not shown on any Google map photos.

The palm branch roof cottage where Mary has walked cannot be seen from the ocean. As they enter the cove, Phil hears distant voices and rises to his elbows. Unconcerned and amused he peeks at the shirtless Hispanic men approaching the beach; *"What the hell is this?"*

They do not notice him lying next to the tree. As the raft glides onto the beach, they toss their bags onto soft white sand. Phil is only about 20 feet away with only the top of his head above the palm tree trunk. He is fascinated that they don't see him; *"These guys are really clueless."*

One of the men begins to pull the boat to the trees, when he is startled by a shirtless man lying there. He falls back onto the water on his ass and in Spanish: "What the fuck!"

Rafta approaches Phil speaking Spanish; "What are you doing here?"

Phil with a broad smile; "Sorry, no Habla Espanol."

Rafta, a second time gruffly asks in perfect English; "What are you doing here?"

Phil shook his head and with a boyish grin; "Enjoying the day, how are you doing?"

Rafta is not amused as he methodically scans the trees; "Are you alone?"

Phil naïvely; "Yes, why..?" As Phil wobbly gets to his feet the other three gather around him.

Swiveling his head around; *"What is going on here?"* Nervously; "Hey, hey guys, I don't want any trouble. I have $20 in my pocket, take it and move along. No harm no foul. Right?" Phil was told to always carry $20 just in case he was approached by unwanted strangers. That is considered a passport for foreigners to pass through unscathed.

With a slight nod of Rafta's head, one of the men grabs Phil from behind, tightly around his neck. As Phil tries to resist; "Hey man what the hell is this, I told you I didn't want any trouble. Come on man cut it out."

The assailant covers his mouth. Then Rafta looks at both and says in Spanish; "End this now."

The assailant withdraws a large knife from his belt sheath, releases his arm and savagely slits his throat. They drag him backward a few steps and lay him back down on his bright white towel.

Phil lies back grabbing his throat; *"Oh God, Oh God what the hell just happened please no please, no...."* They watch as his body writhes, legs kicking as he grabs his throat. Not able to call out he lies there bleeding. Within a a few seconds he passes out and quickly dies. His eyes fixed at the beautiful white clouds billowing overhead.

Rafta gruffly; "Quietly, pick up the boat and move into the dense trees." As he looks at his compass, he points; "That way."

One of the men asks in Moroccan; "What about him?"

Rafta; "I told you to only speak Spanish. I have taught you to only speak Spanish for three months. Are you that **stupid**? Only Spanish..!"

The man nervously replies; "Yes, Mohamad."

Rafta shaking his head exasperated; "Not Mohamad my name is just Rafta. **Rafta**! Brush away our footprints with those palm branches quickly... quietly."

Rafta's lieutenant, now named Jose, looks back and sees Phil's large ruby stone gold graduation ring, glistening on his bloody finger. It's a Rensselaer University Engineering college graduation ring dated 2010. Engraved inside; "PJ - 2010" He aggressively jerks the blood encrusted ring and watch from Phil's lifeless hands and thrusts them into his pocket. Rafta whispers; "Jose, take any money he has in his pocket also. They will think it was a robbery by locals."

The men quickly carry the raft and their duffles and blend into the dense palm forest undergrowth. The last man walks backward, starting at the water's edge erasing any footprints. They silently creep several hundred feet into the palm forest and underbrush.

At one point, Rafta pauses, points and whispers to the men; "Slice open the boat open, deflate it completely, fold it up and bury it, under those branches. Quickly, quickly, leave no traces. **None**! Keep erasing our steps as we go."

Not long after Mary walks back onto the beach. As she strolls carefree, she childishly splashes water before her; "Phil, babe, I got you a few beers and some chips too. She can only see his feet protruding; "Honey..?" As she approaches; "Phil are you napping, it's too early to sleep, and I have some special plans for us."

As she moves around the tree, she sees Phil lying on their beach towel. The contrast of the white towel and glistening red blood in the sunlight is traumatizing. She leans toward Phil to see his oily bronzed chest soaked in blood, a deep slash across his throat. Blood is still trickling across his chest. Holding her face, she staggers backward; *"Oh my God"*; As she drops the ice bucket she tries to scream, but cannot; *"What! No! No! No...!"* The shock is too great as she gasps for air and screams, this time with a horrific howl; "Ahhhhh!" again and again. Treetop birds are startled and scatter into the wind.

Now deep in the undergrowth and far from sight, Rafta

and his group hear the screams. He points in the other direction, fervently, as they move quickly through the trees. He is not at all concerned about the death of another person. Rafta's iPhone compass and map point their way out. He beckons them on; "Quickly a truck is waiting, a short distance. And, none of you forget you must speak Spanish, only Spanish. If I hear one word other than Spanish, I will **cut** your throat myself." The four men and driver glide off quietly in a large dusty SUV. They must drive several hundred miles to the city of Veracruz. There they will hop onto a freight train headed north and blend in with thousands of Central Americans migrants.

The next day in Oklahoma City, reports of the horrific death of the newlywed couple from Greenwich, Connecticut was in the news. The news reporter Elouise Lion was providing a synopsis on the local OKC TV; "Mexican officials have labeled the killing as a robbery by one of the locals that had gone terribly wrong."

Days later, after considerable international media attention, the Mexican national police conduct a thorough search of the entire area with metal detectors. They do not believe at all that it was a robbery. The body was staged. Deep in the undergrowth, they discovered a buried slashed raft with four paddles. On the side of the rubber raft is distinct bloody palm prints. Those facts, however, never reached the media, as the Mexican Government did not want to spread the horrific story. The details of the crime never made its way to the FBI or Interpol.

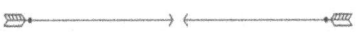

At an isolated railroad yard in Veracruz, Mexico, a slender woman and her young teenage daughter walk cautiously up to a Kansas City Southern de Mexico freight train. The tiny women have difficulty reaching the first rung of the boxcar ladder; "Do not look down Angelina." They carefully reach to the top of the freight car and are greeted by another family attempting the same difficult trek north, to America. They have heard from many friends of a better life in America and are willing to sacrifice everything to get there. While not an easy journey, it must be better than the misery to which they are accustomed. Life has become much more difficult this past year. Carmella's husband, Fernando Ramirez, traveled north for America five years earlier to find work. He would wire money home every month to help, but that stopped abruptly last July, without a word. That was not like him; something horrible must have happened.

Carmela is an impressive 35-year-old Latina. With her slender frame and long black hair, she is quite beautiful. Nonetheless, the years of hard labor on their scratch farm has taken its toll. Angelina, her thirteen-year-old daughter, is still growing but Carmela knows this hard life can no longer be imposed on her child.

Soon after their arrival, the train lurches, then pulls away from the siding. Everything of value has been sold for the trip. Mother and daughter nestle together under a blanket and rock in unison with the train. Not long after, a rotund middle-aged man wearing an oversized tan hat and silver-tipped boots hobbles atop the railcars speaking to many travelers. Carmela leans over and whispers; "He must be the coyote that your Uncle Carlos contracted; he will get us to America."

Eventually, he makes his way to the women, squats down next to them stroking Angelina's shiny black hair; "You two beautiful ladies must be the Ramirez girls. I was expecting you. Your brother Carlos told me so much about you, but he didn't say how beautiful you were." Extending his hand in friendship; "My name is Manuel. Are you the Ramirez ladies..?"

As he strokes her hair, Angelina sees the large, ornate silver bracelet on his wrist. Two exquisitely carved sunbirds are nestled against a large, almost flawless turquoise stone. Troubled by his inappropriate advances, Carmela clutches her daughter closer, tersely; "Yes we are! How long will this trip take?"

Annoyed by her resistance; "Not long little ones. Not long. I will make sure you get there safe and sound. Trust me, ladies... Trust me. Do you have my money? You are required to pay me half at the beginning of the trip and the other half once you are delivered across the border." With grubby hand outstretched: "Do you have my money?"

Carmela reaches into her small purse, turns to hide it from view and counts out $2,000, half the money that was promised. She hastily thrusts it at him then re-clutches her daughter. Manuel does not bother to count the money. He stands back up, towering over them; "Good, if you need anything just ask for me." He turns and confidently points around him with a broad smile; "My men are all around. They will find me, and I will get you whatever you need. Okay." As Manuel wobbles back across the top of the boxcar he leans over to one of his men; "Take special care of these two, I have special plans for them...No one else touches them. Understand..?"

The anxious women sit back and watch as he collects his fees from others on the train. Carmella whispers; "I can see how he can afford such an expensive bracelet. They lie back on their blankets and cover themselves with large black garbage bags to protect them from the intermittent rain. They need to make themselves as secure place as possible for the arduous trip.

Huddled together they are seeing their countryside for the first time. The volcanoes of Mexico are majestic and ominous by contrast. The steel rails slice through the thick mesquite forests that cover the land as far as the eye can see. Occasionally they pass through lush planted green farmland with contrasting snowcapped peaks in the distance. All too often in this country, the measure of one's life is determined by the altitude in which you are born.

Often on long straight runs of the track, it is hard to breathe, as the diesel engine exhaust fumes waft over the train. Most migrant travelers are used to the hard life and just cover their faces for this brief inconvenience.

Angelina beams at two young children galloping on a scrawny horse, evidently racing the train. The audacious slender bronzed boy comically flaunts his father's oversized boots, with legs too short for the stirrups. To make it even more amusing, his tiny sister is riding behind bareback, hair fluttering wildly, holding on for dear life. Their daring rides produce wild cheers from the usually silent throng. But as quickly as the race started it is now over.

Angelina has plenty of time to fantasize and daydream. She grins at the adjacent dry mesquite field, abundant with wild rabbits; *"With my bow and a few arrows there is a lot of meat to hunt."* Often a scrawny rabbit or dove taken by a well-placed arrow was all the meat they had.

Carmella did keep some chickens however until recently they had no money for feed, so they lay very few eggs. The hawks and coyotes ate more chicken than they did. She would joke; "If they could make soup from the feathers the hawks left behind, they could eat very well."

Their journey will take a few days to get to the US border. Every three or four hours the train would stop near a convenient, cool stream. Travelers were allowed to climb down to refresh and relieve themselves. They only had a few minutes, so they had to make the most of it. Always, Manuel was watching.

Peddlers with festively painted donkey carts are routinely positioned at these unscheduled stops. They would throw up bottles of water and small bags of fruit to those willing to pay. It was understood that the coyote would bribe the conductors to ensure these brief respites. No one would discuss this for fear of being thrown off the train. And, on occasion, riders would spot a decomposed corpse only a few yards from the tracks with coyotes scurrying into the brush. A constant reminder of the full price some must pay for the journey. Nonetheless, for most, the rewards of this demanding trip are worth the risk.

Carmela and Angelina are traveling to Oklahoma to find Uncle Carlos. Carmela's brother has promised to give them a dry bed, food and help to find work. That is far more than what they are leaving behind. It is not Carmella's life but Angelina's future she is safeguarding. Local town thugs have had their eye on Angelina for several months. Her budding young figure and inherited sultry gait makes her an attractive candidate for the local whore house. The women have nothing, not money nor standing nor a man, to fight off the gang. Time is not on her side at home or in America. They need to get across the border before there are any changes to the current immigration laws, enabling them to cross the border and stay. They understand that there will be increased border security and possible impenetrable barriers restricting entry. She would rather they both die escaping the hellhole than surrender to that fate.

The next morning at another planned stop, several additional travelers jump onto the train. Every stop brings more and more people pursuing the same destination. Sitting on their precarious perch, Carmella clutches her daughter; *"How many more people do they intend to fit? There is no more room."*

They can hear from several cars away from Manuel's screams; "Come on people move closer together. Do not take up so much room." They see some of Manuel's men are throwing luggage off the train to make more room for riders.

The train company has tried several times by multiple means to thwart these illegal travelers. However, they have found over the years it is easier to just let them sit undisturbed and ride at their own risk. All the travelers understand and accept most of those conditions. The few that do not are thrown off.

As they run to catch the slowing train, Rafta and his three men also seek that same northern destination. They have been avoiding large cities where the Mexican Federal Police may be watching for them. They assume that once they are on board, the authorities will do little to restrict their passage. As the four men climb onto the train, they are immediately noticed by Manuel. Once the train lurches and begins to move, Manuel makes his way to the new arrivals. Standing in front of the four men who were much taller than he, Manuel aggressively pushes to the first and begins speaking Spanish. Rafta has given his men strict instructions to speak to no one. He steps in and interjects; "What is it you want?"

Confidently; "What I want, I want to be paid. I see four of you. Are you all together?"

Rafta in a soft non-confrontational voice; "Yes, we are together, how can I help you?"

"What I want, I want to be paid. I told you that already. Are you stupid or something?"

Shrugging his shoulders; "Why should we pay you?"

He nudges in as his men get into Rafta's face; "Because... If you don't pay me now, I will throw your ass off this train. This is my train you're on."

Manuel turns his head asking for more of his men to join him.

Rafta sees some men on the train walking towards their

car the last thing he wishes to do is to arouse any suspicion; "So my friend, how much money do you need to leave us alone?"

Laughing out loud; "How much money do you have... my friend?"

Rafta has brought a considerable amount of cash with him however hidden in money belts, distributed among his men. The last thing he wants is for this man to take all his money and to put his mission in jeopardy. He always carries a few thousand dollars in his pocket. Reaching into his pocket, he looks at Manuel; "So my friend how much do you need to leave us alone?"

"How far are you going...all the way to the border?"

"Yes...yes we are."

"Well, I have bills I have to pay the train company, the conductors, the State Police, Border Patrol...I have to pay for everyone. You think everyone is on this train pays nothing? I have to pay everyone, for everyone on the train has to pay me. You understand how it works?"

As the train slowly moves out, he sees that the State Police are in the station about a mile down the road. He understands his precarious situation and cannot possibly make any commotion; "My men and I did not plan on paying anything to make this ride."

"So where are you four from? How did you get here, did God drop you from the sky?

Wishing to provide a plausible answer to remedy the situation Rafta gently touches his arm; "Look, my friend, we do not have a lot of money between us. I had to pay the boat captain almost everything we had for him to get us off the boat."

"Boat... boat from where?

"We got a boat from South America, a fishing boat. The pirate took almost all our money to just get us ashore, so we really don't have a lot. I would really appreciate your help and believe me, I will take care of you later."

Manuel shrugs his shoulders; "I'm not a greedy man ask everyone around here, I'm the kindest man on this train. But I do have bills to pay so, I have a feeling I will see you again, and I know you will make it right, for now I will take a thousand dollars each. Does that sound fair?

Rafta being the accomplished actor; "While you're not leaving us a lot, I will give you $4,000, and we will leave as friends." He extends his hand in friendship; *"I will remember you. The next time we see each other, we will not be friends."* In doing so, Rafta's man Pedro standing beside him notices the prominent silver turquoise bracelet and just smiles; *"Very nice."*

Rafta has them separate into groups so as not to attract attention. His second in command, Pedro, has moved to the rear of the train. They walk along, wobbling among the other passengers, seeking an open spot on the overcrowded train. As he walks past Carmella and Angelina, he looks down on them and provocatively sneers; *"Oh yes... Look at these two."* The young women sense his gaze and avert their eyes. The two women sit as stealthy rabbits, eyes transfixed straight ahead, seeking invisibility.

As an ISIS fighter in Iraq, Pedro recognizes and is instinctively attracted to their fear. The two men find an open place on the next car not far from the women. Carmella tugs Angelina closer, sensing the unnerving, persistent stare; *"We shall keep our distance from those animals."*

Pedro has not seen a woman nor had sex in months. He studies all the young women on the train as if there were prey, waiting for his chance. Rules of the civilized man do not apply to him. In only a few days, all will reach their destination. In those days, the train needs to make up the time it has lost from picking up so many passengers. The conductor must reach the border by a specific time. He cannot stop. Usually, everyone on the train would have the ability to relieve themselves and wash up every four hours. On this leg of their journey, there is no time to stop, so all must relieve themselves in place. As one can imagine in the sweltering heat, the conditions become disgusting and unbearable. Several people climb down the ladder just to avoid the stench.

Carmela reaches into her bag and pulls out one of the few remaining oranges, bites off some of the skin and hands it to Angelina; "Little one, peel the skin and rub it under your nose. You will smell like the sweet scent of the orange and not the animals that we must travel with."

After two more days of sweltering dry heat, the train reaches its final stop at the border crossing at Nuevo Laredo, Mexico. It is a bustling city where thousands cross each day legally, from Mexico to the US. This is not their plan as it is too risky to cross the border here. Manuel and his men separate all of his passengers into four groups to assist in their crossing of the river. Other travelers leave the train and disperse quickly so as not to be detained by Mexican State Police.

Manuel guides 50 migrants along some winding paths through dense undergrowth to a semi-secluded area along the river. He has made sure that Carmella and Angelina are in his group. Manuel has been doing this for many years and knows this stretch of river is not heavily guarded. Though the river is fast at this location, he has crossed here successfully many times before. Carmella is anxious and clutches Angelina very close.

With the most challenging river crossing ahead the women realize their arduous journey is far from over. Now they must swim across the swift-moving Rio Grande River to Texas, USA. For safe passage, some utilize inner-tubes; some rent a jet ski for a quick one-way trip or some just take their chances and swim into the strong current. The recent heavy rains have made the river treacherous and unpredictable. As river levels are usually lowest this time of year, most travelers plan to wade part way across then swim the rest. Not today.

Manuel finally stops and orders everyone to just spread out quietly in the dense mesquite and rest before the late night crossing. As the sky darkens, Carmella points to the bright lights down the river; "Look, Angel, there is America, our future." After the long, arduous journey the two women need to clean up. For added privacy, they move away from into the denser brush. They roll out their blankets lay back and relax for what they believe is a secure place. There they will rest as they await word from Manuel. "Rest my child...rest."

Rafta and his men rejoin the throng and walk from the rail yard. They see Manuel from a distance and follow discreetly. Rafta has learned of a caravan of thousands of migrants from Central America that will be arriving in a week, traversing several areas of the border. He is lucky since border security is still not at full strength to encounter the multitude of migrants. They must move quickly to identify the best place to cross. Nonetheless, Rafta wishes to settle the score.

They do not have to see Manuel; they can hear his bellowing laugh many yards away. They cautiously weave their way through the dense mesquite bushes measuring the situation. Rafta has looked at the Internet maps, done his research and believes this is the best time and place to cross. However, for now, they must also wait for the right time. They have done nicely so far on their journey north, blending in well with the multitude of migrants. Their only errors to date are the unexpected encounter with the American on the remote Yucatan beach and Manuel. They do not want any additional diversions for their mission.

Pedro and Jose are two of Rafta's original ISIS fighters taken from Mosul. Both are hardened ruthless murderers that have no problem killing for no reason at all. Rafta has instructed them to rest quietly through the night awaiting his return. The two shadow a small group from a distance still listening to Manuel's laughter as he collects his remaining payments. He has come prepared with his money belt around his waist and has taken it off to be filled. He has slung it over his shoulder for easy access. He does not feel there is anyone among this group that will pose any danger to him.

There is only darkness and the whisper of the flowing river. In the bushes, several feet away, Pedro and Jose hear Manuel whispering instructions to a few migrants.

Angelina and her mother Carmella sit at the river edge, trying to rest after their grungy journey. Carmella needs to pee and wades hesitantly into the river. She covers her waist with a towel and squats close to the bank. Looking back over her shoulder she smiles timidly at daughter; "It is okay, you can come in if you need to." Manuel has not forgotten that he must be paid; plus he has had other things on his mind. Often coyotes extract much more than money from the young unescorted women; an unthinkable price to pay to travel to America. He knows the women must be close and prowls through the bushes seeking his booty; "*Where are you my precious, where are you?*" Knowing all the places to hide, Manuel finally comes upon Carmella in the moonlight, squatting in the river. Looking over her shoulder she notices Manuel gawking at her glistening exposed legs.

She angrily barks out; "Go someplace else, you filthy animal."

Snarling, Manuel lunges out from behind the bushes and grabs Angelina by her long dark hair; "Come here ladies I must be paid and you will pay me now."

Angelina's head is jerked back as he grabs her hair. She screams out in pain as Carmella yells; "Leave her alone, get away you animal." Manuel's bellowing laughter is blended in the night with the screams of the two young women. Angelina's screeches out very loudly and are heard by Pedro and Jose. Manuel pushes Angelina down onto the towel and sits on top of her.

He knows that none of the other migrants will come to help as he gropes at the young girl; *"Oh yes little one, what do we have here?"*

Carmella rushes up and jumps upon Manuel's back. She begins slapping him about the head and face; "Get off her you animal, get off her."

Manuel being much larger and used to feigned strikes, laughs as his hat and money belt fall onto the towel. He is entertained by her hapless blows; "Ha, Ha... You hit like little girls."

Pedro and Jose jump up and dart to the sound of screaming women. Within just seconds they find a partially nude woman struggling with Manuel. Neither has seen a woman in months and are easily aroused, however, they do recognize Manuel. Pedro, a huge man, smiles and thrusts his arm around Manuel's neck and pulls him up off Angelina. Both women sit on the outstretched towels and huddled together.

Manuel tries to get loose, kicking and flailing his arms; "Let loose of me hombre, or you will be in a lot of trouble." Stunned by his unknown attacker, Manuel is quickly thrown to the ground, thrust face pushed down into the sand. Instinctively, Pedro withdraws his sharp knife, pulls Manuel's head back and in one efficient motion, effortlessly glides the blade across his throat. Pedro has also had much practice in Iraq perfecting his technique.

As Pedro stands, Manuel grabs his throat and struggles to his knees. In an attempt to seek help Manuel staggers to his feet, turns and takes a few steps to the river. Within a few seconds, he splashes face down in the river. Manuel lies unconscious bleeding out into the river. Pedro wades into the river to ensure his work is complete. As he straddles over Manuel, he notices the ornate silver turquoise wristband shining in the moonlight. Without hesitation he reaches down, pulls it off and puts it on his hand; *"Very nice indeed. It fits perfectly."* As Pedro rifles through his pockets, $50 and $100 bills pop out, scatter and float down the river. He is unconcerned.

Watching from just a few feet away the women cling together trembling, horrified at what they just witnessed. Angelina quivering; "Mama, Mama, My God what just happened?"

Pedro excited at the blood-sport laughs realizing his trophy hunt is not over. He has not altered his primitive plunder credo and considers these defenseless Christian women as just spoils of war. However, unlike their ISIS campaigns, they cannot take these women as captives. The women scramble across the sand, but Jose blocks their escape. They screech in fright to flee this nightmarish place. The two men tower over the trembling women, hiding the midnight stars. Within moments of Manuel's foiled attack, the women's emotions have morphed from relief to utter horror, sensing the men's intent.

Carmella and Angelina are thrown on their backs and

viciously slapped across their faces until they no longer resist; "No! Please don't, please don't."

Pedro slowly brings his finger quickly to his lips to demand silence; "Shhh."

Carmella, unwilling to accept their fate, struggles violently and angrily slaps Pedro; "Get off me you fucking animal."

To no avail, the slight-framed Carmella is held down with a firm hand pressing firmly into her throat. Her screams are muffled as she gasps for air. In the moonlit shadows she pounds the sand reaching for her daughter. Angelina turns to her mother and can only see a hand with the prominent silver turquoise bracelet thrusting into her mother's slender neck.

The fragile Angelina is ignorant about the attacker's sexual intent as she lays petrified and submissive. Excitedly Jose grunts and rips open her thin shirt exposing her breasts, then pulls off her jeans.

Whimpering; "Mama, Mama," she is thrown around like a splayed, rag doll. As he groans mercilessly on top of her naked body, she is unfamiliar with the incredibly sharp pain. He moans like an animal accentuating his desire. She is too young, and it is too dark for her to understand the purpose of this vicious attack. The pain inside her is incredible, and all she can do is bite her lip to mask her muffled screams.

Carmella tries to see Angelina but with the man pressing down on her neck, she cannot. In an anxious attempt to pull down his trousers Pedro stands and releases his hand from Carmella's neck. He then bends down over to undo his zipper. Carmella reaches for anything in the darkness and finds the money belt in the sand. One last furious attempt the incredibly strong Carmella swings it across Pedro's face; **"No!"** The weight of the compacted money and gold coins is quite forceful.

Stunned he sits back on his heels, shakes his head and just grunts; "Rrrrrr." As he leans forward upright atop Carmella, furiously looks down and withdraws his knife from its sheath. Without hesitation, quickly slashes the side of her neck.

She emits a tormented scream only heard only by Angelina. Carmella grabs her neck in a futile attempt to stop the bleeding. Pedro now has a obedient woman beneath him and finishes the inhumane rape. After a few minutes, the horror is over for both women, Carmella froze in shock, bleeding.

Pedro and Jose have completed their vile attacks. Pedro angrily looks down at the money belt recognizes it and flings it over his shoulder. Without even looking back, they creep through the dense mesquite, to find Rafta.

Angelina quickly tears her blouse and tries to bandage her mother's bleeding throat; "Mama... Mama."

As Carmella lays in shock, motionless she gazes overhead to the full moon, murmuring; "My God, my God my please forgive me my sins and look over my beautiful little Angelina." Understanding her limited time Carmella pulls her daughter close and whispers; "Listen to me child there is not much time... pay attention. There is a large Catholic Church, St. Michael, just across the river in Laredo. Find the tallest building with the cross. Swim across the river and go to the church for sanctuary. The nuns there will care for you. Look in the bag and find money and Uncle Carlos telephone number. Ask the nuns to call that number and contact Uncle Carlos. Stay there until he comes, you.... will be safe with them,... you will be safe with them." Holding the beautiful girls face in her hands; "You must go with Uncle Carlos, you will be safe with him, he is my brother and he is now your family. Promise me you will do this. **Promise me!"**

Angelina's trembling hands tries to cover her half-naked body with the blanket; "Yes Mama I understand... I promise." Angelina has bled out chickens on their farm and recognizes the severity of her mother's wound. She reaches into the small fabric pouch and withdraws the role of money and Uncle Carlos' phone number. The makeshift bandage cannot abate the bleeding. As Carmella's life slowly ebbs away, she draws her daughter close and kisses her face, eyes, and mouth for one last time. Carmella lies lifeless, Angelina sobs uncontrollably.

As time passes, with her head pressed to her mother's chest she can no longer hear her heart beating. She shakes her mother in one last time futile attempt to awaken her; "*Mama, Mama!*"

As the moon sinks below the horizon, Angelina refuses to leave her mother's side. The midnight sky slowly displays its morning colors, Angelina hears distant voices of men yelling and boat engines rumbling along the river. The trauma of the evening has taking an unthinkable human toll. With all that has happened, she barely has the strength to slip on her tattered clothes. She recalls her mother's dying wish; "*Seek out Uncle*

Carlos," in horror at the unknown.

Nonetheless, she is petrified that the men might return to kill her too and trembles, clinging to her mother. She is alone, very alone for the first time in her life. Carmella was the only person Angelina has ever really known, and now she is gone; *"What shall I do? What shall I do?"*

In the pastel light of morning, she hears migrants making their way across the river. Now that Manuel is dead his men have scattered, offering no aid to the migrants. All the travelers must fend for themselves. Dozens of people scurry to the river bank to cross together. Several cling to inner tubes or use makeshift rafts.

Living in the dusty Mexican hill country, Angelina never learned to swim. She does recall playing with her mother in the stream a mile from the house. They would tie water jugs together with a rope to form makeshift water wings. As migrant garbage is strewn everywhere, she quickly finds two empty water jugs along with a discarded belt and ties them together. This will be more than enough to keep her afloat.

She waits quietly behind mesquite, as she hears the sound of another large boat approaching. She has been told that if the Mexican border patrol stops you from crossing, they will send you back to your hometown; *"Her mother told her that was a fate worse than death."* She sits quivering, knees to her chest, reluctant to leave her mother. Downriver the Mexican police have found the body of a man floating, his throat slashed. They recognize Manuel and soon realize they will not be paid tonight.

They will aggressively question other travelers seeking to identify the killer.

She recalls the stories her mother told and her dream to go north to her brother Carlos. Angelina quietly collects her meager belongings and ties them to her belt. For one last time, she gently kisses her mother on her lips and covers her naked body with the towel. Sobbing uncontrollably, she seizes the strap across her chest, water jugs dangling and cautiously inches into the river. The Mexican police are getting too close. As she bobs off, Angelina looks back one last time at the disappearing river bank. The Mexican State Police are close. She hears the roar of the US border patrol boat as it moves to intercept a large group of migrants that have crossed to the US side of the river; *"I must sit still and be silent. Maybe they will not notice me."* In the distance he sees several intercepted migrants shivering on the bank.

A US border patrol agent sits indifferently, arms crossed in his patrol boat, peering down the river. Knowing that he cannot leave those in his custody, he notices two slender arms thrashing about. With radio microphone to his mouth, he watches in amazement at a young girl's frantic attempt to swim to shore. Though she is several hundred feet downriver, he is undecided what to do; *"Look at this tiny creature frantically trying to reach shore. There is no one to help her now, except for God."* A broad smile erupts across his face as he sees an exhausted little girl staggers out of the river; *"If she worked that hard on her own to make it to shore, who am I to stop her?"*

The Mexican police soon come upon the all too familiar crime scene of another unidentified young woman, raped and murdered along the bank. Unfortunately, this scene is repeated almost daily as the frantic migrants try to cross for a better life.

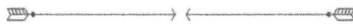

Sr. Carolyn is a diminutive, fragile nun on the slow side of her 80's. Every day she hobbles from the convent to St. Michael's Church to prepare the altar for the 6:00AM mass; today, walking with her is a 17-year-old novitiate.

Rafta and his men had already crossed the river just before first light, paying a handsome toll for a few rented jet-skis. They darted across the river in a matter of seconds to a waiting van. As Rafta stands on the riverbank walking to the white panel van; *"That was a lot easier than I thought it would be. These Americans all boast of their national security, but they leave the back door wide open."* They stayed hidden for a few hours on a residential street, waiting for traffic begin to move.

When the sisters walk at that time of the morning, there usually is not too much traffic. Unfortunately, today a van rolls up beside them with the passenger window rolled down. Pedro sits in the passenger seat in awe of his surroundings. Mosul was nothing like this. Enthused, he cannot pass up an opportunity to torment more innocent women, especially those that are obviously Christian. As the van passes, he makes eye contact with the nuns, as he sticks out his tongue in a vile gesture to the novitiate. He then slides his finger across his throat in an apparent grotesque manner; *"I will pass you by today ladies; but tomorrow, who knows what fate may bring."*

Sr. Carolyn has never seen such loathsome behavior, and

while they appear Hispanic, in her heart, she knows they are not. Not wishing to give them the satisfaction she walks undaunted; "Sister, don't look at them. *Satan, pass me by today, I have souls to attend to.*" It distresses her that such evil men are so close; *"But as sure as I am to receive the body and blood of our Lord of Jesus Christ this day, I am sure that he will strike them down."*

A few hours after wading out of the river, Angelina sits under some bushes, waiting for her clothes to dry. With the early morning heat that does not take long. She hears a few Hispanics walking nearby, so she jumps out and asks for directions to the Saint Michael's Church in Laredo. It requires her to walk a few minutes barefoot, until she sees the shining gold cross of the church. Physically traumatized and exhausted, she pushes open the front doors of the church. It is not long before a priest escorts her to the kitchen to meet Sr. Carolyn. Sr. Carolyn has attended to the sick and displaced for many years. As Angelina recounts her harrowing trip, rape, and the horrific death of her mother, Sr. Carolyn recalls only a few hours earlier the evil men in the van traveling to the highway.

While known only to a devout few, Sr. Carolyn is recognized as a spiritualist, often manifesting clairvoyance. After a hearty breakfast and a change of clothes, she brings Angelina to the side chapel for prayer. She consoles the shivering young girl; "Come child come here and pray with me. God will help you." They kneel below a large statue of St. Michael the Archangel. As they pray quietly, Sr. Carolyn closes her eyes and has a vision; *"Of a young girl not yet out of harm's way. She will be forced to confront satanic evil again in the not too distant future."*

Recognizing the fragility of the child she attempts to craft a prayer to help her overcome her foreshadowed ordeals. With one hand firmly on Angelina's head, and the other beckoning, she loudly extols St. Michael; "He shall defend thee under his wings, and thou shalt be safe in battle behind his shield. Thou shall not be afraid of any terror by night; nor for the arrow that flieth by day. He will empower thee to deliver Satan back into his fiery pit."

Two days later, before Angelina leaves the church, Sr. Carolyn sits next to Angelina, offering final comforting words and a prayer. In her hand is a thin silver chain with a 3 inch elegant silver crucifix. With her visions of what may come, she gently places it around her neck, recalling the prayer that Angelina would somehow find the strength to conquer evil.

Uncle Carlos has driven for several hours and immediately clutches Angelina and embraces her. Sr. Carolyn tiptoes toward Uncle Carlos and whispers of the ordeal that the child had survived. It will take some time for her to overcome the trauma of her rape and her mother's gruesome murder. He has brought her several changes in new clothes.

As she sleeps in the back seat, he wraps her in a large comfortable blanket; "La Niña, you will live in a beautiful house with me, overlooking lush green pastures. I have a good job, and it is a good life. There we will live, and I promise to *always* love you as my own child." While Uncle Carlos' words should be somewhat comforting, Angelina still recalls the horrific loss of her mother and sobs quietly.

It is not long before all are on the interstate highway, headed north to Oklahoma, where they plan to work as undocumented migrants, performing light construction, farming, and landscaping. Rafta must now do his research to locate his targets, the Clouds. The others do not speak any English and must direct all questions to Rafta. After 13 hours of driving the four men have arrived at a remote, dilapidated apartment complex. It is far outside Oklahoma City where they live unnoticed, along with several other migrant families. Their long sharp gardening knives will suffice as weapons for now. Rafta will have plenty of time to observe, prepare and obtain any necessary weapons. Like predatory snakes, they will sit patiently waiting for the appropriate time to strike.

CHAPTER 5
May 2017 -- The Old Watering Hole

After a long and unproductive turkey hunt, John, Daniel, and Grandpa Cloud get to their old watering hole on the outskirts of town. It's been a few months since Col. Cloud's discharge, and he has let his hair grow long and sports a scraggly beard. Even his old friends don't recognize him. Occasionally he cleans up but only when absolutely necessary. John Cloud's condition hasn't improved significantly. His nightmares and flashbacks persist. On most days, he stays secluded, sitting beneath a large cottonwood, behind his mirrored sunglasses, reading. He replays over and over, what he could have done differently to save more servicemen's lives? Once in a while he can have a meaningful conversation but most of the time he sits silent. He enjoys the time he shares with his father and son, realizing that Daniel will be heading to Iraq soon. He often shares his battlefield knowledge with Daniel, however, without the gruesome details.

Grandpa does not understand why his son is so withdrawn. Is it the separation from Crystal, boredom after his military separation, or just drinking too much of Grandpa's moonshine? His symptoms are neither apparent nor consistent; but something is definitely wrong. Since Cloud never shared his traumatic military experiences or the reasons for visiting the VA clinic, his family has no way of knowing he has PTSD.

The rustic restaurant is a throwback to the 1960s, with sticky wood tables, uncomfortable small chairs, and dim lights. But they do have oversized high-back booths. A great venue where the beer is always cold, the pulled pork sandwiches are spicy, and your entire meal arriving in a red plastic mesh basket.

All three men are still clad in their camo outfits, with traces of face paint proudly showing. Other patrons are used to it. Having been up since 4:00am, they are just too exhausted to wash and change. As Grandpa scans the room, he sees Carlos and his newly arrived niece Angelina, waving from a rear booth. Carlos has known the Cloud family for several years and has been working for them as a tenant farmer, doing everything that needs to be done. The farm has been in the Cloud family for almost 100 years. It is too small for anyone wanting to make a living, but just large enough to keep. Any wheat that is grown is enough to pay the upkeep and taxes and, that's about it. As Grandpa walks to the rear booth, Carlos stands and guides Carlos to the front door to speak outside. As they go outside, Grandpa sees that the tarp covering his moonshine stash has come undone, exposing several shiny new mason jars. As Carlos ties down the tarp Grandpa cannot resist getting in one more sip; "This batch we made is probably our best recipe ever, some **really** good stuff. "

After accepting a sip, Carlos' face becomes uncharacteristically somber as he must ask a favor from Grandpa; "Señor Grandpa, my niece Angelina traveled across the border a few months ago, but her mother Carmella did not." He explains in gruesome detail how Carmella was murdered by two unknown assailants in Mexico; "Angelina tells me that she has missed her last two periods and is now getting upset stomachs and is nauseous. I am very worried that she is now pregnant. The only sex she ever had was when the animal raped her. So, I went to the Walgreens and bought a pregnancy kit, and it shows... well, she is with child." Hands beckoning and voice shaking; "Grandpa, as she is a newly arrived with no papers, if we go to a hospital in a few months to deliver the baby they may take them from me. I am her only family. Grandpa, please what should I do? What should I do? I trust you Señor and need your help."

Carlos explains that his sister Carmella had great difficulty and almost died delivering Angelina due to her slender frame and narrow hips. Angelina is built just like her mother and is much younger than her mother when she gave birth. After her ordeal, she has become deeply religious and seeks guidance; "As she is not a full-grown woman delivering a baby might kill her. She needs help; however, she must remain with *me*, protected. You understand?"

Grandpa Cloud hearing the harrowing story, scratches his head. He knows that his granddaughter, Joy, runs a women's clinic in Oklahoma City: "Come on by the cabin tomorrow, and I will give you her address and her telephone number. Tell her I sent you. She will take care of everything. Okay? I promise my friend, it'll be okay."

As Grandpa tries to tie back down the truck tarp, a local troublemaker, Johnny Turner, noisily pulls up with a few of his buddies in his old dusty flatbed. As he slams the squeaky truck door, he turns and intentionally bumps shoulders with Carlos; "Watch where ya goin... beaner."

Grandpa, instantly recognizing his hostility, puts himself between the two; "Sheitt, I haven't heard that term in 50 years. Not since ya grandma passed."

The grungy Turner looks around, feeling that he may have the upper hand; "Y'all talking to me old man? Ya don't want any part of dis."

Looking down and spitting tobacco on Johnny's clay-caked boots; "You know kid you're like a bad fart in an elevator. Nobody wants to be around you. Keep it up, and I'll give you more than ya can handle... you little dip-shit."

Jonny's head lurches back at the unexpected tongue lashing; "...What?"

Daniel noticing the ruckus outside, does not want to include his father; "Dad I got to go outside for a second, why don't you find us a quiet booth." As Daniel walks out the door, he sees Johnny reaching beneath the tarp as he snatches one of the jars; "Well, well... what do we have here?"

Daniel walks up confidently, pries the jar out of his hand and places it back into the crate. He gruffly flips the tarp back over; "Excuse me...exactly what are you looking for ace?"

Johnny leans in and starts aggressively poking Carlos' chest; "I don't like these God-damn wetbacks takin all the jobs from us Americans."

Grandpa nudges his way in; "Exactly whose job is he stealing?"

Johnny leans into Grandpa; "They've been stealing all our factory jobs, and I'm tired of it."

As he thrusts his finger assertively into Grandpa's chest, Daniel firmly grasps his hand and pulls his fingers backward, triggering Johnny to scream; "What da fuck ... let go of me.... Le me go man!"

Daniel pushes him away and releases his fingers. In a slow and deliberate voice pointing at Turner's face; "Boys, I really don't think you have any business here. Why don't you just **move on?**"

Johnny anxiously shakes his cramped hand, again points at Carlos; "This ain't the end of dis, you hear me." He then stomps down the street looking back, grumbling to his friends.

Daniel just stands and watches as Grandpa walks into the restaurant reassuring Carlos; "Come on buddy. Let's go in and get a cold one. I'll buy." Grandpa finds Cloud standing in front of a large circular booth and invites Carlos and Angelina to sit with them. Grandpa pulls John and Daniel aside; "Man I can't tell you the whole story of what happened to this little girl, but it is really a horror show. She was raped and is in a lot of trouble. She's going to need a bunch of help, but we'll talk about it later. Okay?" All five slide into the booth.

The diminutive Angelina is very shy, as she sits next to tall handsome Daniel. Nervously she looks up at him with a slight grin. With an amazing smile in broken English; "Why are your faces painted... and why do you dress funny? Are you natives?"

Daniel tongue-tied; "Why yes, I am or shall I say, yes we are. Part native anyway. We dress like this when we hunt, so we don't scare away the game.

Angelina with chin up, wide-eyed smiling; "I hunted rabbits near our farm in Mexico. I never needed any funny clothes or makeup. And...I always came home with game. You must stand perfectly still and... just don't miss."

Daniel amused, nods; "So *you* know how to shoot a bow."

Angelina was a really good hunter in Mexico, even with her primitive, homemade bow and arrow; "At Uncle Carlos' farm... where we live... I can look across his field and see much game. Hundreds of dove, but they are hard to kill in an open field. So, I hunt beneath the shade trees; that's where the rabbits like to rest in the heat of the day. Across the big field from Carlos' house is a beautiful place to hunt, a small field where he plants beans and corn to attract game. I have seen many, but I usually get a rabbit there anytime I want. But I really don't need to, not so much now... since Uncle Carlos buys all the food, we need. But *I* do the cooking."

Carlos looks around the table with a slight grimace, awkward that it is not really his house but Grandpa's house and food plot she is describing.

Daniel with a wink to Carlos; "That's very impressive young lady."

All the men gaze in amazement at this beautiful shining young girl, who has seen so much tragedy and is showing such strength.

Daniel smiling down on Angelina; "You know there is great hunting, especially in the thick undergrowth around creek bottoms. The animals always come in early morning and late evening to drink." Daniel pauses then looks at John and Grandpa. As he amusingly shakes his head, he slides out of the booth to the truck. Moments later, returns with a new Bowflex compound bow and two quivers of target and hunting arrows. He bought the $600 bow for precision shooting just a few months ago. As he places it gently on the table in front of Angelina; "Have you ever seen a bow like this?"

She nervously shakes her head; "No Señor, that looks funny and very complicated."

Daniel nudges it toward her; "Well, you can borrow it...until I come back. I'll be out of town for a few months, and I would like for it to get some use. I think you will make good use of it. What do you think?"

Cloud whispers to Carlos; "Daniel is being deployed to Iraq as an Army advisor, to train the Iraqi troops in shooting. With all the recent trouble with ISIS, this President decided it was finally time to do something. Fortunately, no combat duty, just as a trainer."

Daniel with his hand on the bow; "Grandpa Cloud can adjust the bow for you and show you how it works." Oh yes, only use these target arrows for practice. If you are to hunt for game use the razor arrows with the bright red tips. Be very, very careful, they are razor sharp.

Angelina points inquisitively; "What is that red tip on the

end."

Daniel touching the nock; "The red tip nock is designed to light up once fired so you can easily find your game in the dark or... the arrow if you miss."

She is awestruck by such a generous gift from the handsome stranger, pulls him over and throws her arms around his neck in appreciation; "Thank you Señor, thank you. I'll take care of it for you and make good use of it too."

After lunch they leave the pub. In typical Oklahoma fashion, the sky turns dark quickly and begins to downpour. In late spring, these rapidly developing storms produce severe thunderheads with an occasional tornado warning. Daniel, seeing that Angelina is only wearing a light T-shirt, runs to his pickup and pulls his old army reserve camo jacket from the backseat. He places it gently over her shoulders, his name CLOUD prominently stenciled on the front, with a silver winged paratrooper insignia pinned on the lapel; "Here you go little one, this will keep you safe and dry."

At first, she is embarrassed by the oversized jacket and tries to pull it off, but Daniel insists; "No you hold on to this for me. I won't need this where I am ongoing."

Angelina blushes then briskly slides her tiny arms into the enormous sleeves. With fingertips barely poking out the sleeves she crosses her arms, looks down and puts her hand over the CLOUD nametag; "Gracias Señor Cloud, muchas gracias."

Grandpa puts his hand on Carlos' shoulder; "My friend, it's a long walk in the heat and I wouldn't want you to make the trip needlessly. I'll keep my radio on my belt, plus I always have my scanner on. Just keep calling me every 10 minutes or so. If I hear any turkey or see deer, I'll let you know when it's good to walk over.

Carlos nods; "Okay Grandpa."

Daniel still grinning at Angelina; "Carlos, I'll be sleeping at the cabin tonight and driving back to OKC tomorrow morning. I wouldn't mind dropping Angelina off at the clinic...it's on my way. I planned to see Joy before I left for overseas, anyway, and I can introduce her to my sister Joy."

"Thank you, Señor Daniel, Angelina, and I really appreciate your generosity."

The next morning, Joy Cloud tiptoes through shattered glass trying to gauge the condition of the building; *"God dammit... this is ridiculous."* A severe thunderstorm came through last night, throwing debris and shattering the double glass doors of the Oklahoma City Woman's Outreach Clinic. A few months earlier, Joy Cloud was appointed to the interim director position, upon abrupt resignation of her boss. As a brassy 23-year-old, with only 18 months working experience at the clinic, Joy soon realizes she's in way over her head. Though she has a lot more to learn, her high energy and boldness will make her an ideal interim director. Her duties are to manage all operating functions. She understands that she must project confidence and professionalism to the public, which includes the government and the media.

To complicate things further, in the past few days, anti-abortion demonstrators have been standing across the street. The job is stressful enough, without dealing with activists and the accompanying media. This is probably the reason why her predecessor resigned abruptly; *"Too much bullshit."* Nonetheless, Joy must toughen up and get things under control. She really wants this job and empathizes with these young women. Her sympathies may have been stoked by her sorority house experience years earlier. Since that incident, she has grown distrustful of most men and has yet to find a suitable male companion. Also, because of her responsibilities, she has built an almost impenetrable façade.

First thing this morning, Joy must figure out who will fix the shattered front doors. Several areas of the city are still without power from the storm. With the front door shattered, the chants from the tireless anti-abortion demonstrators are heard inside the clinic. She wasn't really prepared to supervise any cleanup this morning and had dressed for the scheduled TV interview. With her brand-new high heel shoes, she steps shakily around the splintered floor.

To offer support, she is followed by her brother Daniel and timid Angelina. Daniel walks with his arm around Angelina's, offering encouragement; "Come on Angelina come on in... it's okay. Trust me, my sister Joy will take care of you." Daniel is dressed in Army fatigues, making a striking figure. Once he delivers Angelina, he has to go back to the apartment to finish packing for his pending deployment. With power still out,

Joy sits and prepares for her next patient, Angelina. Self-conscious because of her broken English, Angelina is usually very quiet. They sit in the lobby with no overhead lights as she shivers, recalling what happened to her mother only months earlier.

Joy looks to Daniel and points to the street; "Do they have any idea what we are dealing with every day, *any* idea at all?"

With her arm comforting Angelina, she guides the tiny girl to an examination room, offering reassurance; "Come with me honey, we will take care of you. I promise. Sit up here for a little while. The doctor will be here in a few minutes, and she will explain everything. Okay, honey?"

Shivering not knowing what to expect, the young girl sits with her legs dangling off the exam table, clutching her silver crucifix. Sr. Carolyn had instructed her that she should always call upon God for guidance and strength; *"Oh God please help me I am so scared."*

Joy walks with Daniel back outside to greet the arriving TV camera crew. She has no experience with the public or media and has only watched her predecessor from a distance. She has been given instructions by the Midwest regional office on how to handle herself and on what to say. "Daniel, I'll catch you later. I need to make a statement on TV news. Okay."

Being her dutiful brother; "I'll come out and stand beside you. Is that all right?" They walk to the clinic's front lawn sign. Daniel stands next to his sister, proud and straight, exuding confidence with his stenciled name tag "CLOUD" shown prominently.

Today the MCOKC television news crew is filming. While there is enormous storm damage throughout the city, fortunately, no fatalities were reported. So, the home office decided to dispatch the TV crew to the clinic. Elouise Lion is the new face for the roaming MCOKC TV station. Elouise is aspiring to make a big impression in her new job. Her self-assured, confident style is entirely different. Her predecessor's interviews were getting very stale. So, to attract the new viewership the station decided to project energy, not empathy, even bordering on confrontation.

As Elouise strides confidently, with the microphone in hand, almost projecting it as a weapon, she looks down at Joy and squints; "Say, honey, do I know you?"

Joy having an excellent memory; "I think so. You graduated OU a couple years ago...Communications School, if I recall?"

Leaning over surprised, tilting her head; "Why yes honey. Didn't y'all live in the... Alpha Pi House just a couple of doors down." With a faux smile; "Y'all ready?... Smile into the camera...honey." To gain viewer attention, she thrusts a microphone to Joy's face; "Bringing you today's top news we are here at the Oklahoma City Women's clinic. With us today is Ms. Joy Cloud, interim director. Good morning Ms. Cloud. We see you are trying to keep the clinic open, despite power outage and violent protests."

Joy, appearing surprised; "Yes...Yes, we are here to offer

health services to women that would otherwise have none."

Elouise persisting; "Is it true that a brick was thrown in an attempt to restrict clinic access.

Joy eyebrows compressed, perplexed; "We're... not sure of the cause but... there was a lot of storm damage last night."

"Will you stay open today?"

"Yes... That's our plan."

Elouise leaning to the camera; "There you have it. The Oklahoma City Women's Clinic will remain open... despite the act of some vandals. Elouise Lion MSOKC News."

She has her cameraman scan the small crowd focusing in on anti-abortion signs, to fill her growing digital library; "Well, thank ya darlin'...that was great."

Joy looks annoyingly; "Are we done?... **That's it?**"

Elouise flippantly; "Why yes hon, you're all done here."

The engine hadn't even cooled in the TV van, when they started it back up to go to cover their next story.

Looking at Daniel, Joy shakes her head dejectedly; "One thing I did learn from my boss is that you can never fight the person with the microphone, because no matter what, no matter what... they always get the last word." Throwing her arms around her brother's neck; "You don't have to stay. I've got this covered, and I'll take care of Angelina too. I have Carlos's phone number and will call him once we are done. You take care bro. I love ya. "

The small group of pro-life protesters had arrived just moments before the TV crew. Watching from behind a police tape line is an elderly nun and four senior citizens, shake their heads in disbelief; "Brick, what brick? I just got rotator cuff surgery." Everyone can see the large tree branch jutting out from the shattered front doors.

That evening, in his small apartment, Mohammed Rafta is scanning TV channels watching local news. After several weeks of trying to locate Col. John Cloud he has not been successful. Cloud is not a common name in the Oklahoma City area. Rafta has been looking through old phone listings; however, since Crystal has moved, he cannot find her new address.

Rafta then gets a glimpse of the scrollbar below the screen that summarizes the story. He sees that a woman by the name of Joy Cloud is giving an interview. Rafta pauses and scrolls back and also sees a man in uniform standing beside the young woman. He walks up to the TV screen, leans over squints to see the name CLOUD stenciled on the young man's uniform. Writing feverishly, he notes the military arm patch. It is a US Army uniform, and it doesn't take him long to search Google to find the army unit where this young man is serving in. He then finds on Twitter that the young man's army reserve unit has been called up and is being deployed back to Andar Airbase within days, to train the Iraqi army to fight ISIS.

Smiling scornfully; *"Finally, now I've got two of them."* Looking up sternly he points; "Jose, I want you to go to that clinic, only bring a knife, just a knife and kill that girl."

Barely lifting his face from his chicken sandwich lunch; "What..?"

Agitated; "Stop feeding your face, look at her. Pay attention... look at her. See her face, that girl, the tiny one with the red hair. Only *that* girl. I want you to cut off her head and leave a message. Here is the address for that Clinic. Go there and wait until she is alone and do not get caught. If you fail, I will kill you myself. **Understand!**"

Later that morning, Jason Moore an Oklahoma City police detective strides up to the four demonstrators outside the clinic. A minute or so later after chatting with an elderly nun, gently; "Remember, to stay behind the police tape, OK."

He walks through the shattered front doors, gun and shiny badge displayed prominently on his belt. The slender 6'-3" young man strides confidently through the lobby as the shattered glass crackles under his feet. He moves his sunglasses off his nose atop his short-cropped blonde hair. Not wishing to disturb anyone, he just stands in the lobby waiting for someone to meet him.

Detective Moore is a new hire for the Oklahoma City Police Department. His respectful manner blends well with others in the department. After graduating from the University of Texas, he immediately joined the Dallas Police Department. However, after serving a few years, he realized that there was little chance for advancement and decided to apply for a position in Oklahoma City. With his high test scores, an impressive record and college minor in Forensics Sciences, he was quickly hired.

As he stands and looks about; "Is everyone all right here?" The diminutive Joy Cloud walks up to him quickly and glares angrily; "What the hell do you think? And, where is the police protection that was promised? Your department has known about these demonstrators for days, and these people have been protesting nonstop and, and,... these young women need unobstructed access to the clinic and... undisturbed treatment. "

Jason sensing her agitation tries to calm her down; "And, whom might you be miss?"

Recognizing his placation, Joy stiffens up; "I'm the Director for **this** clinic."

Softly; "Sorry, I didn't get your name miss."

Walking up close, looking almost straight up; "Joy... Joy Cloud"

Jason maintaining his composure; "Well Miss Cloud I..."

Quickly interrupting; "That's **Msss** Cloud."

In a calm, deliberate, voice; "I see Msss. Cloud. The

Oklahoma City Police department and just about all other law enforcement agencies from surrounding towns have been extremely busy attending to hundreds of residents, displaced due to the line of tornados that blew through the city last night. The entire department is pulling 24/7 duty until further notice. We just don't have enough officers to cover routine disturbance calls, at this time."

Head darting, unruly red hair vibrating; "Routine disturbance calls. This is far from a routine disturbance. That is **not** an acceptable answer."

Realizing his efforts to calm her are in vain; "Well my name is Detective Jason Moore and Msss. Cloud, I am sorry, but that is the only answer I can give right now. I will call the dispatcher and ask if they can free up a patrol car to ensure your protection. Not that I think you really need it but... I'll stay here until one arrives."

This is the first time since she has been given responsibility to run the clinic that she has really had to make any decisions. Joy is unusually anxious and is unaccustomed to dealing with people. She tries to muster strength from a quote heard at a women's empowerment seminar; "*I shall not be defined by what is between my legs, I will be defined by what is between my ears.*" She mumbles it over and over as she walks back and forth through the darkened lobby.

Joy irritated, scurries back to Angelina, who is still patiently sitting at in the nearby exam room. Closing the door behind her, Joy sits with Angelina for a few minutes, until the doctor finally arrives. Rubbing her shoulders; "Honey I have to go out for a few hours, but I will come back to see you, I promise. Until then, could you stay here please, the doctor and the nurse will take care of you. Your uncle Carlos will be coming by later this afternoon to pick you up. Okay?"

Angelina is left sitting there on the exam table, the attending nurse offering her some comfort.

A few minutes later Joy darts past Detective Moore; "I have an appointment that I have to attend. I hope you'll stay to provide the necessary police protection…... Thanks." She then tiptoes back across the glass-strewn lobby floor.

Jason observes the arriving squad car; *"Finally, now I can get out here."* As he ambles out the door, he sees Joy from a distance.

Joy walks just a few yards to the adjacent employee parking area. She has occupied the first parking spot labeled Director for the past few weeks. Upon arriving, she soon sees that the front tire is flat. As she stomps to her car; "What the fuck…? I mean what the **fuck**? Can today get any worse?"

Observing and hearing her outburst Defective Moore wanders over to see what the fuss is. Joy sees him coming and shakes her head in disgust me; *"I really didn't want to see this asshole again."*

Bending over looking at the tire; "It doesn't look like you are going anywhere… soon Ms. Cloud."

Joy not saying a word, just glares that him angrily; *"What an arrogant asshole."* As Jason walks nearer, scratching his head; "Listen, I am not your enemy here; I'm just trying to help."

Joy taking her phone out of her pocket; "Really...how can you do that?"

"Sorry, I couldn't get here sooner today, but I am here now. And if you like, I'm leaving now and can give you a lift. Where were you heading? I'll call for a tow truck and have them change that tire for you. Would that be okay?"

Joy with a tight lip, squints at him skeptically; "I have a luncheon appointment at Bricktown, and I'm already 15 minutes late."

Motioning toward his car; "I can drop you off, it's on my way. Just leave the keys with the officer. Your car should be ready later today. Is that okay..?

Joy just cannot abide taking a favor from this "toxic man." Her adversity to men has become overt and needlessly adversarial.

"I can get you to your appointment faster than any Uber. That's if you can get an Uber right now."

Not enthused by her prospects, she reluctantly nods her head as she tosses the keys on the front seat. Jason and Joy walk together until they come upon his red clay encrusted 1993 Chevy El Camino. He stops and pauses with a smile, opens the squeaky passenger side door.

Joy, stares down and gasps at the filthy wreck; "Is this *your* car?"

Eyebrows lifted; "Yes ma'am... my car."

Being ever so skeptical, she tilts her head and squints inside; "This doesn't look like a police detective's *official car*." Looking skeptically at his belt, eyeing his badge; "Are you really a police detective?"

Jason just rolls his eyes and looks at the sky; "It's not my... official car. My police vehicle's windshield was shattered by hail in the storm last night. This will have to do until they get it repaired. Anyway, it's a minor inconvenience considering what other people are dealing with."

Squinting at him skeptically; "You got caught in the middle of that storm?"

He sociably nods his head and motions for her to get in. As Joy uncomfortably slides into the passenger seat, she briskly brushes the fast food bags and empty coffee containers to the floor; "So you're sure this thing's safe?"

Projecting a boyish grin; "This old boy got me through college and every day since."

With a dubious stare and wiggling in her seat, she finds an open place on the floor mat for her feet. She watches intently as Jason walks to the driver side door, taking special notice of his Oklahoma City detective badge. Nonetheless, she brings her knees and feet tightly together not missing a chance to give

Jason another suspicious glance. As Jason slides into the driver's seat Joy looks around and notices small Texas bull horns hanging from the rearview mirror; "So, you didn't go to OU or OSU?"

As the car noisily shakes to start, he puts it in gear and drives away; "No mam, ***TEXAS...!***"

Feeling a bit more comforted; "So, what brought you to OKC from ***Texas***?"

In a bit more friendly tone; "That was actually Dallas Texas. I worked there for some years there then I applied for the job in OKC. May I call you Joy... Msss. Cloud?"

With furrowed brow Joy skeptically nods her head; *"What's he got on his mind?"*

"Well, to make a long story short I was all-state QB in my senior year at the Yukon High School, just outside Oklahoma City.

"I think you know where that is."

"After that, I was recruited and played a few games at Texas though. Then..."

Interrupting; "Were you any good... playing football that is?"

Puffing out his chest; "Not too bad, I had a good arm and completed a few long TD passes. But late in my junior year, I got my knee got torn up and couldn't play my senior year. I could have tried the pros but didn't want to be smashed up any further. I could see a lot of top QB's from other schools that were going to be drafted and figured I really didn't have much of a chance in the pros, so I turned my attention back to my studies and well... here I am."

"So which department are you currently assigned to?"

"I'm new as a detective, only a few weeks. My Lieutenant is moving me around to give me exposure to several departments."

"A detective at your age, aren't *you* pretty young to be a detective?"

"Well, I do have a few years of law enforcement experience. I took the OKC detective exam and aced it. Along with my interview and the fact that the Department wanted a lot more forensics expertise... I got the job."

Feeling more comfortable; "Where do you want to end up?"

"...I want to get more experience before I decide. While I majored in Criminal Justice at Texas, I minored in Forensic Science. I really love the scientific part of the job. It is both interesting and challenging. I want to keep away from the legal side, too much BS paperwork. "

Nodding; "That sounds like a wise decision. Looks like you've got it all figured out."

With an appreciative glance; "Thanks...and you..? I think I can see what you are doing, or at least trying hard to accomplish

. How did you get your position... at such a young age?"

Happily turning part way towards Jason; "Well my boss, Mrs. Harkness just got overwhelmed by everything and just called in one day and quit. No notice or anything. Nobody had a clue. I was her executive assistant, and they moved me right in. They gave me the title of Interim Director, but I might have a shot at Director. I would like to think I do because of my ability. I have been at the clinic now for several months, working 24/7. I got the internship right and out of college and have been here ever since."

Watching Joy's face; "Do you think you're settled in yet?"

Shrugging; "I'm not sure. While I enjoy being the clinic's Director and living here, I have a few irons in the fire and may be moving to DC in a few years if all goes as planned."

"That sounds like a very aggressive career path."

"We all have to do and go where we feel we are needed the most... right?

Nodding; "I hear that....."

AquarianBooks.com

CHAPTER 6
May 2017 -- The Bad News

_A few hours earlier Dawn Cloud was meeting with doctors with her 4-year-old daughter, Samantha. Dawn, Joy's older sister, is a few years younger than her brother Daniel. Dawn is an attractive, slender 25-year-old woman with long dark hair and striking ebony eyes. She grew up modeling herself after her grandmother, aspiring to be a sociable and refined individual. Dawn hasn't changed much since her sorority house days. Today she has her daughter Samantha in tow. Samantha has not been well for several months. She has been losing weight and after dozens of tests the doctors finally figured out what was wrong. Today, after weeks of anxiously waiting for Dr. Sharma is discussing the results of the latest battery of blood tests with Dawn.

Dr. Sharma sitting poised hands clasped behind her desk, speaks deliberately; "We have performed every blood test imaginable and have looked far beyond the routine. We often look at the health profile of the parents for clues of the possible cause for her condition. I see from the chart that there is no name written for the father.

Dawn, listening attentively, leans forward; "That is because Sam's dad was selected."

Dr. Sharma curiously; "Selected..?"

Looking at her daughter; "Yes selected. From a list of qualified male sperm donors based on IQs, education, physical characteristics, personal profiles, that kind of stuff. All men were from this demographic."

Dr. Sharma concerned; "Do we know where the donor is today?"

Dawn becoming anxious; "I have absolutely no idea. Why are you asking? The donors did not want their identities known for legal reasons, and I did not care at that time. That was years ago, and we never met. Why is that so important?"

Dr. Sharma fingering down her health records; "OH, yes I see here it is, in-vitro fertilization."

Dawn leaning towards the doctor in a low voice; "To be clear, the reason I requested and had the in-vitro fertilization was due to my early diagnosis of Hodgkin's Lymphoma, identified a few years before my eggs were fertilized. An aggressive regimen of chemo helped me to overcome that. However, we knew there was a chance that all my eggs could become infertile, so I chose what I considered to be the ideal male donor. Never met him nor saw any photo's but he looked good on paper. Before my chemo regimen, I got pregnant and had Samantha. They also collected, fertilized and froze several eggs,... just in case. Samantha is my first child and probably the last child. My total focus in life is Samantha."

Dr. Sharma speaks very softly; "So you know for sure that you cannot have any additional children?"

Discouragingly; "It was my understanding at that time from my oncologist that except for those additional fertilized eggs, I could no longer bear children."

"Please tell me why **this** is so important."

In a focused tone; "After our last consultation I went ahead and performed a new bank of genetic testing, on Samantha's blood to help diagnose her condition."

"Why hadn't you performed them earlier?"

"With the new health care laws, we are required to go through a specific sequence of tests in a prescribed order. The last bank of tests performed is for genetic disorders, to identify specific gene related markers."

In a hesitant tone; "Well... what did you find?"

Hesitantly; "Well,... Samantha has a very rare disease with symptoms similar to HIV; however, it is not HIV nor was it contracted."

Becoming anxious; "Is there any treatment for this... condition?"

Dr. Sharma's hands are moving back and forth; "Only a gene transplant from a genetically matched sibling has been proven to work. You indicated you had several embryos frozen before your chemotherapy. As you can no longer have additional children do you have someone that could or would volunteer as a surrogate to carry a child...to term. This is the only avenue I think we can take to treat Samantha? Time is essential, and we need to have this accomplished as soon as possible. I must emphasize the urgency of this. Her blood count is getting dangerously low, and there are only so many measures we can take in her weakened state."

Dawn obviously shaken, thinks for a moment; "Yes, I believe I do, my younger sister Joy. She is not married, has no children of her own and we are very, very close. I'm sure she would seriously consider this exceptional request. And, she's Samantha's godmother."

"I must emphasize that we cannot use an aborted fetus for this procedure, only the umbilical cord. Once the sibling is born, we will need the umbilical cord to collect unique T-Cells from the cord blood."

"Once we get the umbilical cord is there is a good chance that it will be a cure for Samantha?"

Raising her hands; "No treatment is 100 percent assured, but I would say it is a good shot. At this time, it's really her only shot for long-term cure. Sorry for this prognosis but we are still hopeful. Let's pray for the best. Keep me informed about your sister; I will move the insurance paperwork along to expedite the procedure. Okay."

As Dawn stands and begins to walk out with Samantha; "Dr. Sharma, thank you so very much. I really appreciate all the research you have done to help Samantha. It just so happens I have lunch booked with Joy in about an hour. I will pose this question to her immediately. How quickly can we get her scheduled for the in vitro procedure?"

Dr. Sharma strokes Samantha's sandy blonde hair; "I'll put a call into an associate of mine in obstetrics and ask her what should be done next... and let you know."

Dawn is running late for lunch, as she had to drop off Samantha, back to daycare. As she was walking through the parking lot at Bricktown, she looks back to the street and from a distance recognizes her sister getting out of a filthy El Camino. She watches, as Joy bends over talking to someone through the passenger side window, with legs crossed, wiggling her butt in a very uncharacteristic girlish, sassy manner. She pauses and stares curiously. This is entirely out of character for her little sister.

Joy peaks back over her shoulder she sees Dawn waiting; "I.... Gotta go."

Jason smiles; "That's not a problem Mss. Cloud. I give you a lot of credit for being so determined. It takes a lot of grit to do what you've done."

Joy with a grin; "Detective ..."

Jason softly interrupts; "Please don't call me detective, just call me Jason."

Joy's nods with a smile; "Well...I think I've known you long enough, you can just call me Joy."

Jason leans across the seat to the window; "Joy, here is my business card. If you do not get the police coverage, you need, please give me a call. Or...if you have any other issues, please feel free to give me a call."

Joy enthusiastically; "Thanks, I gotta go." She spins around and begins to walk away.

Inquisitively with a boyish grin; "Joy, if I'm too bold, would you like to go for a cup of coffee sometime?"

With an unexpected smile; "Sure, I'd like to."

She leans back into the car as they exchange an awkward handshake.

As Jason slowly drives away, he looks into his rearview mirror. A broad smile erupts across his face in disbelief; "*Wow, I didn't expect that.*"

Joy saunters up to join Dawn, with a very strange, satisfied look on her face.

Dawn stretches her neck and bends over slightly to extend her view; "Who the **hell** was that? I thought you were driving here alone."

Joy in a perky voice; "I was,… he was just giving me a ride. It's a long story, let's get a seat, I'm frying my ass off out here. I'll fill you in."

Dawn rushes her sister inside; "Yah, I need to update you, as well."

After being seated and ordering two lime beers, Dawn pokes at Joy's shoulder fondly; "So who's the guy? I didn't get a good look at him, but from what I could see he looks **hot.** How long have you known him?"

Joy, a tad riled; "They all look handsome to you. I'm really not in the market for any guy right now. With everything going on with my job I can't even think of starting any relationship. I've worked my ass off the past several months and think they finally recognize my contributions. It's probably my big chance."

Dawn peeking over the menu; "That doesn't mean you can't have a life after work. You're not going to have your girlish looks forever... honey."

"Yeah, you know how I feel about men. Eventually, you have to deal with their toxic masculinity."

"Honey, a real woman does not have to worry about a man... being a real man."

Joy timidly; "Yeah I know... He did ask if he could call me back...and I said yes."

Dawn winking; "Well there ya go, that's a smart girl. It doesn't hurt to **dip** your toe in the pool every once in a while to remember how it feels. If you know what I mean?"

Joy tersely; "No, I don't remember. And, I don't need your thinly disguised metaphors, either."

"So what does he do for a living, where does he live, I assume he is single."

Briskly throwing her hair back; "He is just an OKCPD Detective. He just came by the clinic for the usual crowd control. There was no uniformed officer stationed because of the severe storms that came through the city last night."

Dawn looking a little bit frustrated wanting more information; "That's it, the way you exchange smiles, I thought there was more to it. That is all great; just keep an open mind,... that's all. By the way, did you get to say goodbye to Danny before his deployment?"

"Yes, I actually saw Danny this morning. He was helping this young Latino girl with a ride."

Innocently; "How about dad, have you spoken to him lately? I think you've only seen him once since he got back."

Getting quickly agitated; "What about **him**..?"

In a conciliatory tone; "Honey, at some point you have to bury the past, let it go. You have all that anger built up inside of you babe. Please let it go for **me...** okay. I spoke to him just the other day, and he was asking about Samantha. He sounded very different, friendlier. I don't know what it is, I can't put my finger on it, but he is different."

Joy puts her head into the menu and grumbles; "I really don't want to talk about him. Can we move on?"

Dawn pauses for several seconds, and as her voice begins to tremor; "Anyway baby, I'm glad we planned this lunch because I really need your help... **seriously**."

Seeing her sister becoming so quickly emotional, Joy reaches across the table for her hand; "What is it, you look shaken. How can I help?"

Dawn's lips begin to tremble; "Samantha is *really* sick. I mean really sick and the doctor says there is only one possible treatment to fix her condition. They've done dozens of tests, and they have identified only one treatment to save her, that's where you come in."

"Honey tell me what I can do? I'll do anything to help. "

Dawn goes on for several minutes and recounts her meeting with Doctor Samara.

Joy attentively listens to her shaken sister, holding her hand as she sobs; "Of course I will help; this is what family is for. I'm her godmother and would do anything for baby Sam, anything to get her well. Okay, I'll do it! I have to get a few things straight in the next few days at the clinic, but after that, I'm ready for this, all of this."

With tears in her eyes: "I really appreciate this Joy, I really do.

Joy squeezing her hand; "I want to do this for you, for baby Sam. You have done so much for me over the years as my big sister. But you know you are more than my big sister, you really brought me up and took care of me all those years. You cared for me when our mother and father forgot me. I will never forget that. So, how soon do you need for the embryo to be implanted?"

Dawn sobbing; "As soon as possible honey, as soon as possible. Samantha is getting weaker every day. In the not too distant future, only transfusions will keep her alive. So if you're available next week for an exam that would be great. God, I'm fortunate having a sister like you."

Joy leans closer; "We are both lucky to have each other. The least I could do is to lend my body to you for a few months and be your surrogate. It isn't as though it is going to be totally out of the action, if you know what I mean? "

Dawn wiping away her tears: "Thanks babe. All this stuff with the doctor has really shaken me up. I'm not feeling that great. Can you come back home with me? Can we forget about lunch? I just need to lie down for a while before Samantha gets home from daycare. Would that be okay?"

Joy motions to the waiter; "Sure, let's go."

As they get back to Dawn's condo, she shows Joy in; "Honey why don't you go make yourself comfortable, have yourself a cold drink and kick off your shoes. I'm just going in the bedroom to lie down for an hour.

"Go ahead and get some rest, you really need it. I can pick up Samantha later this afternoon. I can pick her up about 3:30. That's right isn't it?"

As Dawn walks into the bedroom, she points to the kitchen; "Pour yourself some fresh brewed Cain's ice tea, I made it this morning, it's in the fridge."

Dawn walks softly into the bedroom and partially closes the door. As Joy opens the refrigerator, she pulls out the pitcher of tea. As always, she enjoys a lot of ice and opens the freezer door. There are a lot of frozen dinners in the freezer; she has to move things around to get into the ice bin.

Reaching into the ice bin, she notices a small plastic bag. She withdraws it and inquisitively rubs the frosted label; *"That's odd... I've seen this label before. "Joy - September 4, 2011."* Dumbstruck, she realizes that this was the DNA sample taken years before at the OU clinic. Not wanting to confront her sister, Joy packs it in a small bag of ice and drops it into her oversized purse.

She pours her ice tea and sits on the couch looking out the window. How can she suppress what she has just found? I can't raise this with my sister, not right now, not in her emotional condition. Joy has a faint recollection of what happened at the clinic and no recollection of the chain of events before that. She sits back and ponders her discovery, as well as how to plan for her surrogate pregnancy; *"This shit is just getting too complicated."* Sipping her ice tea, she looks out the window pondering what the future has to offer.

As Joy scans the room, she sees an old family photo showing the happy Cloud family during their last Colorado vacation, taken several years earlier. It was not often that John Cloud could spend quality time with his family when they were all off from school and he was on leave. They had planned this vacation for several months, as it might be the last time that they could all be together, with Daniel going off to college. They had spent about 10 days of their two-week vacation in the

Rockies fishing and camping.

She distinctly remembers that oversized bright white T-shirt with the large red "OU" stenciling. Her brother got it as part of OU freshman orientation days earlier. Joy had soiled a nightshirt a few days earlier, and Jason gave it to her as a convenient alternative. In spite of her diminutive size, she wore it proudly, though it hung down to her ankles. She recalls that unruly mass of red hair that could not be styled. At first, the smile comes to her face, recalling that vacation and then an unusual stark glare comes across her face, as she recalls the chain of events that led to her falling out with her father; *"God dammit."*

As Joy gazes out the window, sipping her ice tea, her mind drifts to that summer night when the family piled into their oversized SUV on that long road trip back from the Rocky Mountain National Park. As usual, the best of plans was waylaid when John Cloud received an emergency call that his leave was canceled. Earlier that evening Crystal Cloud had been partying heavily and definitely needed to sleep off her hangover. They had hastily packed the SUV for the long 13-hour ride home. As usual, Crystal reclined in the front seat, with the three kids in the rear. Over the years, the kids were accustomed to sleeping in the back seat. They could cover themselves with a large unzipped sleeping bag.

When they were approaching the small town of McPherson south of Salina, Kansas John realized that he was below ¼ of a tank and needed to gas-up. It was about 1:30am in the morning, as John slowly rolled into the only open gas station at that exit. He quietly got out of the car, slid his credit card into the machine, and began to pump gas. Unexpectedly, another text message came in, asking that he call the commanding officer at his base in Iraq. Cloud dutifully dialed the number and begins to discuss recent IED attacks and possible countermeasures.

Joy was awakened by her father's voice and the bright lights over the pumps and felt a bit uncomfortable because she had to use the restroom. Sitting by the passenger side window and trying to be considerate to her siblings, she quietly opened and closed the SUV door, not to wake anyone. She had gone to the lady's room alone many times before, with no help.

John had turned his back to the car, watching the digital meter and to muffle his voice. He did not see or hear Joy leave the SUV. Joy saw the sign and scurried to the lady's restroom on the darkened side of the building. Quickly, she opened the stall to find a disgusting mess in the toilet. Nonetheless, she was taught to just do her business, pay no attention and get out. However, as she pulled up her white OU shirt and pull down her bikini bottom, she noticed something very different, something she had never seen before. Her bikini bottom was stained red. The adolescent just started her first period and began spotting; *"Oh God no what is this? What is this? **Oh, fuck no…No….!"***

John Cloud had just finished filling the gas tank and closed the gas tank cover. As he walked to the driver's seat, he could not see through the stained-glass passenger windows, and assumed all were still inside. Not wishing to wake anyone nor wanting to disturb anyone from their sleep he hurriedly got back into the SUV and drove away. As everyone usually covered their heads with the sleeping bag, he did not notice Joy was not in the backseat. Within seconds of him pulling away from the pumps he sees four rambunctious bikers noisily rumbling into the station and appear to have been drinking; *"Perfect timing I'm glad I got the hell out of there when I did."*

Joy being the inquisitive younger sister always queried Dawn about her personal hygiene habits and what she had to do. Nonetheless, she was not prepared for this experience, not here, not now. She needed personal hygiene support, and she needed it quickly. She hopped out of the stall and sharply stuck her head out the bathroom door. She began yelling the top of her lungs for her mother; **"Mom..! Dawn...!** God dammit... where are you guys!"

Undaunted, the resourceful Army brat tries to clean herself as best she could and dunked the bikini bottom in the sink; *"Great, there is no soap."* With only cold water, she couldn't get the faint blood stains to come out. Plus, she did not bring any money with her for the tampon dispenser. Determined, she quickly wadded up a large handful of toilet paper and stuffed it uncomfortably in between her legs. She then wriggled the cold, wet bikini bottom back up her shivering legs, pulling them tightly into place. Then pulling down the OU tee-shirt, looked sternly into the grungy mirror; *"There, that will have to do."*

At that time a couple of the bikers began walking around the corner toward the men's room. Joy quickly jerked her head back in and locked the door. Nonetheless, she realized that she had to get back to the car, and get back there now. With her ear to the door, she listened carefully to men laughing in the restroom next door. She had to make a run for it; *"I have to get out of here, and I have to do it now."*

Joy darts out the restroom door just as the two other bikers were walking around to the men's toilet. She runs directly into them. The diminutive preteen looked up in horror at these giants shadowing over her, obstructing the sky. She panicked; rather than saying, excuse me, she immediately began screaming and pounding on them for no apparent reason.

As Cloud accelerates onto the highway, Dawn awakens and reaches for her little sister. Realizing that Joy is not sleeping next to her; "Mom, Dad... **Where's Joy?**"

"What do you mean where's Joy she's back there with you."

Dawn throws off the cover; "She's not back here with us."

John jerks his head around and grunts and realizes to his horror that little Joy is not in the car; **"Shit..!"** In a heartbeat, he abruptly cuts across the passing lane and descends the steep bank of the median careening through bumper-high wildflowers and again up the steep embankment to the other side. Everyone is jostled, holding on for dear life. As he tries to gain control of the muddied SUV, it slides across two lanes of traffic barely missing a tractor-trailer. With horns blaring, it takes but a few seconds to reach the exit and back into the gas station.

Crystal Cloud is still hungover; "John what the hell you doing?"

Without hesitation he jumps from the SUV and observes the biker's shadowy shapes near the restroom and instinctively reaches for his pistol; however, he did not bring it due to his wife's insistence; "about this being a friendly vacation." Instead on his belt, he carries a black leather Mean Gene coin purse. It was Grandpa's favorite and given to John the day before they left on vacation. The inconspicuous, tear dropped shaped, weighty coin purse can be quite the equalizer. As he walks briskly to the restroom he looks back and points to his family; "Stay in the car and lock the doors."

Nonetheless, Daniel runs from around the SUV to assist: "But Dad..!"

John turns sternly and points; "No! I need for you to stay back with the ladies, just in case this does not work out. If I don't come out, you call 911 and drive off. **Understand..!**?"

Daniel immediately heeds his father and watches from a distance.

Cloud quickly unclasps the weighty Mean Jean from his belt, looks down as it dangles from his hand; *"Better this than nothing."* The glaring lights overhead obscure his view of the shadowy restroom doors. The buzz of the fluorescents and echoing crickets are unnerving, then he hears his daughter's screams. As he runs closer to the glare of the building's lights, his years of military training kicks in and realizes he must adjust his eyes quickly to the darkened condition. He closes one eye to obstruct the bright light and keeps the other open to see where he is going. Immediately entering the dark shadows, he reverses and is prepared for the darkened conditions. Despite his years of military hand-to-hand training, he thankfully never had the opportunity to utilize it. He had to maximize the tools given to him to confront his daughter's attackers; the darkness, and his concealed Mean Gene.

Running to the darkened side of the building, he sees four large men surrounding his petite daughter, raucously laughing. For the past few seconds, the men have been entertaining themselves taunting Joy, lifting her white shirt exposing her slender legs. If she had not impulsively struck them, none of this might have happened. As she spins and turns, she screeches in distress at the giants laughing around her. Her loud shrieks only draw more laughter. One of the drunks effortlessly lifts the tiny 110-pound girl over his head and is amused as she flails about, kicking his face.

With orange hair exploding, pound for pound the slight 4'-7", 12-year-old was a match for men twice her size. She blurts angrily; "Put me down you son of a bitch, or I will bite your fuckin face off."

Within a heartbeat Cloud is upon them; "Put her down... asshole. **Now...!**"

In the shadows of the building, the four large bikers appear formidable. Cloud was never a fighter, but he did remember a few brawling tips from his Special Forces buddies. The closest biker turns and takes a step toward Cloud and laughs out loud; "Yah, okay... Yah man." As he draws his right arm back to punch, Cloud strikes him without hesitation across and the jaw with his leathery friend. A loud **"Crack"** is heard as he collapses unconscious.

The biker holding Joy overhead abruptly drops her to the ground. She hits the pavement and scurries shivering against the dark wall, knees pressed to her chest. She looks up trembling in horror as the three men's attention is turned to her father.

Instinctively, Cloud looks for the largest of the three and stares. Not wanting to take on three at the same time, he quickly beckons with flicking fingers; "Come on" tempting him to move forward. In the darkness they do not notice that Cloud is carrying his equalizer. The man takes two steps forward, raises his hands to fight then garishly grunts. As he does Cloud wildly slams his Mean Jean across the back of the man's left hand, shattering his knuckles. Scowling; "Man, what the fuck" cradling his injured hand against his chest. Cloud strides forward and finishes him off with backhand smash across the jaw. He collapses to the ground unconscious.

The other two men quickly measure their options and instantly lunge for Cloud. The first tries to tackle Cloud as the second grabs at his left arm. In anticipation Cloud brusquely thrusts his right knee up hitting the man in the face. As his head jerks up Cloud whacks him across his head immediately sending him to the ground, stunned. The fourth attacker releases Cloud's arm and quickly takes a step back.

The rotund last attacker stands frozen, weighing his options. Looking at his buddies, he realizes his precarious situation and must get around Cloud to get back to his motorcycle. He sidesteps left then right trying to escape. Seeing his indecision, Cloud mirrors his movement. The perplexed biker raises his hands as if to surrender; but Cloud will have none of that; *"Sorry buddy no prisoners today."* He lunges forward and briskly smacks him across the jaw with his new best friend. **Crack..!** He flops back onto the pavement.

Joy sits quivering against the wall, peaking over her forearm, astonished at her soft-spoken father efficiently destroying her attackers. Cloud looks about, seeing all four men around him, moaning semi-conscious. Leaning over slowly to pick up Joy; "Come on honey, let's go."

Joy unexpectedly jumps up, elbows Cloud aside and runs to the SUV to the arms of her beckoning mother; "Mom."

Saying nothing, Cloud turns and watches his daughter. He emerges slowly from the shadows appearing unfazed, as if he just made a routine restroom visit. As Crystal Cloud embraces her traumatized daughter, she looks up to John shaking her head incredulously; *"You fucking asshole."*

Then the stunned minimart attendant sticks his head out the door to see the commotion. In a calm respectful voice; "Sir, I think you should get back inside and lock that door." He does so immediately.

A huge biker staggers to his feet and wobbles into the glaring overhead lights, displaying a large, shiny hunting knife. Clutching his profusely bleeding mouth, he pauses to spit blood and a few teeth, then mumbles; "If I get you, man, I will kill you and your family."

Cloud has encountered bloodied adversaries before and is unfazed by his threats. Nonetheless, he realizes that his family is far from home and the fact that they have large motorcycles; the bikers can easily overtake them on the long dark interstate. Not seeking another encounter, he pauses for a second then calmly strides to the bikes, raises his arm and with rhythmic precision smashes all four headlights with his Mean Gene; *"You can't drive anywhere fast at night without headlights."*

The mini-mart attendant watches, shaking his head in astonishment; *"Oh Nooo."*

As Cloud stands next to the last motorcycle, he glares at the biker and briskly kicks the first bike over. All watch in as they domino over. Staring with no emotion while pointing his Mean Jean at the biker; "You have a nice night... amigo" and calmly strides back to his SUV where his family has been watching. He motions; "Come on, get in."

Robotically he gets in, flips the Mean Gene onto the dashboard then turns the key and is ready to drive away. Realizing his initial error, he hesitates and looks back; "Joy...Honey are you okay? Sorry, babe, I thought you were in the back before I drove off. I'm very sorry..."

Dawn's arm is clutching her little sister, trying to calm her down. Joy is trembling, trying to comprehend the incredible chain of events she just experienced. Totally puzzled by her father's placid demeanor, she angrily kicks the back of his seat three times; "Fuck you man, fuck you. Get me the fuck out-a-here."

While they had heard Joy's profanity-laced tirades

before all were dumbfounded by this spontaneous outburst, directed at her father. The family would not find out until the following day the graphic details of her first period and how she was taunted and groped by the four bikers. Although she was not physically injured her emotional trauma was considerable. Though Cloud quickly returned to rescue her, Joy nonetheless believed her father abandoned her. None would realize that this confluence of events would leave an indelible mark on her psyche and affect Joy's relationship with Cloud for many years to come.

That night, Cloud's Post Traumatic Stress symptoms were just burgeoning; displaying him as dispassionate or distant. It was difficult for him to transition from military to civilian life, then back again. In this particular encounter, his rigorous training was effectively triggered to protect those he loved. Regrettably, he could not project empathy or affection when most needed. Cloud would often replay the details of that dark night; but what resonated; *"How he protected and defended his daughter."* Unfortunately for Cloud, that is not how Joy remembered it, not at all.

Later that afternoon Joy got a taxi back to her own condo. She opens her purse and examines the sample vial found in Dawn's freezer. She places it deep within her own freezer. She never asked nor mentioned what she had seen to Dawn.

The following week Joy meets with Dr. Sharma. She verifies the diagnosis for Samantha and emphasizes that only T cells collected from the umbilical cord can save her niece from what might be certain death; "Time is of the essence." Joy spends several minutes filling out dozens of legal forms. Recognizing the urgency, she quickly schedules a visit to have the in-vitro fertilization performed, utilizing Dawn's frozen saved fertilized eggs.

Not knowing what the future may hold, Dawn has also given permission to sign over extra frozen embryos to Joy, just in case. The following week, the in-vitro procedure is performed on Joy, and now all she has to do is wait. As she is sitting there, she asks that the OB/GYN doctor to turn over a few of the remaining frozen embryos in a freezer bag. The doctor knew better than to ask why. Joy brings them back home for safekeeping and places them beside the rape test kit vial in her freezer.

CHAPTER 7
June 2017 – Consequences

Cloud, now unemployed, tries to keep occupied performing odd jobs around the farm. There really isn't much for him to do; reinforcing the tree stand and clearing brush, the kind of mundane work that requires no planning or thinking. Cloud continues to get occasional anxiety attacks and nightmares. Dr. Fellows' prescriptions have had some effect in dulling his visions; however, there are undesired side effects; they have made him even more introverted.

He was not given a pistol when he retired from the Army. Nonetheless, he wished to maintain his proficiency and decided to purchase his familiar 9 mm Beretta pistol; *"I must stay sharp, just in case."* He decided to keep only a small amount of ammunition in the cabin and would only purchase 100 rounds at a time and practice against a stone cliff backdrop, setting up targets. Along with his new pistol, he purchased acoustic ear protection to muffle the muzzle crack; *"No need to trigger my symptoms."* That day, he had almost finished an entire box of ammo leaving only one in his gun; *"No time today to clean the gun, it can wait till tomorrow."*

That evening when Grandpa came home early, he found Cloud passed out drunk in bed. He spotted the half-empty jar of moonshine next to Cloud's notebook, pressed open to a blood-stained page with his loaded pistol; *"What the hell is going on here. What's the matter with you boy?"* As Grandpa examined the pistol, he set it aside and began to finger the tattered pages. He could not help but notice indiscernible ghoulish doodles in the margins. These sketches could not have been drawn by the son he knew; *"What the hell have you been going through all these years?"* While Grandpa had seen his fill of combat as an Army sniper during the Vietnam War, he was never close to anyone he killed. The loaded gun and troubling sketches alarmed him so much, and he decided to eject the last bullet from the pistol and place it back down. Grandpa had no way of knowing that it was not the gun that was causing his son harm; it was his horrific recollections. Cloud never asked about the gun, and they never spoke of it.

The next day he was sitting at the table looking out the window and spotted a flock of turkey crossing the access road. At first, he saw two male toms and a hen followed by a dozen chicks, then another gobbler and another hen. A faint smile crossed his face; *"Now that's how you take care of your family."*

Rhythmically tapping the 50-caliber cartridge on the table; *"Today is the first day of the rest of my life. Today is the first day of the rest of my life."* He realized he had to break from the past and to focus on the future; but what future? He wrote in his notebook, the only item he brought back from all of his tours overseas. The only family photos he had were lost. He realized that for the past several years, he had few if any fond memories of his family and only harbored horrific memories of Iraq. While Cloud's written reports are their usual impeccable quality, his face to face interactions with fellow servicemen becomes increasingly difficult. Those problems continued into civilian life.

Nonetheless, he decided to drive to town where he could get cell coverage and make a call to his daughter Dawn. "Dawn honey,... It's your dad.... How are ya?"

"Hi dad, how are you doing? I spoke to mom, and I was hesitant to give you a call, not knowing how you were."

"Goddammit take a deep breath and just talk." "Yeah...Your mom and I... didn't get along the last time... we were together so... I decided to spend some time at the farm.... Get reoriented."

"So dad, how are you doing?"

Biting his lip; *"Stay focused, stay focused;"* "I'm okay... I guess. It gets kinda quiet out here,... not much to do.... Would love to see ya... anytime, maybe even see that beautiful granddaughter of mine.... Any chance of that?"

Without hesitation; "Sure, it would be great to see ya, and I could use a break from her once in a while. For a four-year-old, she's an awful lot to handle. Just let me know when it's convenient for you, and we'll work something out."

Cloud was incredibly frustrated by his evidently flawed speech. He did not wish to draw attention to his problem. He has to grind through it, despite his disability.

Despite Crystal Cloud's vehement objections, Dawn agreed to have Cloud visit and even babysit for little Samantha. After seeing Cloud for the first time, Dawn was alarmed at his unkempt appearance and suggested that Cloud clean himself up. The excessive drinking and poor hygiene had taken its toll. So he went to a local barber and got his customary high and tight haircut and once again clean-shaven. That and a hot shower made him look almost normal.

Cloud and Samantha really get along, and after a few brief visits, he can't get enough of her endless hugs and kisses; *"Incredibly therapeutic, better than any meds the doc could prescribe."* To allow his family to penetrate his emotional fortress, he decided to cut back on his medications. While it seemed like the appropriate thing to do, the doctor told him it could make him vulnerable to unanticipated stimuli and trigger a manic PTSD episode. For Cloud, this was not a difficult decision to make. He has been so isolated from his family that he would do anything now to reconcile.

Cloud never attempted reconciliation with his wife Crystal; her last emotional outbreak was enough. Nonetheless, he tries to build bridges with his children. He drives to OKC and spends as much time with Dawn and Samantha as he can. He stays away from Joy out of respect for her wishes. With reduced medications, he still gets unexpected "mental lapses." He would inadvertently pause during conversation, unable to find the appropriate response. He perseveres; *"Today is the first day of the rest of my life."* He's still in relatively good physical condition but is trying everything to regain mental acuity. He regularly drives to town to the local library and reads every article he can about PTSD. Few researchers have clearly defined his symptoms or have meaningful treatments for his persistent nightmares. But it still attempts to carve out his new path. There are a lot of fences to mend and has all the time in the world to mend them; *"Select your target, choose the desired strategy and implement aggressively."* He starts with the easiest target his: granddaughter, that already loves him very much, move on from there. He lavishes all the love and attention on Samantha that he could never give to his own children. It is not long before his Dawn welcomes him back, but she notices that there is still something different.

Sadly, when he gets back to the cabin, he reverts back. Every morning he sits embracing his cup of coffee at the rickety window table, doggedly opening his notebook to revisit his notes and sketches, seeking fresh solutions to old problems; while rhythmically tapping the ever-present 50 caliber cartridge; *"What else did I miss? What could I have done differently?"*

As suggested by his VA psychologist Dr. Fellows, he should try to visualize new friendly images such as the faces of his children and granddaughter. It would work for a short period; but ultimately, he would revert. He realized that for him to project warmth and empathy, he must reduce his psych meds. But of course, this had undesired side effects. Nonetheless, Dr. Fellows keeps emphasizing; "Dissolve the troubling images of the past. Today's the first day of the rest of your life."

AquarianBooks.com

CHAPTER 8
Then Came Jason

A week later, Jason gives Joy that much-anticipated call and they have dinner at a pricey, secluded restaurant. Despite their initial barbs, they become comfortable. She is especially pleased that Jason did not attend Oklahoma University and does not have that *"obnoxious frat-house persona."* For several years, she consciously avoided any man that attended OU. Jason projects casual confidence, but when Joy probes deeper about his family and career goals, he is much more serious. Joy begins to believe that he is the genuine article; *"a real keeper."*

After dinner, they drive back to her condo and while standing at her front door; "Well Jason, I have to say I've had a surprisingly good evening. By the way, just for the record, I was more than happy to split the bill."

"Sorry Joy, I just wasn't brought up that way. I hope that won't be a problem? "

"No, it's not a problem I'm just a woman that wants to stay you know… independent."

"Joy, you project enough confidence that no one would ever question your independence."

Tilting her head and looking up at the much taller Jason; "You really think I project that kind of image?"

Smiling and leaning up against the wall; "Joy, it's not in dispute what you project, it's who you really are. People can

161

sense that."

Gazing up with a curious grin, she slides the key into the door; "Like to come in for a drink or cup of coffee?"

"I wouldn't want to trouble you, to put you out or anything, plus it's getting a little late."

Shoving the door open as an abrupt push from her hip; "Trouble... it's no trouble at all, com-on in."

Trying to contain the erupting smile; "Sure, I can come in for a little while."

She flippantly throws her keys and purse onto the table, walks into the kitchen; "Like me to make you some coffee?"

Jason looks around "Wow, nice place... Naa that's all right, I need to get up early in the morning, and that stuff keeps me awake. But I will have a beer, if you have a cold one."

Opening the door, bending over with a grin; "Sure... Here you go."

They walk into the living room as Joy flips off her shoes and sits on the couch. Jason sits on the sofa, but not immediately next to her. He wishes to make sure that there is an appropriate distance between the two; *I don't want to appear too eager.*

Joy notices but doesn't say a word; *Most guys would try to be on top of me already. Is there something wrong with me...*

or with him?"

Jason realizes how wary she is and doesn't want to proceed too quickly; *"This just might grow into a long-term relationship."* After continued chatting for a half an hour he glances at his watch; "Wow, it's getting late… I gotta go."

Joy a little surprised and a bit disappointed; "Yeah, sure,… Me too."

Forgetting her shoes, she is easily a foot shorter than Jason. As they walk to the front door. "Well Jason, I thought this was an enjoyable evening."

As Joy extends her hand up to him in an awkward handshake, Jason gently grasps it, and pulling her close, gives her a kiss on the cheek; "I agree Joy, this has been an enjoyable evening, and I hope I can see you again… real soon."

Taken aback by his slow show of affection, she awkwardly shrugs her shoulders; "Yeah sure,… sure."

"See ya, good night."

No sooner did Jason leave, than did she get on the phone to her sister Dawn, who is anxiously expecting a progress report. They spend several minutes going over every small detail of the evening.

Dawn blurts out; "and then he kissed you on the cheek? I don't know what to make of that. He seems too nice. I wonder what's wrong with him."

"Sis, it's getting late, and I gotta get up in the morning... a whole bunch of stuff going on. Do you need anything from me?

"No, I don't think so. But thanks for the offer. Uh...I have a quick question... Do you have any issues about me having.... sex... when I'm carrying the baby? "

Dawn hesitates; "Joy you're my sister, and we both know you're not a lesbian. So, at some point, you have to... give it up. And to answer your question; no... I don't think so. You have access to more doctors than I do. That's a question you should really take up with them. When and for how long? But I feel comfortable with you exercising appropriate precautions, considering how important this baby is to Samantha. Okay..? If it's all right with you, it's okay with me. Have a good evening babe."

After just a few minutes Joy sits beneath her covers with knees up, ready for her phone. It does not take long for her fingers to begin messaging; "Enjoyed tonight would like to do it again soon."

Jason had been home for only a few minutes and was exhausted after a long day. After throwing off his clothes and washing up, he turned off the light and jumped into bed. As usual, Jason placed his phone and gun on the nightstand beside the digital clock. The lights were out for just a few minutes and he hears the buzz, indicating a text message. Texts this time of night are usually ignored. But, tonight is different and he curiously decides to gaze at it with one eye.

Seeing it is from Joy, he takes a deep breath, knowing he should ignore it, and sits up; *"How do I wish to respond to this? I don't want to be too eager, then again I don't want her to feel I am ignoring her."* After a minute he responds; "How about my bringing dinner over tomorrow night to your place? Your choice: Western, Chinese, Mexican,..."

Within a few seconds; "Sounds great. I like everything, you surprise me. How about 6:30?

Jason takes a deep breath; "6:30 it is."

The next day Jason reviews several online menus and decides upon a new Taiwanese restaurant. He has heard a lot of good reviews, especially from some of the female officers in the squad, so; *"Why not."*

He arrives promptly at 6:30 and Joy was waiting at the door.

She was quite surprised at his dinner selection, as she had also been thinking of going to that very same restaurant; *"ha simpatico."*

The two enjoy the meal, and after a quick table clearing, they sit on the couch together. Jason recognizes her desire to be in control, just like in the office and gives her the opportunity. Then out of nowhere Joy jumps up and excuses herself for the restroom. She sits on the toilet with the cover down and begins to ponder past experiences with men; *"What the hell am I supposed to do now? Damn, I wish Dawn was here to talk me through this."*

Most recent experiences with men were at work, with very few social interactions. Though well-educated Joy would often become tongue-tied and blurt out profanities. She thinks to herself; *"Can't do that tonight."* She recalls her short temper and not taking no for an answer; *"Can't do that either."*

Some of this stemmed from her not bonding with her father as her primary male role model, and could be a reason why other male-female relations become difficult. Her recollection of being groped by the bikers and her sister's assertion of being raped at this sorority house makes her dubious of any man seeking affection; *"I gotta get over that too."*

While never giving into her desires, she feels emotions now; *"I do like this guy... a lot ."* She dated a few guys at the brother frat house, but never long enough to get physically close or emotionally attached. Plus, all they wanted to do was; *"Feel me up, those horny assholes."*

For the past several months, her communications have been emailing or text messages. Plus, the vast majority of people she deals with are women. When she does have an exchange with a man, she never sees his facial expression or hears voice inflections. She has no personal archive to gauge male-female interaction. While working at the clinic, she is intimately familiar with the female anatomy but... not guys.

Despite her expectations of having Jason touch her, it comes with considerable apprehension; ***"Oh God... I am such a fucking mess!"*** She stands and walks out of the bathroom then into her bedroom yelling out; "Be out in a minute..."

Jason just sits patiently on the couch thumbing his phone. He dare not turn on the TV he knows; *"How that turns women off."*

The embryo incubated for a few weeks, Joy took a home pregnancy test, and the results tested positive.   She reported the results to her doctor and to Dawn.   She was given the green light by both to proceed with her big evening.   In anticipation she decided to wear the sexy copper color, satin chemise nightgown, purchased that afternoon. Incredibly hard to find in a size 4.   Tired of her dowdy flannel nightshirt, Joy wanted to wear something suitable for her wild expectations.   Turning and glaring in the mirror; *"Maybe a bit long... but better too long... than too short."* She takes a deep breath, then fluffs up her uncooperative red hair; *"Common kid, you can do this. What's the worst that can happen?..... **Oh shit!**"*

Slowly opening the door, she walks stiffly back to the living room, making eye contact, gauging his response; *" Oh shit... Oh shit... Oh shit... Can he see how anxious I am?"*

He did not wish to spook her and overstate her appearance, nor did he want to be ungrateful of her efforts. Nodding his head with a broad smile; "Very nice... Wow you look great."

She plopped herself into the couch next to Jason and wriggled a bit anxiously. Jason just sat there waiting patiently for her to get comfortable; *"Don't rush or you'll scare her off... Her house... her rules."*

After a few minutes of idle chitchat, he leans towards her to speak, as she was leaning towards him, squinting, curiously judging his intentions. She has had no intimate experiences with a man, so this is a first. Remembering her sister's words; *"If you like the guy... just let it go."*

With their faces close, she leans in wide-eyed to offer a hesitant kiss, then pulls back to see his response. Based on her stiffness, he presumes she had minimal experience; *"Do not rush anything."* They sit on the couch awkwardly contorted, trying to embrace. Both seek the connection. Then he gently coaxes her to lie across the couch, cradling her in his arms. Gently massaging her lush red hair, they begin to softly kiss. They embrace for an hour on the couch, both thoroughly enjoying this first romantic experience. Joy; *"Wow he's really...really good. I never realized a guy could make me feel this way."*

Jason knows he could have gone further, but decides to slow down; *"She could be the real thing, I don't want to make any mistakes"* and eases up.

Joy, however, becomes incredibly aroused, and wants Jason to continue. Wanting him to be a man, she squeezes him closer; *"...Don't stop now."* He gently coaxes her closer cradling her head. With Joy's inexperience, she takes a breath and nudges him away. But Jason lightly persists. As they are kissing, she becomes even more engrossed, as Jason begins to stroke her legs gently.

Wanting to maintain control, Joy pauses, looks up and puts her hand on his throat, and squeezes; "Will you stop if I ask you to?"

He nods and mouths; "Yes." Passionately kissing, he senses her deepening breath.

Becoming increasingly aroused, trying to remain in control, Joy pauses again, gazes up. She places her hand on his throat and gently presses her fingernails in. She whispers; "If I ask you to stop... will you stop?"

Staring wide-eyed with a grin, softly; "Yes."

After several minutes of passionate necking, he gently fondles her breasts through the satin gown. As her breathing deepens, he tenderly rubs her inner thigh. Carefully, he lightly massages and moves his hand higher and higher.

As he slowly slides his hand into her satiny, white panties, she places her hand on his throat, pauses for a moment... then puts her hand on his heart. Remembering her sister's words *"let it go"*... she does.

At some point, she trusts this man with her heart. As he paints her body with his gentle caress, she is totally captivated, aroused like never before. After several seconds, Joy's body begins a deep repetitive shuttering. Jason does not rush, but lingers there. With legs fluttering wildly, her entire body stiffens, as she convulses into an orgasm; again, and again and... again; *"Oh God......"* as she exhales deeply.

Joy's first orgasm was totally unexpected and intense. After several seconds, she starts to breathe normally. As she exhales slowly to regain her composure, Joy's eyes begin to well with tears; *"Are these tears of joy or regret for not having done this sooner?"*

He chivalrously covers her legs, brushes back her disheveled hair, to gently stroke her face. Looking into her beseeching eyes; "Honey are you okay?"

Bashful, it takes her a few more seconds to come down. As she exhales; "Yes,... I'm okay, I'm okay." Then, out of nowhere, a blushing glow erupts across her face and timidly covers her flushed face; "Don't look at me."

"Why not... you're beautiful."

This was not just her first orgasm; this is the first time she had a deep emotional connection with a man. This first time was the beautiful experience that she always dreamed it could be. She is fortunate that Jason is a loving and trustworthy man, worthy of her.

He appreciates the physical and emotional barriers that she has torn down for him; *"Shit, I didn't realize how much I like her."* He does not want to take her first sexual experience any further. He wants it to sink in, and be properly absorbed, and to ensure Joy is emotionally prepared.

From his prior dalliances, he learned that deep sexual arousal of a woman should not be undertaken without considerable forethought. He did not want to initiate what could be a clingy relationship, unless of course, he wanted it for himself. The fact that Joy is a gorgeous, well-educated, and an incredibly determined woman makes this a unique opportunity for Jason as well. Then unexpectedly; "Joy honey, you may not be the first girl I have ever loved... but I want you to be the last."

She is totally stunned by his remark and enthusiastically wraps her arm around his head and forcefully kisses him.

Soon there are no barriers to their sexuality. They love, make love, and absorb each other completely. They bond physically and emotionally and, soon become inseparable.

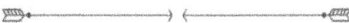

Jason and Joy do not hesitate and have sex at any opportunity. They are both mature and recognize what they want and what each has found. Since Joy never dated before, she has issues relinquishing control over day to day matters. Nonetheless, Jason realizes what a sweet girl she is; *"Even though she can be quite a handful, at times."*

Now that Joy is pregnant, she becomes nervous about how to maintain their fledgling relationship; *"How the hell do I tell him about the surrogate pregnancy without losing him?"* She recognizes what is at stake if she tells the truth, but also realizes what will happen in a few months if she lies. Jason has noticed how Joy becomes deeply introspective and uncharacteristically silent. She was totally not prepared for this relationship and did not foresee it in her future when she agreed to be a surrogate for her sister. She struggles to find the right time or the right words to reveal her incredibly difficult situation.

As they sit on the couch watching TV Jason gently massages her feet; "Joy, can I ask a question? It's kind of personal."

"Sure... what is it?" As she tilts her head.

"Well, we have been together for a few weeks and have, you know... **done it**... several times. I really enjoy making love to you."

Scrunching her eyebrows, perplexed; "Done it?"

"You know... sex."

"**Yah!**... So, is there a problem?"

With an apologetic grimace on his face; "Well, you never asked me to wear any protection, and that seemed to be a bit..."

"A bit what?"

Hesitantly; "Well....a bit different..."

Reverting into her aggressive-protective; "**Different**! Different than all other the girls... Different how?"

Realizing he may have opened Pandora's Box; "Well, I haven't really slept around much, especially since I got back to OKC.

"**Much..!**"

"To be precise... not at all since I met you... Okay..? But

when I did... with other girls... there was usually a requirement that I wear protection. And, you never asked me to wear any ... **protection**. I don't want to and appreciate that you haven't asked me to. That's what I mean by different."

Joy quickly cools and leans over to stroke his arm; "Jay, yes I know, and that's okay."

Still puzzled; "I know you are director of the woman's clinic and probably have a handle on all types of birth control and I just wanted to make sure that you are... well taking care of that on your end. Are you?"

Joy with a whimsical look; "Well yes... and no."

Perplexed; "What, No... why?"

Joy, realizing the fortuitous direction this conversation has taken, reaches out to him; "I don't need to any longer. I was taking care of it before... but now I don't need to."

Jason leans back and shakes his head at the encrypted message; "Then what **are** you doing now? You really have me wondering. I don't understand what you're talking about. I like you and want to continue our relationship."

Becoming uncharacteristically playful; "I didn't realize we had a **relationship,** nor had any problems with... sex."

Tersely, becoming uncomfortable; "We don't. I haven't dated a lot because most often it has been a total waste of my time. Seriously... you are different. You are...very special. I connect with you. I really like you and don't want to make any mistakes, to say or do something idiotic to jeopardize that. I know we have seen each several times and want to make sure we are... on the same page. Do you understand where I'm coming from?"

Joy knows she must get this right the first time; "Jay, it is great that you want to talk about this subject because I needed to **talk** to you as well, about something important to me... very important. And, I really didn't know how to raise the subject, but I got a text from my OBGYN a few weeks ago."

Jason stiffens and turns; "A few weeks ago.... What... What the hell for?"

Focusing deep into his eyes; "Jason no... Wait a minute. You wanted to talk, so pay very close attention to what I am about to tell you. This is very **important** to me...all right?"

He takes a deep breath and shakes his head; "I guess I didn't realize what I just started. What is it? Doctor's visit, why?"

"I'm going to have a baby."

Startled; "What... a baby?"

Joy in an uncharacteristically soft tone; "I believe I am pregnant, but had to wait a few more weeks to be sure."

Dumbfounded, Jason grabs his head; "Now I am really confused. Are you telling me you are pregnant?"

Joy leans again to touch his arm, but he pulls away; "Well yes, but not from having sex with you. That is why this is so very... very hard."

Jason stands up abruptly, flipping her feet off his lap; "So you have been having sex with someone else and me at the same time? How the hell can that be, I've been with you almost every night. I'm not sure I understand what the hell you're telling me."

As she taps the sofa, speaking softly; "Jason come... Please sit. You wanted to talk so sit, please be patient and allow me to explain. Please... Come on...sit." Jason sits with his head in hands; *"What the hell did I get myself into?"*

"I also like you an awful lot. And, if things keep going the way I hope they will go, I want us to stay together. I trust you more than any guy I have ever known and want to be honest with you from the get-go."

In an attempt to get his answer; "But... but."

"Jason, no secrets, no misunderstandings and hopefully no misgivings."

Jason looks skeptically at the diminutive feisty redhead; "But you want to have someone else's baby?"

Joy taps his leg again; "Jason, please listen carefully and please don't interrupt. I didn't want to have it... the baby...But I have to. You see my sister Dawn, you haven't met her yet, has asked me to have a baby for her, and she doesn't have any time to find another surrogate.   Sit back, and I will pour you a bourbon and let me explain the entire situation from the beginning."

Jason sits gripping his filled tumbler of Woodford Reserve.   After several minutes of excruciating medical mumbo-jumbo, he finally understands Joy's perplexing situation. He leans forward, sits the empty glass on the table and places his hands on her face. He scrunches her rosy cheeks; "Joy, honey, I think I understand and am willing to help in whatever way I can. I think I know you well enough already from your work and from our being together that you have thought this through and that this is your only solution. A lot of those gold-diggers out there would lie and tell me it is mine and want me to pay for everything. I respect your candor."

Joy focusing on his expression; "Jay, **Wow!** I didn't expect that from anybody. I had no idea when Dawn asked me to be a surrogate that I would be sitting here today with someone that I truly care for. I thought I would have to go through this alone. I want for us to be together and not begin any relationship based on a lie."

Stroking her leg; "Honey, I have no idea where this relationship will end up, but I am here for you right now and will support you all the way with your decision."

Obviously shaken; "That is more than any person can ask."

A few days later, Joy and Jason are riding to the hospital for another doctor's exam to check the embryo and any faint heartbeat. Joy is sitting in the front seat texting her sister and laughing. Jason shakes his head; *"Probably more meaningless chatter about things that don't matter. I guess she can communicate very well when she wants to."*

All goes well with Joy with her ultrasound, and within another month, she begins to get the all too familiar pregnancy symptoms. She and Jason have grown closer and he has moved some of his clothes into her place. He becomes very supportive and doting, to a fault. Likewise, Jason is the only man that she has had willing sex with, loved and can confide in.

Days later at the morning breakfast table, her little knee tucked beneath her chin, Joy looks up and asks; "Jason, you really never tell me much about your mom."

"There really isn't very much to tell. What do you want to know?"

"I'd like to know just about everything, about you and her before you met me."

Pondering; "Well you already know that I was born here, but raised in Texas. My mom got married to an oil company guy, a roughneck and he died when I was really young, so I can't remember too much about him. We lived in Midland for a few years then, when she needed a good paying job, we moved to Dallas. My mom got her degree in microbiology and got a job in a DNA lab. She was the one that got me interested in science and biology and, that is where I got my first exposure to forensics."

As Jason pauses, Joy asked inquisitively; "So that's it?"

"Yeah pretty much, without getting into too much detail."

"So your mom... she lives here in OKC?"

"Back when I relocated from Dallas, she moved to OKC a few months later. Yes, she was able to get a great job here in OKC. She runs a DNA lab at a Bio-research company just outside OKC."

As they continue eating breakfast, there is an extended silence. Joy jerks her head up from her iPhone; "Can you ask your mother to run a DNA sequencing test for me? I could have it done at the clinic, but with all the paperwork, there are too many nosy people. I want to keep this 100% confidential."

Distracted, munching on his morning cereal; "What? Sure.... Why? Are there any details you can share?"

Raising her eyes up from her iPhone; "Easy detective, no, not right now. But I will fill you in... in due time... I promise."

Walking back from the freezer, she slides a frozen bag containing a vile into his hand; "I would really like to know who the dad is. After the embryos were implanted, the doctor had a few left over that they were going to be discarded. My sister signed them over to me, so I asked, and the doctor and she allowed me to keep them. I kept them frozen. Is there any way to compare DNA results to identify the father in the national data bank? I don't want to get anyone in trouble; I'd just like to know just in case there are complications."

Finally showing some interest; "Sure, I can drive by my mom's office and ask her if it's okay for her to run the tests...discreetly. She has all the sequencing equipment and access to all the national DNA databases."

"You sure she won't mind? I don't want to get her into any trouble. By the way, you never told me her name."

With a curious look, he gently examines the vile; "My mom's name, Barbara, Barbara Moore. Maybe she can find more information about your niece's condition too. Would that be okay?"

Joy smiles, pauses a second and scurries barefoot across the floor back to the freezer, rummages around for a second, then pulls out a second bag from the freezer; "Can I ask a second favor, just an itty-bitty one?

With his eyes tracing her steps around the room; *"Oh shit, what did I just get into?"*

"While she is at it, can she do another DNA sequence on this second vile? If it's **too** much trouble... I'll just throw it back in the freezer."

Squinting he carefully reads the two labels, sees the first that is dated 2012 and the second was her name dated 2011; " Hey, a quick question; the first vile is dated 2012 has Dawn's name on it, but the first vile dated 2011 is your name on it with a swab inside, how come?"

Joy standing behind him, rubbing his shoulders; "Honey, remember what we discussed a few weeks ago... that we had to trust each other. This is part of that **trust** thing. Okay? So, you're bringing them to your mom today, right? Here's a small freezer bag you must keep them frozen. You must keep them frozen.... Understand? "

Jason looking back around to see Joy's face; "Sure, I guess. What is the second vile for?"

Joy walks away, so Jason cannot see her blushing; "It's kind of personal and I would really appreciate it if you don't ask any detective, probative questions. I told you, I cannot give you any details,...not right now anyway, if it is that difficult then forget about the whole... thing."

Apologetically; "Okay, okay... I got it... **no** more questions. I'll drive them to her office right after breakfast. Do you want me to see the results of the search or do you want them to be kept confidential as well?"

Joy turns around ankles crossed, leaning up against the fridge,; " Jay, please... for now I would really appreciate total privacy and your discretion. I don't know how I will handle the information, once I get it and wouldn't want you to get involved... Is that okay?"

"All right, I understand. I will do exactly as you ask."

Joy runs back and throws her arms around his neck, hugging him aggressively; "You're the **best.**"

Jason nods and continues to crunch on his breakfast cereal. About a half hour later Jason is driving up to a single story building on Northwest Highway outside OKC. There are about two dozen cars lined up in the sweltering parking lot. He walks to the reception desk and asks to see Barbara Moore. The young receptionist looks up with a big grin on her face. Jason seeing her smile, shakes his head; "So what is so amusing?"

Receptionist with a big smile; "Well I have heard about you from your mom. She speaks glowingly of you. The photo of you on her desk... doesn't do you justice. I'm sure she can see you. Just walk through these doors and to the end of the hall. You will see the door marked DNA lab. That's her office."

Jason walks back to the lab and sees his mother with her back turned to the open door. As he enters, he knocks and looks around; *"This place is quite elaborate. A lot bigger than the other cubicle she had in Dallas."*

She slowly swivels around, sits up erect, and offers a broad smile. Even hidden under her professional lab coat, Barbara is still very attractive, an athletic woman in her late-40's. Her long sandy-colored hair is tucked to one side, held back by a blue rubber band in a feeble attempt at control. As a fully occupied lab professional, with no man in her life, she spends little time caring for her looks. Nonetheless, the blue-eyed beauty shows through.

Barbara beaming up at her son; "Well, what brings you to this part of town? This is not like you to visit me at the office. Is this a social visit or for business?"

Jason with his hands behind his back; "Both, I wanted to see if they took care of you all right, with your new office, and I figured it's way too long since I've seen ya."

Disbelievingly; "Wow, you really do need something special. Don't ya?"

Uncomfortably rocking; "Well, sort of. I have a friend, and she needs some DNA tests. Specifically, DNA sequencing performed and doesn't want to go through any legal hassles, to get the results. Can you do that for me... us?

Inquisitively; "Sure, I believe I can. Why not run the test through your OKCPD, DNA lab. They have the equipment, don't they?"

Jason walks over and inquisitively fingers through the lavender colored DNA data sheets on her desk; "I don't want to fill out any tedious paperwork to send up any red flags through a government lab. I don't know those guys well enough yet. Is this what the results look like for DNA sequencing, identity test?"

Barbara annoyed; "Yes... please put those down, that's confidential information. Don't change the subject; is she someone special to you? You haven't dated anyone special for quite some time. Not since Dallas."

"*Special*...well sort of special. We kind of like each other...a bit. While we haven't made any commitments, I do see Joy a lot. We enjoy being... together. You know..."

Rolling her eyes; "For kids your age today...that says a lot. And, a lot more than most married couples I know. Yes, of course, I will do the test. How quickly do you need the results? Can you share any information about the samples; where and when they were taken and under what circumstances?"

As Jason reluctantly hands them over; "The first is a frozen embryo from her sister, taken in 2012. It's a long story, but her niece is very, very sick and needs to have Joy... the girl I am *seeing,* **to** have a surrogate baby... to help save her niece; identical DNA and all that stuff. I guess some very special stem cells can only be taken from a newborn's umbilical cord that can save her niece."

As she slowly leans back, open-mouthed; "Wow, it looks like she is a *very*, very special, unselfish person, willing to give her body for her sister. That's really unusual today, without meeting her she sounds like a keeper. What does she do?"

Sensing a mini-inquisition; "Please, can we keep this on track mom?"

Barbara rotates and inquisitively examines the second vile; "At first glance, it appears to be a rape kit sample, taken in 2011 at the OU campus clinic. That goes back a few years." Peering up at him; "Is there anything you can tell me about this one?"

With a playful sneer; "I have no idea of the circumstances surrounding that sample. She didn't want to share *any* details. All she gave me was the vial. That's it.... Nothin else... However, she seemed embarrassed to even ask me, and I didn't want to press it. She has been very honest with me I'm sure she will share the details when the time is right."

Lifting her chin; "You're a good detective, why don't you take down the sample serial number and information and see what else you can find, I will do the rest."

"I know that's a good idea and obviously I can do it, but I promised her that I would stay out of this. And, a promise *is* a promise. Right, mom... that's what you always taught me."

With a broad grin; "So Jay, when will I meet this impressive young lady, any time soon?"

Turning to leave; "Pretty soon mom, I'll try to schedule lunch or dinner or somethin soon. Okay. No pressure, right mom..?"

Standing as he leaves; "So, where are you off to now?"

Jason leaning up against the door; "After the extra storm duty, I have hours of comp time coming, so I signed up for special marksmanship training, and my first class is scheduled for this afternoon."

"I thought you already qualified as a marksman at Texas."

Taking a step backward to leave; "I did, I just wanted to get a refresher. Let me know when you get the lab results. Thanks, mom, you're the best. *Luv ya*.."

CHAPTER 9
Family Ties

As Grandpa Cloud walks out of the sweltering cabin with his bow, he sees Cloud on a creaky rocker reading a book; "You have been moping around here for weeks. When are you going to get off your ass and do somethin?"

Head in the book; "Yes pop. I'm actually teaching a new marksmanship class at the police academy later this afternoon."

Grandpa reaches into his pocket for a fresh dip of Red Man snuff and puts it under his lower lip; "Great, it's about time that you got out of this God damn cabin and get on with your life. Take it from an expert, women aren't everything in life, even though they would like for us to think so."

Still focused on the book; "Okay pop, got the message."

Grandpa stands for several seconds peering into the trees; "Heard a couple of gobblers the other day, so I'm going down to the tree stand to sit with Carlos. Today we have some cut corn thrown out to attract turkey. They've been hiding in the thick cedar, and we're trying to coax them out."

Cloud glancing up; "Yeah, I saw a flock crossing the road just the other day. By the way, how is Carlos' niece...Angelina? How she doin? Is she OK... Ya know?"

Just shaking his head; "How can any girl be okay after what those animals did to her and her mom? But she seems to be adjusting, as best a young girl can."

"Did you ever adjust and teach her how to shoot Daniel's bow?"

Exhaling with a whistle; "Wow... I'll say... You should see that little girl shoot. She has an incredible eye and feel. She's a natural. A few weeks ago, she won the target shooting competition at the summer camp, beating all the boys...easily. And, they were a lot older and bigger than she was. It was embarrassing to watch."

With a grin; "Has she taken off Daniels' jacket yet?"

Shaking his head; "Nope. Not even in this wretched heat. Damn, she looks funny. It goes all the way down past her knees. I don't think she'll ever take that off. She always asks when Daniel is getting back home."

Head in his book; "Well pop, good luck. Try to remember some old Indian tricks and bring us back something to eat... for a change."

Grandpa comes out of the cabin with a handheld short-wave radio in hand; "Carlos, you there, buddy?"

After about 10 seconds; "Si, Señor, I am on my way to our tree stand now."

"Is Angelina joining us today?"

"No Papa, she is doing her target practice today, again. Practice, practice, practice that is all she ever does. She is wearing out that target and the arrows you bought her."

Walking off the front steps; "Okay I will meet you in the stand in a few minutes."

Cloud slowly raises his eyes from his book; "By the way Pop, how many batches of your special recipe did you make this time?"

As Grandpa strolls to his battery-powered ATV, he looks back; "I can't really say I have several cases aging down below, ready to sell. I'm just waiting on some orders to come in."

Cloud yells back; "Listen, just don't get caught. Only carry a few out at a time. You know it's still against the law."

Cloud rocks back and listens to the country-western music on the radio. He raises his ear to hear an old Charlie Rich song Behind Closed Doors ♪; "Did you happen to see the most beautiful girl in the world. ...." Cloud can become easily emotional, especially with the imbalance in his meds and reminisces of a time when things were less complicated. A few minutes later, he looks at his watch, jumps up and drives back to Oklahoma City to teach his class.

Grandpa and Carlos meet at the base of their favorite tree stand. It is a sturdy hunting platform that comfortably seats three. Well-hidden, 30 feet up the tree, it overlooks the entire area. The 100-year-old oak with a 10-foot trunk at the base has withstood every storm during its lifespan. Their camouflaged platform is built into the outstretched 2-foot-thick limbs, providing excellent support and cover. Even in daylight, it is difficult to see the men in their perch.

Below the platform stretches a lush growing 5-acre food

plot. It is hidden from other hunter's eyes by surrounding trees and thick undergrowth. The Clouds have planted beans, beets, various greens, and even some feed corn. The crops are selected to attract deer and wild turkey.

The back side of the old oak reaches over a trickling creek that continues down a quarter mile to the cabin. Through countless years, stormwater runoff has washed out the red clay embankment, leaving roots exposed. The meandering creek carved a half-moon shaped wash around the tree, creating high, steep slippery banks; making it very difficult for any animal to escape. Grandpa dips more Red Man chew then reaches into his carry bag and pulls his trusted wood turkey call. He gently whittles out a few calls, and within a few seconds he gets a distant response from a Tom turkey.

Eyebrows raised; Carlos looks at Grandpa; "I think we will be lucky today Señor Pop."

Grandpa continues the turkey call; "You never know what will show up around here do ya? Ya just never know."

It's about 1:00pm, as Jason makes his way to the Oklahoma City police firing range. Only three officers are waiting to receive instruction. John Cloud, while military erect, is unkempt, not at all projecting a professional instructor. His stay at the cabin has taken its toll. Cloud hasn't interacted with many outsiders for a few weeks, so his communication skills are rusty; "So, who here has any marksmanship training, other than what you received at the academy?"

Only Jason raises his hand. Cloud, gesturing at Jason; "Son, why don't you set up at the end...over there. Go ahead and zero in at 100 and I'll get to you in time, after I get these boys set up. All right?" Cloud has realized for some time that the loud crack of gunfire could trigger an anxiety attack, so he quickly dons his acoustical headphones. Nonetheless, getting back to what he knows is a good way to reacclimate.

Jason, always respectful, just nods his head; "Yes sir. Thank you." Jason works his way down to the last firing station of the line and unrolls his firing mat. Carefully unzipping the rifle case, he carefully checks all of his gear. He is in no rush to assemble his AR rifle, bipod, scope and targeting scope. And, oh yes, he has plenty of magazines and ammo. After assembling his rifle and scope, Jason lies belly down and turns his hat around. This is customary with anyone who shoots, as it keeps the hat brim out of their way of the scope. Once he gets his rifle and scope mounted, he begins ranging in his weapon. *Pop! Pop!* In the background, you can hear the crack of several other rifles going off. After about a half hour, and once the other students have completed their lesson, John Cloud ambles his way down to Jason. He sits at a table behind Jason peering through a targeting scope. He watches as Jason squeezes a few rounds off.

Cloud first looks over Jason's firing position trying to identify any apparent errors. Seeing none, he looks through the spotting scope; "Son, you're not that bad at all for 100 yards. Why don't you take it out to the 200 yards and take three more shots, and see what you can do? That's the red circle target out there to the right."

Jason looks back and nods respectfully; "Yes sir."

After adjusting his scope for the new distance, he again checks the wind and exhales slowly. He then squeezes off three more shots in slow rhythmic succession. Jason turns his head around and looks back to Cloud.

Cloud nods affirmatively; "That is pretty good, pretty... good. I like your technique. Now, why don't you take it out 350 yards, let's see what you got. All the way out there... That small white target in the center. See it..?"

Cloud watches as Jason adjusts his rifle scope again for windage and distance. Cloud peers through the spotter's scope. While not hitting the bull's eye, 10-ring, all shots hit the center mass of the target.

Cloud; "Considering that's a semi-automatic rifle and you have no spotter, that's damn good shootin... **damn** good shootin son." With his clear Oklahoma twang; "Have you trained here before **son**?"

As they both remove their ear protection Jason spins around and sits up facing Cloud; "No sir. This is my first time shooting in Oklahoma, as an officer that is."

"Explain?"

"Well sir, I learned to shoot at UT where I got my degree in Criminal Justice. I moved to OKC in the past year, filling a detective position. I used to shoot along with my grandpa though he lived in Yukon, just outside OKC."

Cloud leaning toward Jason; "Did you ever consider joining SWAT as a sniper? You are a natural and they could always use someone like you. I would only need to give you a few pointers to tune you up real good. Some of those other clowns want to join SWAT but can't hit the 10-ring at 100 yards. I have to say you have it, you're a natural."

"No sir, I'm really not interested in SWAT. My interest in college was forensics, and that's what makes me tick."

With a perplexed; "So if you don't want SWAT and can shoot better than anyone I've seen in a while, what really brings you here today?

Jason stiffens his back; "Well sir... you."

Tersely; "Explain!"

Dropping his head bashfully; "Well sir, …. I'm dating your daughter and wanted to meet you. I know a little about you from the others in the department and just wanted to meet you myself."

With a broad smile; "Which daughter, **Dawn**?"

"No, sir... Joy."

Cloud just shakes his head; "Son, I sure hope you know what you are getting yourself into. She is one sharp girl, but she can create a whole **heap** of trouble,…. really fast. But you look like a resilient fellow, strong, smart. I guess she could do a lot worse. Did she ask about me?"

With a slight grimace; "Sorry sir, no. The other day when I asked about her family, she told me about her mom, Crystal. She also mentioned about her brother Daniel and her sister Dawn, also her niece Samantha, but only in brief passing about you."

With sinking voice; "So, what **did** she say about me... or can't you say."

Jason hesitates to speak.

"Come on boy... spit it out."

Dejectedly; "Well sir, I wouldn't have brought it up. Please excuse me for saying, but it was something like; 'I wouldn't piss on him if he were on fire.' Or something to that effect. Sorry, sir, I wouldn't have said it, but you asked. Excuse my bluntness. Please don't ever tell her I told you."

Throwing his head back with a loud chuckle; "Yep... that's my baby girl. Sounds like she hasn't changed a bit. Now I understand why you are here. You probably want to know what kind of a son-of-a-bitch could generate that kind of response from his loving daughter. Well, it wasn't easy and took a lot of years. Do you want to know the details?"

Jason apologetically; "Well, yes sir, if that is all right with you? But I won't tell her we spoke."

For some reason, whether it's Cloud's sober state or Jason's amiable personality, Cloud feels comfortable opening up to the young stranger. As they sit at a nearby shady table, he takes a deep breath; "Well *son*, that is good because if you do, she will probably kick your ass to the curb. Back years ago, when I met her mom, I was graduating college and going into the US Army. Her mom Crystal really took to me, and she had big plans. Back then, she was drop-dead gorgeous, I mean Hollywood beautiful. Way above my pay grade. But her father was a General attached to the Pentagon, and she figured that he could pull some strings and have me move quickly up through the ranks. She loved the brass and the glory but not the dedication and sacrifice, if you know what I mean. After a few years we settled in, and I got a desk job at the Pentagon as a planner. I hated it, I fucking hated it. So, with 911, guess what happened? Because of all the huge defense cuts made years earlier, we were short on manpower and equipment to fight two wars, Iraq and Afghanistan. Is this interesting you... *son*?

Jason leans in; "Yes sir."

"I was attached to an armored unit during the Iraq invasion. We saw some action, but I never fired my weapon. After a few years things kind of calmed down, then all hell broke loose. Remnants of Saddam's elite Iraqi Republican guard began setting roadside bombs or what is known as IED's. Initially, there was little that we could do. As an engineer with considerable knowledge of our equipment, I volunteered to help retrofit up-armoring to the existing vehicles. They would bring back the equipment after an IED attack and my job was to evaluate the damage and make recommendations."

Recalling the horror, pauses and in a shaking voice; "The carnage... I observed... was horrific. Not just the equipment but the body parts blood and bandages were everywhere. I was never trained for that. I had never seen anything like that, and I hope I never will again."

Cloud bows his head, takes a deep breath and tightly clasps his hands not to show them shaking. He doesn't speak for several seconds; "Son, people back home have absolutely no idea what that hell was like. You recall a soldier you saw that morning, then see what IED did to him. It was a fucking slaughterhouse." Taking a moment to regain his composure; "...Before I left Iraq, I had the opportunity to take out a major player in those IED attacks. We almost got the son-of-a-bitch that day, but he never showed up. Some other nasty shit happened that I wish I could forget. I knew I had to come home, but not in the condition I was in. I didn't want what was happening over there to affect my family. So, I stayed overseas as much as I could, not only to protect them, but to try to rehab, to exorcise my own demons. I don't think I succeeded on either count."

Jason respectfully; "Sir, I've never seen combat and hope I never will, but what I do know is you can't take everything that happened upon yourself. Things... Unthinkable things do happen, but that doesn't mean it's your fault. At some point, you have to let it all go."

With the scent of gun smoke still in the air, Cloud closes his eyes for a moment. He cannot help but recall the face of the Iraqi baby held in his bloodstained hands. Shaking his head, as he brings his hands to his face; "Let it go, I wish I could. It's easier said than done. So many vivid images are right there, every day."

Cloud again pauses to regain his coming composure; "All my experiences have taken their toll on our marriage and family. My wife and my children don't recognize me. I don't even recognize myself when I look in the mirror. It wasn't just the physical separation, but the emotional distance created. The Army shrinks tried to help me reconcile, but some things are just too hard... to fix... and I guess I have to learn to live with it...."

Jason allows him to vent and only interjects after a long pause; "Sir, I think by recognizing these things you've already come a long way. You may have to give it a bit more time. Not that I'm a shrink, but I think you're on the right track, not only with yourself, but with your family as well."

As he looks deep into Jason's eyes; "Son, one of the problems with my condition is you have no idea where you are on this road; the beginning, the middle or the end. You're a good listener *son...* I can see why Joy likes you."

With an opportunity to change the subject, Jason smiles; "That's another story for another day."

"So aside from Joy, have you met the rest of the family yet?"

"Not yet, sir, I don't want to push things, you know how Joy can be. Joy does share a few things with me about your family. I look forward to meeting your daughter Dawn and your wife, Crystal. I understand both are quite attractive women."

Growing a smile; "Crystal my wife... is an intelligent

woman that wanted things I never could give her. She was Hollywood beautiful, but not an extraordinary woman. Deep down, we were never a good match." Sneaking beneath his sunglasses, as he wipes the tears from his eyes; "Don't repeat what I said. **Understand!** I've already said too much."

Sympathetically; "No sir, what is said here stays here."

As Jason pauses with a smirk; "Curious, I do not believe I ever heard that term used when describing a woman, extraordinary. Have you ever met an extraordinary woman in your life?"

Pondering for several seconds; "... Yes, once."

"So why didn't you end up with that woman, the extraordinary woman?"

Raising his eyebrows; "Son, sometimes you have to play the hand you are dealt and make the best of it."

As Jason begins packing away his equipment; "Well sir, I really appreciate our meeting here today and our discussion. I won't tell Joy that we met nor recount our conversation, ever. I hope to see you again soon, possibly under more agreeable circumstances, with your entire family."

Cloud stands stiffly and shakes Jason's hand; "Me too, keep in touch and good luck with Joy, son. She's a **handful**."

CHAPTER 10
June 2017 - Too Much Blood

While driving from the station, Jason hears the dispatcher requesting any available car to go to the OKC Women's clinic. They got a call from the Director that no officers have been stationed in front to control the demonstrators...again. He recognizes the address, and responds to the call. Jason finishes his Grande coffee and parks in the rear lot. He hurries through the rear door to use their men's room. As he rushes past Joy he motions; "I'll be right back."

Motioning to her office at the end of the hall; "See me when you get out, I have some good news." Today, Joy is wearing a light blue spring dress, in celebration of her good news about her recent obstetric appointment.

For several weeks, Rafta's man Jose has been watching for his chance to murder Joy. He has been waiting for an opportunity to sneak into the clinic unobstructed. As José arrives, it appears no police will be guarding the front door. Rafta has grown increasingly aggravated with Jose, and his inability to kill Joy.

Seconds later Jose walks briskly past the peaceful demonstrators and warily opens the front glass door. As he walks down the shiny hall, he unbuttons his jacket and slowly withdraws his large shiny blade. Hiding the knife, the 6'3" attacker slyly scans all the rooms, searching for Joy. He passes by the men's room knowing she cannot be there. Frustrated, he shoves open the door of an OB/GYN procedure rooms.

At that moment the doctor peers up past the woman's spread legs and sees Jose gawking in the doorway. Startled, the doctor drops an instrument to the floor; "What are you doing here? Get the hell out of here, immediately."

The attending nurse screams upon seeing the enormous intruder, displaying a large knife; "**Ahhh...**"

Hearing the screams, Joy scurries into the procedure room from the rear door. Jose and Joy lock eyes immediately. Jose slowly moves around the room toward Joy, knife waving; "***Joy Cloud,... Sí.***"

Immediately spotting the knife, Joy freezes; ""Oh shit... what now?"

The doctor and nurse stand fixed, beside their awakening patient. The young woman on the exam table is confused, just stirring from anesthesia. She stares wide-eyed, tracking Jose's cautious steps around the table" *"Huh..."*

Upon hearing the screams, Jason is stunned and fumbles to hastily zip his fly...but gets jammed; *"God damn thing always get stuck."* In seconds, he yanks it up, hopping out of the restroom door. Hesitantly he withdraws his Glock pistol, stepping cautiously, listening for any sound. The last thing he wants to do is to enter a procedure room at an inappropriate time; *"What the hell is going on here."*

Jose, now focused on the tiny woman with the perfusion

of red hair, quickly lunges around the table, but slips on the fallen instrument, landing hard. His knife becomes dislodged, skidding across the floor.

Realizing she can't move in her high heels, she instinctively kicks off her shoes; *"Gotta to move fast, gotta to move quick. Where do I go? Which way do I move? Oh shit...!"*

With just a few feet between them, Jose watches Joy as he drops to his hands and knees, frantically looking for his blade; *"Where is it? Where is it?"*

Joy does not grasp the gravity of her situation; nonetheless, seizing the opportunity, picks up a heavy stainless instrument tray, draws back and swings it wildly. Like a superhero character from her youth she provides her own sound effects; "EeeYaa..."

Jose focuses curiously; *"Qué."*

The little barefoot woman bounds left, then right, then aggressively thrusts the edge of the tray squarely onto his nose. With a scornful smile; "Take that **asshole!**"

Jose clutches his face and grunts in pain; "Rrrrr." Staggering up, hunched over holding his nose, he cannot see clearly.

Joy instinctively runs up and kicks him square in the groin; *"**Hee Yahhh!**.*

Jose grabs his crotch and falls to his knees; "**Ahhhhh..**"

As the onlookers watch, Joy tries to hit him again, but Jose intercepts her swing, grabs her arm and flings her against the wall like a rag doll. Joy bangs her head hard against the wall, dazed, semiconscious; **"Owww."** Defenseless, she sits with exposed splayed legs.

Seeing José searching for his knife, the doctor, nurse and semiconscious patient rush out the main door; **"Hurry... get out! Get out! Get out!"**

The abortion procedure completed just minutes earlier; with the tiny fetus in a stainless-steel bowl, covered by a white towel. Jose is disoriented, nose bleeding profusely, staggers back to his feet. Angrily flailing his arms, he grunts; **"Rurrr."** he abruptly jerks at the nearby white towel to wipe his face. This sends the stainless bowl airborne and the examining table light swaying.

Joy sits stunned, trying to gain her senses, watches as the stainless bowl rise up and slowly tumbles above her. The bowl lands upside down between her splayed legs.

José is still dazed, eyes watering, struggles to see past the towel. He searches across the floor for his knife; *"My knife, I must find my knife."*

Groggy, Joy lifts the bowl, immediately screams at the sight of the tiny, bloody fetus, nestled in her lap. *"**Yaaa, Yaaa, Yaaa**..."* Her screams are horrific and uncontained.

As Jason recognizes Joy's cries, he enters the room as the others escape. At the moment Jason comes into the room pistol in hand, he makes eye contact with the Jose; *"What the fuck?"* and sees Joy against the wall.

Jose looks at Jason with steely resolve, robotically moves toward Joy, shining knife in hand; *"I must complete my task."* Profusely bleeding from his nose, he towers over her tiny body; *"Finally...the lamb to the slaughter."*

Jason carefully raises and sights in his Glock, yells; **"Freeze!"**

Jose viciously grabs Joy's disheveled red mass, exposing her fragile neck. As he raises the knife, Joy stares up petrified, neck stretched, hyperventilating. All she can do is just watch; *"What..? God no!* **God no..!"**

Jason yells loudly; **"Freeze...! Drop the knife...!"**

Jose has been trained for this. He is resolved to his fate and glares over his shoulder again at Jason, rears his arm back in preparation for the execution; **"Rurrr."**

As Jason hears; ***"Allah Akbar"*** two shots rapidly ring out, hitting Jose in the back of the head, killing him instantly. Blood and brain matter spray everywhere, across the wall and all over Joy. Jose body collapses in a hulk, engulfing her.

Jason rushes to pull the bleeding, dead giant off Joy; "Get the hell off."

Joy, horrified, patterned in blood, sits quaking with the aborted fetus still nestled on her lap; *"What,.. what... what... is..*

happening.. to.. me?"

Jason astonished at seeing the fetus, quickly kneels down opens the towel and delicately picks it up, places it onto the bowl. Instinctively, he pulls out his radio and makes the call; "Shots fired, shots fired, Oklahoma City woman's clinic."

Joy sits eyes open yet, unresponsive. Realizing she is in shock, he opens a nearby cabinet, grabs clean linen and attempts to wipe away the mass of blood and matter. She continues to quiver uncontrollably, unresponsive to his presence. As he tries to bring her gently back, whispering; "Joy honey... honey, it's me, Jason."

Minutes later, the entire facility is surrounded by dozens of police cars. Jason carefully cradles her in his arms and carries her from the procedure room to the reception area. Kneeling, Jason tries to clean the blood from her face and hair.

Detective Lieutenant stands warily beside Jason, holding Jose's knife in an evidence bag; "What the hell just happened here Moore? The press is already outside, I need some answers."

Jason still kneeling in front of Joy, looks up at him; "I wish I knew. I'll try to get you a report ASAP, as soon as I take care of Miss Cloud." He looks at the Lieutenant and with darting eyes tells him to get the knife away from Joy.

Voice quivering; beginning to regain her senses, Joy instinctively slides her arms around Jason's neck; "Geeet... mmee the ffuck outa hhere. Ttake me home."

Jason gently carries her to his car; "Joy, I'll take you back to my place to clean up. Okay, babe..?" He brings the shivering young girl to his apartment and walks her to the bathroom. He turns on the shower and runs for a minute; turns to her; "Go ahead babe, get out of those clothes."

Hands still trembling Joy has trouble undoing her dress; "Let me help you with that." As he helps her out of her blood-drenched dress, she gently reaches for him, eyes beckoning; "It's OK, I'll stay here with you. You are safe now."

Joy is still on the edge of hysteria, but the warm, comforting shower begins to calm her. She has difficulty cleaning the encrusted blood from her unruly red mass, so Jason slides open the shower door; "Let me help you with that." Seeing the blood leaching from her hair, not wanting her to become even more alarmed; "Babe... Keep your eyes closed."

Though he is getting drenched, he massages copious amounts of shampoo, rinses, then starts the process all over again. It takes three cycles to clean, but it's more therapeutic than cleansing. He covers Joy's tiny body with a huge towel, then instinctively rolls another on top of her head. With only her flushed red face showing, he carries her into the bedroom. Throwing back the covers; "Come on and slide in."

Sitting next to Joy, Jason receives a text message; "Officers are outside. We will guard the unit."

Jason texts back; "If a female officer is available, have her come in" A female officer enters his condo and stands at the bedroom door, making her presence known. She scans the area and notices the blood-soaked dress on the floor in the bathroom, shaking her head in disbelief.

Sitting beside Joy still shaking, looking into fluttering eyes; "Joy...Honey, I have asked a few questions. Are you able to answer some for me?"

Joy nods, mouthing; "Okay."

"Do you remember what just happened?"

Joy nods; "Not sure."

"Did you recognize the guy at the clinic; the guy that attacked you?"

Joy unable to speak just shakes her head, mouths; "No"

"Was there anything that you may have received in the mail or over the phone that might shed light on the attack?"

As Joy tucks her knees under her chin, just shakes her head; "No"

At that point, the Detective Lieutenant is also standing at the door. Jason looks back; "This is crazy, a total stranger just walks in with the huge knife trying to kill her and yells Allah Akbar. I have absolutely no clue what the hell is going on here, but I will find out, I promise you. Ms. Cloud... Can you stay here for a few days?"

Joy just nods yes, then reaches for his arm.

"It will be fine Joy; we will have a female officer stay with you."

Looking at the Lieutenant; "Can you arrange that Sir?"

The Lieutenant nods his head, directing Jason to come with him; "Yes, I will take care of security."

When they get outside the room, the Lieutenant takes him aside; "Okay... Tell me what you know."

Jason, standing there in his still in dripping clothes, stained with blood; "Sir, I was driving about a quarter mile from the clinic when I heard the dispatcher over the radio. Ms. Cloud... Joy Cloud and I have been dating for several weeks now.

The Lieutenant looks at him skeptically; "What..?"

"Sir, she is the interim director at the clinic. And yes, we have been dating for the past several weeks. But that has nothing to do with the situation."

With a bewildered; "Go ahead Moore, keep explaining."

"When I got there, I had to take a leak. In the restroom, I heard screams and I ran out. When I got into the examination room, I saw the assailant standing over her with that knife. You have that knife. I ordered him to freeze and drop the knife. He yelled Allah Akbar raised the knife and I shot him."

"He yelled what?"

"That's right Sir... he yelled Allah Akbar."

But I shot him twice. I might be able to fill in more blanks if I can get back to the clinic, if that's okay with you sir."

With an affirmative look; "So far your recollection jives with the doctor and nurse. I will let you stay on this case. However, since you were involved in the shooting, you must keep me completely informed. Understand?"

"Yes, sir."

As Jason sticks his head back into the bedroom doorway; "Okay Joy, I'll be back later this afternoon. They will have an officer assigned to sit with you, all right? I'll be back later; you just try to get some rest."

Joy just nods her head.

Jason returns to the clinic not long after. Clothes still stained with José's blood, there are now plenty of onlookers and news crews covering the story as Jason walks under the yellow police barrier tape. With blue foot booties and disposable gloves, Jason slowly walks noting every smudge and mark. He moves past one of the offices and sees another detective taking statements from the doctor, the nurse, and the female patient. Jason just nods at them and walks to the procedure room. He sees Jose's body covered by a sheet and recalls his last words and attempts to reconstruct the scene. Squatting down next to José he looks up his friend, Jimmy the forensic field tech; "This guy was no anti-abortion activist. They are harmless; old folks that just make a lot of noise. This guy was here on a mission."

He kneels down to look closely at Jose's hands and recognizes a distinctive large ruby stone ring on his pinky. Curiously looking at Jimmy, he asks; "Can you take a photo of this hand, please? I am going to take off the ring and examine it." Examining the ring up close; "Rensselaer Engineering, 2010 inside inscription, PJ." Believe me, this guy was no engineering school grad. Jimmy, direct the lab to run a DNA genealogy on him immediately."

"DNA genealogy. What? Why?"

Jason takes out his iPhone, takes a few photos of the ring and returns it to the tech; "Just do as I ask and don't raise any suspicions. Oh yes, I need to get the results ASAP."

Outside the clinic our friendly MSOCK reporter, Elouise Lion, stands before a TV camera, microphone in hand; "Today there was a brazen attack by anti-abortion activists. Recently, there have been heightened tensions between the activists and police. Earlier, those tensions exploded when an activist attempted to kill the clinic's director, Ms. Joy Cloud. Fortunately, she was unharmed; however, the assailant, whose name is being withheld, was killed by an undercover officer. We will keep you fully informed. Elouise Lion, reporting live from the scene."

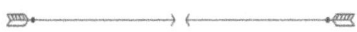

Rafta has been waiting anxiously for several days, scanning the news for information about his associates in Venezuela who were waiting for his notice to proceed. He hears of the botched attempt on Joy Cloud's life by José and decides he must prepare better for future operations. With this botched attempt, Rafta must relocate until the heat dies down. He rents a few shabby mobile homes further outside of town. Rafta texts his other men, suggesting that they move up their travel plans to America. Realizing he may be under surveillance, he encrypts his message; "So, when will I get my package and how many are included? That is good, there are eight more coming in two separate packages, and it should arrive in a few days. Excellent!"

Rafta is angered by José's failure to kill the diminutive girl. He now begins to plan his next attack; *"This time, we will not fail, and we will get all of them."*

Each evening, like clockwork, major thunderstorms explode throughout the area. Rafta watches the TV and tries to anticipate which towns might be vulnerable to extended power outages. He must also determine which of the gun shops in the area would be good candidates for firearms. There are plenty of gun stores to choose from in central Oklahoma, so he has several candidates. But they need to be reasonably large stores, stocking several automatic rifles. Just northwest of Oklahoma City, he hears warnings that the power distribution grid was being stressed by the prolonged heat wave and that the approaching line of thunderstorms could compromise the electric grid, and all the towns in that area could go dark.

He watches patiently, as predicted, the line of storms pass through on time. Rafta notes the reports of the towns hit by the storms and anticipates those that will be without power for hours. With the loss of power, security alarms go off at AJ's Gun Shop. It's a common occurrence for store alarms to be ringing out when the AC power goes out. Rafta has methodically planned this operation for weeks. He quickly drives his men in a van to the rear of AJ's Gun Shop. His men pry open the rear door, alarm already blaring, strobe lights flashing from the power outage. Rafta's men steal several ready to shoot AK's right off the rack along with thousands of rounds of ammunition. He also takes an inoperable war memento RPG, a trophy of the Iraq war, just hanging on the wall. Not a problem for Rafta, an expert in weapons repairs. Before he leaves, he opens a glass case containing several pistols. After scanning his selection, he grabs a shiny 38-caliber snub-nosed revolver and a nearby box of shells, and slides the revolver into his pocket; "I will keep this close and make sure it comes to good use." This is a veritable candy store for terrorists. He just looks around shakes his head and smiles as they exit; *"This could not have been easier."* No one noticed them breaking in and getting out of the gun store that night; the police rarely ever drive by to check it out.

The town Sheriff and State Police were called the next day to investigate the theft. With police blocking the road, lights flashing, they have no reason to connect the robbery to the shooting at the Oklahoma City Woman's Clinic days earlier.

Outside the police rope line, our friendly MSOCK reporter Elouise Lion is busier than ever, standing before a TV camera, microphone in her face; "Last night with the power out, an Oklahoma gun store was boldly robbed, several automatic weapons were stolen. Informed sources indicate it was perpetrated by Right Wing affiliated extremists, stockpiling automatic weapons. Elouise Lion, reporting live from the scene."

It only takes a few days for the details of the clinic crime scene report to come together. Jason studies the DNA genealogy results and is mystified. The Rensselaer Engineering School ring, taken from the assailant at the clinic belonged to a Phil Johnson of Greenwich, Connecticut; who graduated Rensselaer in 2010. Phil was killed in Mexico several weeks earlier. Also, the DNA genealogy results from the unidentified assailant is even more troubling. It designates the primary ancestral regions of North Africa and Middle Eastern.

Jason utters to himself; *"What the hell is going on here? A ruby ring stolen from a recently murdered college grad, weeks earlier at a Yucatan Mexican resort 2000 miles away. So, buddy, you have been really traveling quite a long distance and have been a very busy guy. Why are you here and why now? And, what does Joy Cloud have to do it this?"*

Jason immediately picks up his office phone, and calls other law enforcement investigative branches. First the State Police; they indicate it is not their jurisdiction. He calls the FBI and Homeland Security and schedules a visit at the local FBI OKC office for later that morning.

"I'm here to see FBI Agent Matthews." Agent Matthews has the unenviable job of evaluating extraneous crimes and evidence from local law enforcement agencies, to determine if they are linked. As Jason walks down the brightly adorned walls with plaques, he knocks on Agent Matthew's door; "Agent Matthews you and I spoke earlier today about information that I thought you might be interested in."

Agent Matthews barely raises his head from the paperwork on his desk; "We are inundated daily with hearsay rumors about terrorist attacks. Detective Moore, do you have any additional, actionable intelligence?"

Detective Moore extends a folder to Agent Matthews; "I had a DNA test performed on the assailant, on what I believed to be a terrorist attack. It indicates that the geographical origin of the attacker is North Africa and the Middle East. Plus, before I killed him, he screamed Allah Akbar."

Agent Matthews annoyed, discouragingly opens up the folder, scans it for a minute then shakes his head; "Do you realize how many leads we get every day about North African or Middle Eastern terrorists coming into this country? Dozens. Detective, I really appreciate your initiative." Points to a pinboard with dozens of Post-it notes atop photos and evidence sheets; "Please take a look at my wall. Those are but a few of the cases that we are overseeing with our eight other agencies like ATF and narcotics."

As Jason tries to interject, Agent Matthews disparagingly closes his eyes and just waves his finger; "A couple of days ago we got a report from ATF that a bunch of right-wing extremists broke into the local firearms store and stole about a dozen AK's with ammo, and if you can imagine, a fucking RPG...That's enough to start a small war.... Then we got a report from DEA that they intercepted the tractor-trailer shipment of methamphetamine from Mexico headed for OKC. If you can imagine, the traffickers cut open hundreds of cantaloupes and filled them with bags of meth then glued them shut. *Cantaloupes... fucking cantaloupes!*"

Detective Moore, I'm sure you have done a thorough investigation, tracking down a few valuable clues, but there is nothing to indicate that this is a wide spread conspiracy or that there are others involved. As far as we are concerned, this guy is just a single nut-job going after an abortion clinic. He was just an unaffiliated disgruntled individual. That is it. If you can find additional evidence that points to a larger organization or conspiracy, please call me immediately. Other than that, I can't help you. "

Pointing to the door, he hands the folder back to Jason; "Good work though. Keep us informed if something else comes up. Thanks."

Jason slides the folder under his arm and walks dejectedly back to his overheated pickup, for a slow ride back to his office.

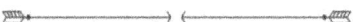

Locked away for days working on a backlog of DNA test samples, Jason's mother Barbara Moore is isolated from the outside world. Deep in the building stacked with test equipment, she cannot get radio reception. With earbuds firmly in place, she listens to her favorite Pandora playlist.

Humming to a favorite Garth Brooks song, The Dance ♪ "Looking back at the memories of the dance we shared.." becomes silent as she reviews the forensic test results requested by Jason. She sits at her desk, at first inquisitive, then a perplexed look comes across her face; *"What the heck...?"* She compares the three sequencing tests in front of her; the first labeled Dawn 2012, the second labeled Joy 2011 and the third of person that matches both DNA samples. She meticulously examines the sheets, then frantically hammers at the computer to verify the labeling, testing sequences, and protocols. *"Everything is in order. This cannot be. How the hell can this be?"* As she is about to make her call to Jason, the phone rings. It is her son Jason; "Mom, it's Jason."

Barbara anxiously; "Jay, we need to talk. I..."

Not wishing to waste any time, Jason interrupts; "Mom... give me a second to explain, please. Something terrible happened the other day. Didn't you hear about it? It's was really a horrific scene. I had to kill a guy. Didn't ya hear about it on the news?"

Anxiously; "***Kill*** a guy.. are, are you okay?

"I'm fine, but Joy is still a mess. She just sits there with her knees to her chest...shaking. I need to take care of her right now. I was just talking to the FBI and wanted to let you know what happened and that I'm alright. Sorry I didn't call you sooner. "

Shaking her head; "FBI..? Who was this guy that you killed? Can you tell me anything?"

Hurriedly; "Sorry mom I can't talk now, but I'll get back to you soon as I can, all right."

"I'll talk to you later Jay. But we need to talk later, promise... Be careful. "

Barbara slowly hangs up the phone and looks down at the test results again. As is standard procedure, DNA tests are screened against everyone in the national DNA database. Shaking her head, she hurriedly folds three lavender colored DNA test-result sheets and places them into her purse.

John Cloud finally got through to Dawn, and was hoping to join them for the next hospital appointment. She is always so busy with work and caring for Samantha, she rarely finds time to see her father. Cloud anxiously wanting to see his sick granddaughter; "Dawn... Honey, it's dad. I'd love to see you and come by and see Samantha. I got a letter from Danny, and he mentioned something about Samantha's health problems. You never told me she was sick. What is it? Is there anything I can do?"

Looking at Samantha with a happy face; "Well dad, I would like to fill you in on the phone, but it would take a long time, so I guess the best thing would be for you to meet us next week, when I have a 1:30 appointment at the hospital with Samantha's doctor. We can fill you in then. Mom has already promised to drive, and I said that would be fine, plus Joy will be meeting us as well. Maybe we can all go out and have ice cream afterward or somethin. Would that be okay?"

"That sounds great. I'll plan on seeing you at the hospital's front entrance, next Wednesday around 1:30."

After several days, Joy is recovering and decides to move more belongings out of her condo into Jason's. She feels a lot safer there now. She and Jason have been spending every evening together, just cuddling and watching TV. Jason keeps his off-duty pistol always close, but just out of sight, as not to alarm her. The fact that she was almost beheaded has made the once effervescent, fiery redhead incredibly defensive and paranoid. Plus, the reality of her now being pregnant is taking a physical toll. Nonetheless, she is gritty and slowly pulls herself together for her ultrasound appointment, scheduled for 11 o'clock. Jason is standing beside her today at the entrance to the hospital.

After he missed his opportunity to kill Joy Cloud, and now unable to locate her, Rafta seeks out other members of Cloud's family. When Mohammed Rafta coordinated the ISIS recruiting in Iraq, he heavily utilized the Internet. He relies on several social websites, such as Facebook and Twitter. When he looks up the name Cloud on Facebook, it is not long before he identifies Dawn Cloud. Dawn has several Facebook interests, especially for her daughter's health. She was greatly alarmed that her sister was attacked. There were no details given; *"I need more information, more information."* She is overjoyed with the progress Joy is having with her surrogate pregnancy and shares some scant details on her Facebook page. While there is no information about Dawn's home address, it does not take long before Rafta tracks down an important tidbit. Dawn inadvertently mentions her 1:30 Wednesday hospital appointment on Facebook where many family members are gathering: "That special day." Rafta sees this is an incredible opportunity to either track or to kill many in the Cloud family; *" On that special day."*

By this time an additional eight men have arrived in Oklahoma City to prepare for their mission. He has them stay inconspicuous and out of sight. Rafta's third in charge Pedro is waiting close to the main hospital entrance. Rafta sits unnoticed across the street with binoculars and a handheld radio. He recognizes Dawn Cloud with her beautiful long dark hair, holding Samantha's hand along with Crystal Cloud; *"Oh what a beautiful family."*

Cloud planned to get a few things done in the city that day. He had an appointment scheduled with Dr. Fellows and once done, planned to drive over and see Dawn and Samantha and the rest of his family. Once Cloud got off the elevator, he saw Dr. Fellows standing in the lobby just outside her office. She greeted him with a smile, and he just asked; "What's up?"

"Come on John follow me down the hall." Dr. Fellows had been listening attentively to Cloud for several weeks and realized that he was internalizing so much guilt and did not realize how much good he had accomplished, so she decided a more direct approach was needed. As the two enter a meeting room, five men are sitting in a circle with two empty chairs left for Cloud and the doctor. Not being very communicative, Cloud looks anxiously to Dr. Fellows; "What's this all about? You know how I feel about group discussions."

"John, you are just going to have to trust me on this one, have a seat."

Seated in the circle are five Army veterans that have obviously had traumatic injuries. All are about Cloud's age however he does not recognize anyone.

Dr. Fellows asks; "Could everyone please just give me their name rank and the unit they served in, in Iraq.

"Hello, my name is Sgt. Desmond O'Brien, 9th Cavalry Regiment." As they go around the circle, the man sitting next to Cloud says; "My name is Staff Sergeant Patrick Mulvey, 215th Brigade Support Battalion."

Cloud begins to get nervous; *"I don't know these men, but I do recognize these units. They served in Iraq when I was there, and I even recall studying the damage of some of their vehicles."*

Dr. Fellows; "Is there anything you men would like to say to Col. Cloud while he is here."

Cloud becoming very anxious, stands; "Doctor, I told you I didn't want to go through any of this I made it quite clear when we first met."

Grasping his hand; "John just please sit and have the trust me for a minute."

"Okay, Sgt. O'Brien, you asked to have the opportunity to address Col. Cloud directly."

"Yes, thank you Dr. Fellows. Colonel, I never had the opportunity to thank you when I served. I was in a convoy, and it was struck by an IED. I just wanted to let you know that if it wasn't for the additional shielding that you had installed on my Humvee that I wouldn't be standing here today. Yes, I did lose an arm, and it took several months for me to rehabilitate, but if it weren't for you and your hard work, I would've never seen my wife and two kids again."

As others take their turn to speak directly to Cloud, he becomes emotional not realizing that the work he did had saved lives.

The man next to Cloud stands, looks at Cloud and, placing his hand on his shoulder; "Colonel, again my name is Patrick Mulvey. Our convoy was also ambushed, and the Humvee that I rode in was heavily damaged by an IED. While all in the vehicle were immediately stunned by the blast, we were all able to get out and fight off the ambush. I did take a hit in my leg from an AK round, but I survived. My Lieutenant told me after the battle that steel shielding that you recommended had been installed and if it were not for that, I wouldn't be standing here today and be the proud father of a newborn baby girl."

Dr. Fellows turns part ways and looks at Cloud, her hand on his knee; "You see John you did help people, dozens and dozens of servicemen and women over the years. You may not have known them or have seen them, but they are out there, and these are just a few of the thousands that you did help save. I'm sure if others had the opportunity, they would be praising you for your efforts as well." As Dr. Fellows stands; "I want to thank you, men, all of you, for being here today and for speaking to Col. Cloud. I know he is not a man of many words, so I will speak on his behalf today."

Cloud stays seated and very somber, as each of the men comes up to him to shake his hand and thank him. After all of the men have left, Cloud and Dr. Fellows are together; "You see

Colonel, I know you hold considerable guilt for what happened in Iraq, but you did serve your country very well and honorably, and there are hundreds, if not thousands of men, that would stand and thank you today for helping to save their lives. When you begin to reflect, I want you to include that on the scales of your conscience. Hopefully, that will help bring things back into balance for you. On a final note there is that adage, it's always darkest before the dawn. I just want to add, that every sunrise is uniquely beautiful and different. But you will never know unless you give yourself the opportunity to see it."

Cloud is too emotional to speak. Any recollection of his work in Iraq distresses him greatly. Nonetheless, he does take some solace from Dr. Fellow's words and the words of the men he met; "Thanks Doc I appreciate it. You're right I really do have to try and balance things out."

Cloud goes to the cafeteria to just grab a quick sandwich and a Coke before he drives to the hospital to meet his family. For the first time in so many years, he is comforted by the words of his fellow servicemen and the advice from Dr. Fellows. He no longer sits there dispassionate; he is actually able to generate a smile. He is now reconciled and looking forward to meeting his family; *Today is the first day of the rest of your life and the future just got a lot brighter."*

As they amble to the hospital's main entrance, John Cloud drives by, lowers the window and in an unfamiliar cheery voice; "Dawn, why don't y'all wait in the cool lobby. I'll go park the car, and I'll be there in a few minutes. Love ya...."

Standing at the entrance, protectively next to Joy, is

Jason. This morning, Joy had to get out of the house quickly; losing patience with her hair, so she just washed it and tied it back in a long tight ponytail. Joy watches, as the three slowly walk up the long sidewalk to the front entrance. At 1:30 in a midsummer's day in Oklahoma City it's already stiflingly hot. The two women and a young child stroll slowly towards the main entrance.

Before today, Rafta had no specific plans until he saw so many members of the Cloud family. He needs time to prepare his new arrivals. However, over these many weeks, he has grown very impatient. His original plan was to track them and possibly even follow some of them home. As Rafta sees the three women, from a distance, strolling, he orders Pedro; "Start your engine quickly, quickly. There's been a change of plans. This is too good an opportunity... we must take it."

Pedro races the engine of his huge SUV and hears instructions from Rafta over the radio; "The two women and young girl walking together, 100 feet in front of you. See them?.... See them there? They are your target. Use your vehicle, use your vehicle now, run them down... run them down **now**. Do not fail me."

As Joy slowly steps out of the hospital lobby in anticipation, Dawn, Samantha, and Crystal are only a yard away. Joy and Jason step out to the curb to greet them. "There's my beautiful little niece."

Rafta becomes excited, as timing is now critical. He observes all of Cloud's daughters, flocking toward the hospital entrance. He blurts to Pedro over the radio; "There is the other daughter, the redhead with them. Hurry, drive... drive now, fast, fast, **fast!** Put your foot to it, man!"

Pedro guns his engine and careens onto the sidewalk. As Joy is walking away from him, Jason immediately sees the oncoming SUV, instinctively reaches for the only thing he can, Joy's profuse ponytail. With outstretched arm, he grasps for it and pulls Joy back from the oncoming disaster. Pedro continues at full speed at the hapless women. They are horrified, frozen together, unable to move. A moment before contact, Dawn instinctively clutches her daughter, but at that incredible speed, their fate is all but sealed; *"Oh my God."* The sound of the collision and screams are sickening. In a second all the three absorb the full force of the murderous, vehicular attack and are hurled several feet into the air. Moments later the women and child lying motionless and bleeding. From only a few feet away Joy watches in horror, clutched in Jason's arms. She feverishly tries to go to her sister's aid but is held back. Jason, recognizing the danger, restrains Joy and immediately calls in the incident to police dispatch; "10-33, 10-33, Emergency assistance. Entrance, OKC Hospital. 10-33. Large, black SUV speeding from the scene. "

As Cloud is parking just around the building, he sees people running to the entrance and hears the bystander screams. He sprints to the front of the hospital and sees the carnage. Cloud has not seen his wife Crystal for months; nonetheless he recognizes her bloodied face and mangled body lying motionless; her fate is certain; "Oh God what the hell just happened." He runs beside Dawn, broken and bloody, yet conscious; begging for her daughter; "Samantha, Samantha... Daddy, save my baby." Seeing his young granddaughter a few feet away he slides across the grass and sees that she is unconscious and bleeding but still breathing; "Somebody get a doctor; somebody get a doctor." He immediately takes off his outer shirt, tears away his white undershirt and, instinctively presses it hard against her wounds to stop the bleeding."

Dawn absorbed the brunt of the SUV attack and is severely injured. Looking up, with makeshift bandage compressed on Samantha's chest, it is as if he is willing her to live; *"God, please help them."* His PTSD symptoms are immediately triggered, and he begins to shake uncontrollably, sweating profusely. He closes his eyes and beseeches; *"How can this be, how could I be reliving this horror again?"* Within seconds they are surrounded by dozens of nurses and doctors. Emergency and police vehicles pull up from all around.

Rafta observes the chaos with a scornful sneer; "Finally, I will get my vengeance."

All three receive immediate care, as a traumatized Cloud is reluctantly pulled away. Within a few minutes all three are wheeled to the emergency room with Joy, Jason and Cloud following. The scene is a frenzy of medical personnel, with police dashing everywhere. In the midst of the madness, Joy spots her father, sitting alone shirtless, bloody hands over his face, shaking uncontrollably. At first, she does not recognize him, until she sees his face masked with anguish. Jason persistently hovers over her, as they stand from a distance, watching Dawn and Samantha rolled into the emergency room. Joy peaks through the observation window, astonished at the expanding pile of discarded bloody bandages. Jason tries to restrain her, to spare her this ghastly image, but Joy's love for her sister is too strong, and she thrusts them away; "No... I need to stay."

Despite their frantic attempts, Crystal's head trauma is massive and she is quickly pronounced dead. Dawn and Samantha Cloud barely cling to life.

After the attack, Pedro casually drives down the main road, as if nothing had happened. No one has identified him yet, no one is following. After only a few minutes, he abandons the dented, bloodied SUV in the rear of a minimart and casually walks away. No cameras are there to record his face. This method of high-speed ramming of innocent civilians, endorsed by ISIS, has worked again. Rafta, after seeing the result of his improvised attack, scornfully smiles. He will drive back leisurely to his squalid mobile home; in front of his TV, he waits for the results of his plan.

Dawn and Samantha are both in extremely critical condition. As the family sits in the waiting room, a dejected doctor comes out; "I am very sorry Ms. Cloud, but your sister Dawn has died on the operating table. We were unable to stop her internal bleeding."

Joy collapses in Jason's arms; "Goddamnit no, *Noooo*,."

Jason tries to calm Joy but cannot and drags her over to a seat not far from her father. She looks at her father sitting there stunned she is mystified by his emotional detachment; *"What a coldhearted bastard. He hasn't changed one bit."* Neither Joy nor anyone else recognize the signs of his mental breakdown.

Jason looks up at the doctor; "What about the little girl... Samantha?"

The doctor shakes his head fatefully; "If it is any consolation the fact that a mother was holding her, shielded Samantha from more serious injuries. However, she is still in very critical condition, we may know more by morning."

In the early morning hours, all are still waiting. Despite the heroic attempts by the doctors Samantha dies. The doctor stated; "Because of her weakened immune system and the severity of her injuries, we just couldn't save her. There was nothing we could do."

John and Joy Cloud sit at opposite sides of the waiting room, both overcome with grief. Joy is unable to contain her grief. Cloud is on an emotional roller coaster. Just an hour earlier, he was finally on the path to resolving some PTS emotional issues and is now whipsawed back into his private hell. Cloud's grief is inconsolable, seeing baby Samantha's blood on his hands... ***"Not again."***

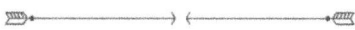

Mohammed Rafta sits on a grungy couch surrounded by empty pizza boxes, crafting an encrypted text message for his overseas partners; "That is correct, you have our permission to slaughter the calf for Ramadan."

As Rafta watches, a TV news report; "Earlier today a drunken driver jumped the curb at the OKC Hospital killing three. The driver, thought to be an illegal immigrant, is being sought by police. Any information that could lead to the apprehension and arrest of the individual should be directed to the OKC police. Elouise Lion, MSOKC reporting."

A few hours later, on a firing range at the Al Andar airfield, the primary base for US trainers in Iraq, Lt. Daniel Cloud stands over a line of Iraqi riflemen overseeing their marksmanship training. His name, CLOUD is conspicuously stenciled on his jacket. A new Iraqi recruit stands in line, attentively watching Lt. Cloud. He affably smiles at the young Cloud offers instructions. Earlier that day the same Iraqi soldier was given a martyr's mission. The only questions remaining where, when and how.

As the Iraqi soldier watches attentively, he sees someone come up to Lt. Cloud take him aside and, whisper the devastating news about the deaths in his family. Lt. Cloud did not have to be there. As a petroleum engineer, he had been quite busy over the past few years. He was doing quite well financially and was planning to get married in about a year. However, drilling activity across the state has slowed considerably, with the recent fall in oil prices. His company has to give him fewer field assignments, so he decided to ask for leave of absence. Daniel was in the Army reserve and saw the postings and decided to volunteer for a six-month stint as a marksman trainer. He had a good job and was planning on getting engaged; a good life lay ahead.

Head down, he now appears obviously shaken. He turns to move away slowly from the firing line. The alert Iraqi recruit realizes he has only one chance to accomplish his mission. He robotically walks up to the firing line, yanks a loaded M16 from the hands of an instructor and while yelling *"Allah Akbar"* fires three shots into Daniel Cloud's back. Wearing no body armor, the assassination is certain and young Lt. Cloud dies right there. The deadly Iraqi assassin is killed straightway by other US advisors. It all happens so quickly; the attack could not have been thwarted.

Neither the CIA, US Army or FBI conducts an investigation to connect the killings. The media is blatantly negligent, with no interest. Their story is that it was just another unfortunate incident of friendly fire.

CHAPTER 11
July 4, 2017 – So Many Lost

Joy arrived at the cemetery in Jason's clay caked pickup, at his insistence. As they stand at the gravesite, anxiously waiting for John Cloud's arrival, Joy clutches at Jason's supportive arm. Before them are four caskets, the last covered by the American flag. She leans to him and whispers; "How could this possibly happen? It is as if God is seeking revenge on our family."

Jason has held back the intelligence information he received yesterday and has been waiting for the right time to share it with Joy; "I didn't want to distress you further, but there is more information about the killings. I did some research on the guy that tried to kill you in the clinic."

Looking bewildered; "What does that have to do with all of this?"

"Joy honey, he was Middle Eastern."

Shaking her head; "What the **hell** are you talking about? How do you know that?"

Jason clutching her hand leans over and whispers; "Days ago I had a DNA test done on your attacker's blood, and it indicated 95% probability he was North African and Middle Eastern. FBI also got back to me with a fingerprint match. He was Moroccan and arrested there a few years ago for being an ISIS supporter."

Joy looking out over the caskets; "Moroccan... **ISIS**! So, why would he want to kill me or any of my family?"

Jason compresses his lips then looks at her with a wide-eyed blank stare. Joy thrusts her arm out and tries to pull away from Jason; "My father, my fucking *father*! He's the reason they're all *dead*."

As he restrains her; "It is only a theory, but it all makes sense. Also, I did some research on the ring worn by your attacker. It was a Rensselaer University ring taken from a Phil Johnson of Greenwich, Connecticut. He was murdered in Mexico several weeks earlier. His throat was slashed on a remote Mexican beach resort."

"Mexico... Why Mexico?"

I am theorizing that a man or men encountered Phil Johnson on a remote beach in Mexico and for an unknown reason, killed him. But they came here for a reason, a *specific* purpose. Finding him in your clinic is no coincidence. Also, do you remember what he said before he tried to kill you?"

Joy head down, listening attentively; "No not really, I was dazed after hitting that wall."

"Well, I was there and heard him clearly. He screamed *Allah Akbar*."

Joy looking incredulously into Jason's eyes; "*What..!* Why didn't you tell me this sooner?"

Staring; "I couldn't until I knew for certain. But it all now makes sense now. When I got the DNA results, I contacted the FBI, but they blew me off. But then they got a fingerprint match from Interpol. Honey, I think they were after not just you, but your entire family."

Staring irately at the coffins, attempting to pull away; "I **cannot** *hate* **my father more** than I do now.

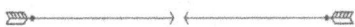

Mohammed Rafta has been planning this event for weeks. He knew that if he killed one of the Clouds that the rest would attend the funeral. He fits perfectly into his disguise and blends into their culture. Wearing mirrored sunglasses, Rafta stands relaxed by the road with a few of his men, disguised as grungy gravediggers. Pedro and the others stay at their condo awaiting instructions. No one, not the FBI, CIA, Homeland Security or any police would expect that they would be bold enough to attend the funeral of the people they just slaughtered. But here he is, making mental notes, planning his next move, whispering to one of his men, in Spanish.

They watch, as the crowd cowers around the grave. Moments later a man nonchalantly walks and attaches a small magnetic GPS tracker onto the sidewall of Jason's pickup. With all eyes on the gravesite, no one notices his actions. Rafta is now able to track Jason's car from miles away on his iPhone. Joy will be targeted next to die, then finally Col. John Cloud.

Mourners continue to migrate to the gravesite. Col. John Cloud, while no longer on active duty, stands in full dress uniform. As he walks alone to the graves, the local FBI Station Chief walks briskly up to him and gently grasps his arm. They pause for a moment; "We have Mohamad Rafta's recent Honduran passport photo. So, if he shows himself, we will get him."

Cloud, semi-lucid and overmedicated, looks at him, bewildered; "Who... what the hell are you talking about?"

FBI Station Chief; "Mohamad Rafta; didn't you get the information? Detective Jason Moore put it all together a few days ago." Since the killings, Cloud has taken all his PTSD medication and gulped it down with Grandpa's moonshine. When he begins to visualize the horror, he swigs more moonshine. The two combined, help Cloud repress his uncontrollable PTS symptoms. Cloud, unresponsive, stands motionless shaking his head; "No... Who..? Jason Moore... I met him once but... he never mentioned Mohamad Rafta... or that anyone was trying to kill my family."

FBI Station Chief; "We put it together a few days ago once we got the fingerprints back from Interpol. That was a week or so after your daughter Joy's, attempted murder."

Cloud was barely able to stand shakes his head; "Joy! My Joy..? What attempted murder?"
FBI Station Chief; "They didn't tell you? Homeland Security has no way of knowing how many others crossed the border with Rafta or where they are. We have no actionable intelligence. There may be a few, there may be dozens. We have no new information."

With a dejected look, Col. John Cloud jerks his arm away and slowly walks erect to the row of chairs at the gravesite and sits rigid at attention; *"When I thought it could not get any worse; it does. The deaths of my family are my fault, all my fault."* Cloud seize upon his training, what he knows, despite what others say or thinks; *"I must stay calm and try to think."*

Grandpa finally walks behind him and sits next to Cloud with Joy noticeably a few seats away. Before them are four caskets; three adorned with red and white roses the fourth draped with an American Flag. The attending crowd of mourners has grown very large.

The FBI Station Chief walks up behind Jason and draws him close; "After the ceremony, you have to get Col. Cloud and his family the hell out of here. Don't go home, find a secluded place and stay there. Every US intelligence agency is combing their records to find Mohamad Rafta or others that may be involved. We have no way of knowing who they are or how many there may be. ***Do you understand***? No one must travel to their homes. I'll call you when I hear anything." Jason stands behind Joy, hands gently on her shoulders, offering support.

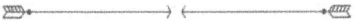

Barbara Moore, Jason's mother, is also attending the funeral today out of respect for her son's girlfriend. She has been secluded for weeks in her office, listening to her Pandora music. Other than the funeral time and location, Barbara has heard no details from her son. Arriving at the funeral a bit late, she has trouble getting a close parking place. She never got Joy's full name and only intended to express her condolences to

Joy, then leave. Barbara is astonished by the number of people attending the funeral. She had no idea the funeral is for four people.

A woman accompanies Barbara on the walk to the graves, gently touching her; "It is so sad, so very sad, so many killed."

Barbara; "How many were killed?"

"Oh my God... Four members of the same family all died within a day of each other. Did you know any of them?"

Puzzled; "No not really, I am here because my son is a good friend of a family member."

With so much distance between Barbara and the gravesite, she cannot hear the priest or eulogy. All that can be heard are the shots from the military honor guard. As part of the traditional military funeral, a flag is presented to Col. John Cloud. Stone-faced he sits trembling in his chair. Despite his personal struggles, he had so much to live for and now most of that is gone. Now realizing that he is the possible cause for all their deaths; *"My fault, it's all my fault."* He sits weeping uncontrollably, veiled behind sunglasses.

Grandpa Cloud gently taps on his leg; "Son there are some people over there I haven't seen in quite a while. I'm gonna walk over and speak to'm."

Over the previous several weeks, Cloud's PTSD symptoms had been somewhat under control. Reducing his meds and controlling his drinking had worked. Also, being with his family had been very therapeutic. However, this tragedy thrust him into a suicidal state. All he can do now is sit and reflect. He brought his 50 caliber casing in his pants pocket and gently taps it, trying to maintain composure; *"Today is. Today is the first day..."* It is unbearable for him to say the rest without his family being there.

Mourners begin to pass by the caskets, laying down roses, offering their condolences. Col. John Cloud sits unresponsive. Standing tiptoe, Barbara is searching for Jason who is standing protectively behind Joy. Barbara leans her head to see the uniformed man in the front row. As Jason scans the crowd, he makes eye contact with his mother and shakes his head discouragingly. Col. John Cloud finally raises his head to the sky beseeching answers; *"What have I done to cause so much death? What could I have done differently?"*

Barbara finally sees the profile of the Army officer in the front row, it is unmistakable. Barbara stares astounded, recognizing the seated Col. John Cloud. It is the first time in 30 years that she has seen him. Immediately shaken, Barbara quickly turns her head away, and walks back toward her car. She fumbles for her keys as she walks briskly past the observing gravediggers. Immediately, as she starts her car, the Pandora music mix begins to play a favorite, song ♪ by Dolly Parton, "I will always love you." "I hope life will treat you kind And I hope that you have all that you ever dreamed of. And I wish you joy and happiness but above all of this I wish you love And I will always love you, I will always love you."

As the music plays, she looks back to the gravesite and yells; *"No!"* She listens on as tears explode, lips trembling. She glances back at the throng of mourners leaving, listening to the song until it ends. She ponders and ponders and ponders her next move. She angrily turns off the car and walks briskly back. She elbows through the departing crowd, nudging her way to the gravesite.

From a distance, the inconspicuous Mohammad Rafta still watches coolly. He pulls from his pocket John Cloud's helmet photos. He scans the Cloud family photos including; "Crystal, Dawn, Joy, and Daniel." However, there is a second weathered photo, glued with dried blood to the others. As he pulls them apart, it reveals a much younger John Cloud with another young girl, however, not his wife. Rafta again moistens his fingers to clean the photo of blood, revealing the face of the other woman. It is Barbara Moore and John Cloud embracing in their swimwear, during their college days.

Barbara stands to the side hesitating to move, lips trembling. She makes eye contact with her son Jason with an unrecognizable expression. Emotions churn from decades earlier and well up. She sees Cloud sitting alone, shaking, sobbing inconsolably, ceremonial flag clutched in his rigid arms. With four roses clutched in his hand, he cannot let them go. As the mourner's hover over the coffins, Barbara nudges her way up closer. She passes by Grandpa, unrecognized as he slowly walks away. Without making eye contact, she walks past Jason and Joy.

With her back to the caskets, she stands in front of Cloud for several seconds, unable to talk or to touch him. Finally, Cloud looks up, his face contorted. He does not recognize Barbara. She kneels down in front of him gently cradling his face in her hands; stares and makes eye contact; "John it's me,... it's me."

Bewildered at first, then instinctively he clutches onto Barbara. True love once parted can never be extinguished. The flowers and flag are enveloped.

Rafta and his men can now see them from a distance. Despite the local, state and federal agencies mingled with the mourners, he is unfazed by the extraordinary security surrounding him. The master of disguise is hiding in plain sight. With a wry grin; *"Finally you know the sorrow you have caused me. But this is not over, not even close to being over."*

Joy watches as Barbara clutches Cloud's hands; wondering how odd it is for a total stranger to be so comforting to him. Joy looks at Jason; "Who is she, do you know her?

Awkwardly; "That's my mother, Barbara Moore."

"What is she doing? She doesn't know my dad?"

 Feeling uneasy Jason walks over and leans down to help his mother stand; "Mom, let me help you up. Do you know Col. Cloud?"

Barbara does not respond to her son and brushes him away. Instead, she stands briskly and in a single abrupt move pulls the rigid John Cloud up from his chair. Cloud stares around for a few seconds in confusion, oblivious. As she begins to escort him away, he stops, takes a few steps back and gently places a rose on each of the coffins. Barbara wraps her arm tightly around Cloud, guiding him back to her car. They walk through the slowly moving throng. They pass in front of the disguised Mohammed Rafta and several accomplices. Barbara helps John to the passenger side door, quickly opens her driver side door and abruptly sits. As she angrily slams it closed; "John... get in. **Get in!**"

Jason baffled by what he is seeing, runs up and leans into the car; "Mom what you doing... what the hell you doing?

"Jason, get the hell away from my car."

"You just can't come here and take Col. Cloud away; you don't know him."

"Son I can't talk to you right now. Just get the hell out of my way."

"Mom please listen... before you drive off. All of us have to get you out of here, **now**. They're after all of us, and we don't know how many of them there are."

Cloud semi-lucid spinning his head; "**Joy!**, Where's Joy? Is she in danger?"

Jason taps on the roof; "John she is with me she's okay, but we have to get the hell out of here. **Now!**"

Cloud agitated, staring at Barbara; "We will all drive to the cabin... we will be safe there... no one knows of its location. Tell Joy and Grandpa to drive there **now**,... Joy knows where it is and how to get there.

Jason leans in again; "We must leave now, I mean **right** now, be careful. We will follow behind you."

One of Rafta's men tries to walk quickly up to Barbara's moving car to attach another magnetic GPS; however, Barbara accelerates quickly almost knocking down some onlookers.

Even though there is a national manhunt for Mohammed Rafta he stands there coolly, glaring at everyone from behind his mirrored sunglasses; "*It is only a matter of time now... only a matter of time.*"

As Grandpa gets into his truck with Carlos and Angelina; "Carlos my friend, today we buried my family... and the Cloud name."

Carlos looking confused; "Señor Pop, you still have your name and your family."

As Grandpa stares out the window to the gravesite, voice trembling; "No my friend, my grandson Daniel was the last male to carry the Cloud family name. Our family and our future will end."

AquarianBooks.com

CHAPTER 12
The Approaching Storm

Three cars speed perilously, north, uncertain what their futures may hold. Cloud sits indifferent to Barbara, still not fully grasping the situation. It has been 30 years since they have seen or spoken to each other. After several minutes the effects of the moonshine and drugs begin to wane. Cloud's eyes blink erratically as he starts to look around. He turns to look at Barbara, grasping if this is another bizarre dream. Fumbling to find the words; "Is this a dream or.... is that really you?

"No..., unfortunately, this is not a dream."

"Barb... how is it that you are here, now. I don't understand."

Dejected; "John,... Jason told me..."

"Jason... Jason who?"

"Jason Moore... he is my son."

Blinking his eyes, trying to clear his head; "Jason Moore,... Jason Moore. I think... I met Jason Moore... a few weeks ago. We were... at the firing range and... Are we talking about the same Jason Moore, the police detective?

Cloud's impeccable uniform and polished appearance suggest a confident military officer. However, Barbara is puzzled by his unresponsiveness; *"What is the matter with him why can't he speak?"*

Taking off his hat, sluggishly shaking his head; "Jason, Jason Moore is **your** son?"

Barbara is dumbfounded at what she is seeing; *"Oh God, was he injured in the war? Did have some kind of brain damage? What the hell is going on here?"* While trying to focus on her driving, her head darts to see Cloud's face to learn what is wrong; *"Is he right in the head, is he on drugs, is he drunk? This is not the man I knew so many years ago."* "Yes, Jason is my son. It wasn't until I walked to the gravesite that I knew that he was dating your daughter."

Cloud's PTSD symptoms vacillate, and his mood abruptly changes. He panics and snarls; "How could you **not** know… Joy is my daughter."

Seeing Cloud's sudden agitation, Barbara attempts to calm him down. Softly; "They have only been dating for a few months, and I only spoke to her on the phone once. With our schedules, it's difficult to get together for dinner at night. Plus, these kids today are very private… short three-word sentences, you know. I never got her last name."

No one around Cloud realized the full extent of his PTSD. They knew he was having problems adjusting to civilian life and that moonshine was his medication of choice, to help adapt. With his mood vacillating; "Didn't you hear their names on the TV or radio? It was all over the news."

Cloud becomes paranoid, with flashbacks of the deaths

of his family, now realizing that Rafta may be following him. He jerks his head around looking over his shoulder. Awkwardly, Cloud withdraws the service weapon from its holster to check if it is loaded, however, it is not.

Barbara has not seen Cloud for decades and realizes he is no longer the affable, vibrant man she once knew. Looking at Cloud, in an attempt to calm him, she places her hand on the gun and points it to the floor; "John... Please put that away. No... I've been locked up in the lab for several days, no news or anything. I work all day just listening to my music, that's all I have for enjoyment. John, I am sorry, so very sorry for your loss. I wish there were something I could do or say to help you through this."

Cloud turns and stares at Barbara, then looks back out the side window, tears rising in his steely eyes. The seasoned veteran fights his greatest battle, to gain control. The tragedy of the past few days has resurrected those gruesome images, now too vivid to suppress. His condition fluctuates. Clutching his hands and taking a deep breath he exhales slowly to regain control; "Barb, do you know where you are going? Do you need directions?"

"**No,...** I don't need help I can find that old cabin with my eyes closed." Then in an attempt to affect Cloud's mood, Barbara turns on her car Wi-Fi. For a few moments, it is just silent with only the Pandora music playing another of Barbara's selections. In an attempt to take his mind away from the tragedies, she thumbs her iPhone to find one of their old favorites; Garth Brooks, ♪, If tomorrow never comes; "Will she know how much I loved her?...." Clenching his fists and breathing deeply, he cannot stop the tears from rolling down his face. Once the song ends, Cloud slowly reaches to turn down the volume.

In an awkward attempt to connect; "So John, I have not heard about you or from you for 30 years. I see from the number of ribbons on your uniform that you have served in quite a few places."

Cloud does not respond. The effects of the psych drugs and moonshine are beginning abate.

"John, so you met my son Jason?... **John!"**

Cloud does not respond, transfixed out the window, trying to regain lucidity.

"John, can you talk? If you want your space, I'll leave you alone."

Finally gaining control, he wipes his face and, with another deep breath, looks at Barbara; "Yes.... I believe so."

In a soft tone; "John, can you explain to me what happened to your family. Do you have any idea why all this happened? I saw several State Police and FBI cars at the cemetery. Why? I'm sorry that I have to ask such dumb questions, but I've been locked up for several days in a lab, with no news or anything. Had I known it was your family, I would have attended the wake. I am not here to make you uncomfortable."

Cloud in a sharp tone; "Barb, there is some *serious shit* about to come down... right now and you shouldn't be anywhere near me. This is a real shit storm, and I'm in the middle of it. It's my fault... all of it! Everything that has happened is a deep, indelible mark on my soul. I'm not even sure if God can forgive me."

Anxiously; "What, **no!** You didn't cause all this. This was not your fault. The car was just an accident; not an act of God."

In a deliberate threatening tone; "Not God, a **devil**. They were all reprisal killings."

"The **devil!**... **W**hat the **hell** are you talking about?"

"Yes, the devil. He followed me back from Iraq, and now he wants to exact revenge."

"Revenge... for what?"

Agitated; "Things that happened years ago... in Iraq. Things I was part of...things I did...and things I helped do."

Barbara does not know if she can believe Cloud or if he is having a psychotic episode; "Who is after you? **John..** who..is..after.. you?"

Stone faced; "**ISIS..!**"

With the sudden jerk over her head; "**ISIS!** Are you fucking kidding me, the cut off your head guys? I thought they were wiping them out in Iraq, Syria. Here..? Not here?"

"Well... they are here now, and they are after the rest of my family and me. That is why, once I get to the cabin, you need to drive the hell away and don't look back."

Realizing that she could cut the tension with a knife, Barbara attempts to calm Cloud, recognizing a reminiscent favorite song, raises her Pandora volume 🎵; BREAD's, Everything I own; "You sheltered me from harm Kept me warm, kept me warm. You gave my life to me Set me free, set me free. The finest years I ever knew, are all the years I had with you…"

Barbara's lips stiffen; her emotions can no longer be contained. The man she loved over 30 years ago sits here next to her and is about to walk away, possibly never to be seen again. Cloud sees Barbara's emotions welling and touches her arm; "Barb, you have nothing to fear they're not after you. You'll be fine, you will be safe. All you have to do is drive off…"

She angrily yanks her arm away; "Drive off..! Drive off! I just cannot do that, not again. It's not that fucking easy John."

Perplexed at Barbara's emotional shift; "Why not… why the **hell** not?"

Voice trembling; "I did not plan on being here today, or to see you again. But now I am… I have a few questions… questions I have had for too many years. I will not leave until I have an answer, from you… a ***truthful*** answer."

Confused: "An answer… for what? What the hell is it that *you* need to know?"

Barbara explodes; "Why did you leave me those many years ago? **Why!** "

Emotions churning, trying to find the right words; "Is that why you are here... for an overdue apology? Do you have any idea what I the fuck I'm going through, what I just lost?" Pounded the dashboard; "***God dammit,...*** do you have any idea at all? I don't need this **shit** right now. Not from you, not ***anybody....***"

His explosive response startles her; "John, I cannot grasp the depth of your loss. I'm not sure anyone can. I am here solely by chance I may never see you again. But now that I am here, I have questions. But before I drive off again... possibly this time forever... I just need to know."

As Cloud and Barbara's eyes meet; "John, we were close, probably too close for kids our age..., you know what I mean. I need to know before I leave."

Barbara's voice shakes, apologetically; "Was I not good enough for you?"

The recollections of their days together come flooding back. Powerful memories begin to rush back of their first encounter at OU, studying together under the shade trees. An innocent glance and shy smile started it all. They were both kids focused on their education. However, after 2 ½ years of arduous studying, both sought emotional relief, a glimpse of the future, of what their life could be. They were both in their prime, mature enough for an unencumbered sexual relationship. However, neither sought nor anticipated the bond that would develop. Before long the two became inseparable. Though neither spoke of it, both presumed that they would ultimately marry. The two dated through to their graduations.

Then a situation arose, with unanticipated consequences they could neither envision nor alter.

The weight of the past few days is overwhelming, both are emotionally spent. Tears well up again in Cloud's eyes, he has difficulty looking at Barbara. Then they make inadvertent eye contact, and he reaches out and gently grasps her hand.

 Eyes locked his voice shaking; "Not good enough for me... Barb, you are the most complete woman I have ever known."

That flame between two people who were once incredibly in love is reignited. They can sense that sudden emotional rush, once lost, now rekindled.

Expressionless for several seconds, she is stunned. Resurrected emotions explode and memories churn, then burst; "***After 30 years, after 30 fucking years*** you say you feel this way, you still feel this way? ***You sorry piece-a-shit..!***"

Surprised by her outburst; "It is the truth, the God honest truth."

Shaking her head in disbelief; "I just need to understand what happened, why you walked away."

Head bent; "Barb, it's a long story, a long and difficult story."

"We have time right now tell me...If you truly felt that way...please explain to me ***why***!"

Realizing he has no place to run, pauses and takes a deep breath; "Barb, right after I graduated when we were still... together, I had to go into Army Officer Candidate School at Fort Benning, Georgia for 12 weeks.

Tersely; "I already know that, *then what*?"

"When I was in OCS, I met another woman. I wasn't looking for anyone else or anyone different, but I met her...Crystal. At our OCS graduation party, she came up to me and asked for a dance. I had a few drinks, then a few more dances. We were both feeling pretty good, so she introduced me to her father. He was a two-star General from the Pentagon, the dignitary guest for dinner. Well... I guess I had a lot to drink that night, celebrating my commission and all. She kind of liked me because we went to her room that night... and well...things happened."

"...Spare me *those* details."

Somberly; "After graduation, I had to go through additional training, for six more weeks. Crystal and I didn't exchange any calls or letters or anything. However, the last week of training I got a phone call from Crystal telling me that she's pregnant. She begged me to help her. She didn't want to cause a scandal with her family and begged me to help. For her, the only acceptable option was to get married. He...the general had a reputation for being a real asshole. She made it quite clear that if her father found out, that he could be quite vindictive. Her plan was that if we got married her father would help my career and accelerate me through the ranks. That was her plan...." Pausing to reflect; "....Barb, I really loved you but,..."

Barbara does not understand the erratic PTSD symptoms, annoyed by his meandering response; "You made this decision 30 years ago, and you're telling me now, that it was the wrong decision. It's a bit too late for that, *ya think?*"

"But...."

"Did you ever think of *me*? Ever once... of me and my needs, what I may have needed? *Huh, even once?*

Cloud rambling; "You just don't understand.... If I did... get married...... I would be with her... If I walked away.... I would get shipped off to some shithole overseas... and probably killed. Neither was a good choice? Barb...I was young, inexperienced and well... really stupid.... I made some terrible mistakes."

Clenching her steering wheel; "So when *did* you decide to never speak to me again?... **Huh...?** to never explain. You're not a macho soldier, you really are just a *fucking pussy.*"

Eyes blinking erratically, Cloud cannot see straight; "You're right... I should have.... said something back then."

"Yes, ...*anything!*"

Shaking his head; "How could I...? What would I say...? I could not find the words... I still loved you *too much*."

While the discussion has nothing to do with their exodus north this frank exchange helps get his mind off the tragedy. Cloud, in a conciliatory tone; "Barb, it may sound like bullshit but... it's the truth. I would understand... if you drove off and never saw me again."

Lips quivering, emotionally helpless, she pauses to find the right words; "Did you really love me... as you said...back then? **Really...?** John... look at me. Tell me the truth, and we don't ever have to speak of this again. "

She looks hesitantly at him for the answer, as Cloud turns his head. Peering deep into her eyes; "Barb, I never stopped loving you."

Stunned; **"Really...why?** Why are you telling me this now?

He understands that he cannot change what happened, but he atones; "I have to tell you now... because, once you leave... I may never see you again."

Not a word is spoken, not an utterance, just silence, as they both try to measure the weight of their words. They drive north along the heat-shimmered highway as familiar landmarks begin to appear. The tranquility of the rolling fields is calming and a much-needed distraction. Nothing complicated here, good land, good people, a simpler life. They listen to Barbara's Pandora selections, both trying to regain control of their emotions.

"Barb, tell me about Jason. Looks like you raised an incredibly thoughtful young man."

"Well, Jay will be 30 next month. After I graduated OU, I

moved to Texas. Jay's father was an oil rig foreman and roughneck. His father, James or Jamie Moore was a very hard worker and made a good home for us. Jamie died when Jason was around ten in an oil rig explosion. He was trying to cap a runaway well when something went wrong, and it blew. He died instantly.

Texas is where Jason was born, and where we both lived up until a few months ago. Though I had a good job in Dallas when Jason moved back to OKC, I moved back up to stay close to him. Over the years his grandfather helped keep Jason in line... Believe me, that wasn't easy for single mom."

"I'm sure you had a lot to do with it."

"No, Jay wasn't really that much trouble. He was a good kid... an energetic kid."

"You can be very proud...he's really a great guy."

"It took a few months, but when a job opened up at the bio-lab in OKC, I took it. It's a long commute, but I don't mind. How about you and your family?

Cloud takes a deep breath to reflect; "Not sure if we have enough time. The short version... About seven months after we got married Crystal had Daniel. Ya know...? After that... we had Dawn, then Joy a few years later. In the early years, I was stationed in several stateside posts."

Cloud gets choked up and pauses again, recalling the beautiful family he lost; "Dawn was the real deal, she had it all together. Smart... really smart, good looking, nothing could hold her back. Daniel is... was a great son. He couldn't wait to serve his country. He got a job as an engineer out of college, then decided to join the reserves. He didn't need nor want a commission. He just wanted to serve. He planned to get married in about a year or so. He was a vibrant, mature person, a natural leader. Recently the Army needed trainers to go back into Iraq and he immediately volunteered."

Pausing to maintain his composure; "He... they... had their lives in front of them. Samantha, my granddaughter was priceless. She was so thin and fragile... but the spitting image of her grandmother. She was an incredibly beautiful baby with sparkling blue eyes. She would have been something...." Cloud begins to choke up; "I have to stop."

Barbara takes her hand off the steering wheel and gestures toward him; "John, we can catch up later."

Rafta is following about a mile behind the three-car caravan, with his iPhone GPS tracker in hand. He sees that Joy and Jason's car is heading north on I-35. He calls Pedro in the van following; "Tell the others to follow us north on I-35. We will give you more details later. Stay a few miles apart, drive slow and do not attract any attention. Make sure the batteries in the video cameras are charged. We will be taking a lot of trophy films for the world to see."

Weeks earlier, when Rafta was planning the attacks, he walked into a local superstore to get ideas on equipment that they might use. He purchased six mobile CB two-way radios, flashlights, and other gear. Even though they only have a range of a few miles, they could prove invaluable in coordinating his attack.

He stares out the side window, and in a large open field, he sees a young boy and his father flying a small remote-control airplane. Too often in Iraq and Syria, the Americans used larger drones, such as these, as surveillance instruments for killing. He points out the window; "Look at how the Americans teach their children to fly drones, to kill from a distance. We teach our young to kill up close with a gun or the edge of a knife. That is honorable." He shakes his head thinking of what the future may hold.

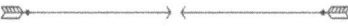

Jason and Joy are not far from Barbara and Cloud; "Joy, where are we going?"

Joy sitting rigid in her seat, points; "We are following my grandpa and my father to our farm and old hunting cabin."

"Can you tell me about it?"

"We use to come up here when we were kids and camped in the nearby woods. There was also a farm pond a quarter mile away, where we would catch bass, bluegill, and crappie. Dawn and I would swim on hot summer afternoons. I knew that farm by heart, every spruce, willow and cedar tree...... It seems like only yesterday."

Jason, trying to lift her spirits; "So what is the cabin like?"

As she relaxes; "Well, unless grandpa has made some major improvements... which I doubt, it is a rather small log cabin that sleeps four people, eight in a squeeze. An old raunchy indoor toilet... that was really scary. It got electric in the 1960's so they could get running water, radio and a few rabbit ear TV stations. A really primitive place, but that's probably why we loved it. It stands at the end of a long meandering dirt road, hidden by dense trees and hills. They never wanted to improve it because it would just attract kids that might ransack the place. Oh, yah.. there's a mine shaft."

Jason amused; "A mine shaft..?"

"Yah, a really cool mine shaft."

"What was that for?"

Animated, waving her hands; "The cabin... before my grandpa fixed it up, was abandoned. I think it was an old lead mine. It dates back to the 1890's, right around the land rush days. The old mine was dug out beneath the cabin floor and winds about 200 feet into the mountain. It's not really a mountain, but a 100-foot hill behind the cabin. As little kids, we use to climb it. We named it Grandpas' Mountain, really cool. Since the mountain was a high point on the property it would get hit by lightning quite often, scared the shit out of me once."

Inquisitively; "So what's the cabin used for... now?

"My grandpa has been using it for years as a hunting cabin. They have planted some crops in a nearby five-acre plot to attract deer and turkey. It is really secluded, a great place to hide out. No paved road, address or mailbox, really off the grid."

As he continues driving, Jason glances at her and sees tears begin to well; "Joy, it is not his fault. It is the fault of those ISIS animals. All they want is an excuse to kill people. They are looking for some fantastic media events. We should be safe there until these guys are found and killed."

Joy wiping her eyes; "I hope you are right, for all our sakes, I hope you're right."

Joy cannot contain her emotions, stirs in her seat; "I was just thinking about Dawn and little Samantha. It's just not fair, **dammit!** I could have saved Samantha. Now that she is gone, what do I do.... about this baby?"

He turns his head surprised; "What do you mean... about the baby? You have... it of course."

Sobbing, agitated; "It's not that simple, it's a lot more complicated now. It is only seven weeks since I got the embryo. I have to think about this. I have options,...I have the rest of my life to consider. Dawn was going to take the baby, care for the baby as her own, once it was delivered. That was our *deal*. I was just the surrogate. I was still going to have my life ahead of me."

Jason reaches for her hand; "Joy honey, this is a living piece of your sister inside you, not an unintended cluster of cells. You are carrying your sister's baby...a piece of Dawn inside you."

Tearfully; "You don't think I don't know all that already...that I haven't considered all that are ready."

Pressing her hand making eye contact; "And, now it is *our* baby you are carrying."

Becoming animated; "You don't understand, I have to think about the big picture, what am I gonna do about the rest of my life. I have a great job; I have a career I have to think of. I have to take all those things into account. I see this situation every day at the clinic for a lot of other young girls, but I never thought I'd put myself into that situation. It's not that simple... *it's not that simple.*"

"I'm sure these decisions are never simple, never easy."

"You're a guy... you don't understand what it's like for a young girl to go through this. To make this decision... you just don't understand. How am I supposed to go to work in a woman's clinic, giving women support for their reproductive rights with me carrying a baby?"

"But that is exactly the point isn't it? Reproductive rights...**you** are making the decision to reproduce or not to reproduce. It doesn't mean that because you work in the clinic, you're forcing yourself to abort."

As Joy breaks down crying again; "*It's a boy*. Dawn never found out it was a boy."

Jason leans toward her; "Does this mean you want to keep it? I want you to keep it. I want **us** to keep it."

Staring at him; "Jay, this is not your baby, you can walk away, I would understand, that was my promise to you. You do not have to be tied to this... to me..."

"Joy, other guys may take you up on that, but not me. I already made my decision, I just want us to be together, **all** of us... a real family."

"I was thinking about having this... this baby. If you don't have a problem, I will name him Daniel after my brother. Dawn would like that."

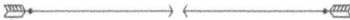

As Cloud sees they are getting close to their exit, he gives Grandpa Cloud a call; "Pop, before you drive to the cabin could you go to the convenience store and you pick enough supplies for six people for about a week?"

"Six people, for a week why? What the hell is going on Jason?"

"Pop, I'll fill you in when you get back to the cabin. Really appreciate it, thanks. Oh yes, drop off Carlos and Angelina after that... if that's okay?"

"Sure son, anything else?"

"Oh yeah, give Joy a call and have her follow you to the

store. Ya know...only guys have been living in that cabin for the past several months and honestly, it stinks like shit. Have her pick out some toiletries for the ladies, to make it livable for them. I'll try and square the place away before y'all get there."

It is not long until Joy and Jason are following Grandpa to the store, while Cloud and Barbara drive to the cabin and park in the nearby dense undergrowth.

Rafta watches his iPhone GPS tracking app closely. He notices his phone begins beeping, and is losing power fast. From the GPS tracker, he sees their vehicle has gotten off the highway and is moving at a slower speed; *"This damn GPS app uses a lot of power and I don't have a phone jack in this van."* Soon thereafter, he can no longer track the target.

Abruptly, he calls Pedro; "I can no longer track the GPS signal. We must wait until my phone is recharged. Until then we must communicate on the handheld radios. I know they are close; we will find them in a few hours. Get off the highway at the next exit and find a convenience store. Purchase some food, water, a cigarette lighter USB power jack for my cell phone and, oh yes, toilet paper for the men. Don't forget that jack and do not arouse any suspicion. Also, when I hang up the phone, give a few CB radios to the others. Turn them to CB channel 25–5, understand? I will let you know when I regain their GPS signal and give you further instructions."

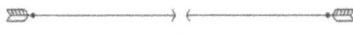

Johnny Turner is also pulling into that same town in his brand new red Dodge Ram pickup truck. All tripped out with huge chrome exhaust, he decided to attach two American flags to the pipes so everyone in town would notice him coming. He's finally got a good paying job as a roughneck working for the fracking company about 30 miles away. No sooner did he get his first paycheck, than he thumped down a deposit and drove off with the truck. Johnny's two buddies stand conspicuously in the rear of the truck. As dust rises from his skidding stop in front of the local convenience store, they all rowdily jump out for a cold pop and chips. Jumping from the passenger side door is his beautiful 17-year-old girlfriend, Mandy, for her first ride. Her long curly brown hair cover-ups her tied tank top shirt. Trying to make a good indelible impression on Johnny, she is not wearing a bra and has considerable cleavage showing. Walking into the store she enjoys flaunting her frayed low rise denim shorts, with teasing white pockets.

A minute or so later, Grandpa pulls up to the same convenience store, a few spaces away, and begins writing down his list of needed supplies. Jason and Joy pull up next to Grandpa soon after. Unknowingly, Grandpa is just feet away from Johnny Turner's red pickup. As Grandpa writes his list, Carlos notices Johnny and his friends' rowdy actions in the store. Not wishing to provoke an altercation, he reaches over to Grandpa and nods. Angelina, sitting between them, just sits and watches attentively. They both lower their hats over their faces to not get noticed. Grandpa waives his palm to Jason and Joy, indicating for them to stop and wait. Joy sits curiously waiting for Grandpa to get out of his truck; "What the hell is he doing, why doesn't want to get out of his truck?"

Jason, gently grasps her knee; "Joy honey, just sit back and wait a minute I'm sure he has a good reason."

Several seconds later, Pedro pulls into the same store parking lot on the far side of Johnny Turner, with the second van full of men sliding in beside him. Rafta did not let Pedro know the model of the pickup that is holding the GPS or a description of his targets.

All five vehicles are parked in a row, Johnny Turner in the middle. Two of the men accompanying Pedro slide the panel door open and quickly jump out; they stand around stretching their legs. Pedro has them wait as he goes over the carefully prepared list dictated by Rafta. His men pause, standing next to his door.

Johnny and his girlfriend playfully stroll out the glass double doors with melting ice cream cones in hand. Two of Pedro's men are immediately dumbstruck, never having seen such a seductive long-legged beauty so provocatively dressed, walking directly to them. All the insurgents have been locked away for months with only TV, pizza, and cola to keep them occupied. As Mandy moseys to the passenger side door the two men nudge together to obstruct her path. One of Pedro's men looks down with a brown-toothed, broad grin playfully tugging at the bottom of Mandy's tank top.

Johnny Turner anxiously runs around to rescue Mandy, quickly forcing himself between her and the men. Loudly; "What the **hell** do you think you're doing here? Step the hell back... or I'll kick your **ass**."

Through their hat brims, Grandpa and Carlos intently watch the altercation between Johnny and Pedro's men.

Today, in an attempt to bolster his manliness, Johnny is carrying his granddad's old 38 police special pistol, under his shirt. Driving such a conspicuous red truck, he feels the need for added protection.

Face-to-face, Johnny thrusts his chest into the intruder and pulls his shirt up exposing the revolver; "Do you want some of dis... **amigo**?"

Pedro, inertly observing the altercation, calmly pulls an AK-47 from between the seats slides, it onto his lap, then briskly pounds the barrel against the window. Johnny startled by the loud **tap, tap, tap...** pauses in wide-eyed awe, recognizing the distinctive barrel of an AK-47 pointing at him. With a stone face Pedro stares, raises his eyebrows and nods his head, directing that he move on.

With discrete hand gestures, Grandpa gets Joy's and Jason's attention. They all casually turn their heads to not be noticed.

Johnny abruptly jerks Mandy's arm and pulls her away. All four hastily jump into the pickup and speed off. Looking back, dust billowing; "I guess these guys are really desperate for jobs."

As Johnny accelerates down the road, Pedro lowers the rifle back between the seats. Grandpa and Jason have been slyly observing what just occurred. They both recognize the AK-47, not often used in this part of the country.

Angelina has been riveted on the entire confrontation, peering through her sunglasses. As Angelina stares at Pedro, she is petrified to see that unmistakable silver turquoise bracelet. It has been only a few months but her memory of that event is still vivid and she recalls the bracelet indelibly. Carlos, seeing her stunned expression; "What is the matter... Angel?"

With trembling finger, she reluctantly points; "Uncle Carlos that is him the man that killed mama. That's the bracelet worn by mama's killer."

Carlos casually glances; "Are you sure? How can this be?"

Angelina, shivering, looks again steely-eyed; her glance catches Pedro's attention and he looks back at her. He puckers his lips with a repulsive kiss. He does not recognize her wearing sunglasses, seated between the two men.

Angelina recoils into her seat, anxious; "That is him, I know his face, that is the silver bracelet, I remember it exactly, all of it. That's him... *he is the animal!*"

Grandpa still doesn't know the details of the Mexico killings. They wait a few minutes for the men to come out of the store with their supplies. They all scrutinize, as the men loaded with supplies climb into the vans. They observe, as both side doors slide open, with the outstretched hands grabbing drinks.

Grandpa is astonished at the number of men in the vans

and their appearance. They are all fairly young, similar appearance, wearing the same new, department store work clothes; *"This is no coincidence."*

Once the two vans are far out of site, Grandpa, Joy, and Jason quickly run into the store and purchase all the needed supplies and rush out. Grandpa immediately calls Cloud on his shortwave radio, with Jason standing beside him. Hands shaking; "Son it's me. Listen, Angelina just ID'd one of these guys that killed her mother. Something is definitely wrong here... definitely wrong."

Cloud quickly responds; "What?... Is she sure?

Jason, anxiously shaking his head; "Also, we just counted eight guys in two-panel vans. It could be a total coincidence but it looks awful fishy. They are all about the same age, dressed in the same clean workman's clothes. They definitely do not look like local farm or factory workers."

Grandpa barks; "And...one had an AK across his lap. Son, migrant workers don't carry **AK's!"**

Cloud tersely; "Drop off Carlos and Angelina and get back here ASAP. It may not be anything, but we just can't take any chances. I don't know if or how they found out where we are, but we can figure that out later. Get back here quick and make sure no one is following you."

"Son, what the fuck is going on here... Somebody fill me in?

"I'll do when you get back to the cabin pop."

"Okay Son."

Joy has been sitting quietly next to Jason, listening to the details. Hearing everything, she becomes very anxious. As they drive off, Jason sees that she is shivering; "Joy honey, are you all right?"

She sits shaking, hands clasped in her lap; *"What the fuck is going on here, what am I doing here?"*

Jason; "Joy, Joy look at me, are you okay?" Joy just looks at him, shuddering, unable to contain her fear. She continues to shudder all the way back to the cabin.

A few minutes later, as Grandpa gets to the farmhouse and Carlos and Angelina get out; "Carlos leave your radio on, stay close my friend. I will call if I need anything."

Carlos nods uneasily; "Si' Grandpa, I will wait for your call."

As Grandpa drives off, Carlos turns on the TV to get a weather alert and hears of an approaching line of severe thunderstorms, heading toward their county, planned for later that evening; *"That is just great, what next?"*

As they walk onto their front porch, Carlos stands next to Angelina and draws her close: "Angel... Grandpa is like family to me...to us. He gave me get this job and this house for us to live in. No one else would give me work or a roof over my head.

We owe him much. If he calls, I must go to help him. Do you understand?"

Uneasy; "Si Tío Carlos... Si"

Grandpa and Jason speed toward the obscure dusty access road to the cabin. They park three abreast in the dense Cedar pines. Jason and Joy walk in quickly and drop all the supplies onto the table. Without looking at her father, Joy walks over to the bed, sits and begins rocking anxiously. Jason sits next to her, rubbing her arms, trying to calm her down. Cloud is resolved to his daughter's hostility and knows he must focus on the more important matters at hand; *"I have to get things organized. I only have one chance to get this right."*

Not knowing where to store food and supplies Barbara goes about cleaning things up. She also notes the various pill bottles scattered across the table. Disturbed she immediately sees John Cloud's name on the prescription bottles and the names and dosage of the pills that he has been taking; *"Oh my God, I can only imagine what kind of problems he has, for him to be taking so many meds."*

Joy looks up head shaking sees Barbara; "Jason, why is she here? How does she know my father?

Shrugging his shoulders, he stands and walks up behind his mother; "Mom. Mom, why are you here? How is it that you know John? John Cloud?"

Barbara turns her head part way around, not wanting to show her son her eyes or her anguish; "John, John and I are old college friends. We haven't seen each other in over 30 years. I recognized him at the funeral and just wanted to help. That's all."

Jason sensing her discomfort and not wanting to make a scene just rubs her arm and sits back down next to Joy; "Joy, they are just old friends from college. That's it."

Grandpa walks into the cabin, furiously throws all his supplies onto the table making quite a commotion. Looking at Cloud; "Someone please explain to me what the fuck we are doing out here and who the fuck these people are?"

Seeing that Grandpa is really agitated, Cloud walks up to him; "Pop you gotta calm down, it doesn't help our situation with you getting anxious"

"Anxious, I'm not anxious I'm *fucking furious!* I just buried four of my family... that I love... and nobody's telling me what the *fuck* is going on. I want answers... I'm not going to calm down until you tell me what happened... And... who are these people?"

Turning around looking at everyone; "One thing. I guess I owe all of you an explanation. Today, an FBI agent approached me at the funeral and explained what has been going on. About six years ago when I was stationed in Iraq, I was part of an operation that went bad. Things happened that was not my fault and I could not control. A woman and young baby were killed during an operation to get the IED builder. They were his wife and son. Years later he joined ISIS and for whatever reason, he is here now to get revenge. That's all I know."

All in the room are stunned, hearing it from Cloud in such a calm tone. Jason has not had the opportunity to speak to Cloud and walks him outside; "Sir, I need to apologize to you for a bunch of things, I really fucked up. I'm really very sorry that I didn't inform you about these guys; and not calling you about the attack on Joy. It was really stupid and inconsiderate of me. I was just thinking about Joy and trying to find the identity of the guy that almost killed her."

"Son, everything happened so very fast. If I were in your shoes, I'd probably have done the same thing. From what I understand, absolutely no one could've put all that information together to stop this. At least you saved Joy and I appreciate that."

Grandpa crisscrosses the cabin floor trying to put the supplies away, grumbling to himself.

The grief and anger from the funerals have taken their toll on Joy. Her emotions vacillate wildly. Jason notices and draws her closer; "Babe why don't you lie down and rest for a few minutes maybe you'll feel better."

Joy, incredibly anxious; "*Feel better? Feel better*? How the **hell** can anybody *feel better*? This morning we buried half of my family and now those fucking animals are minutes from here....and coming for us. We need help...Or we need to get the hell out of here."

Grandpa, also agitated, stares around the room; "Son, this is the real deal son... a real shit storm. We have to think of something to end this and kill the sons of bitches. *I'm tired of talkin*. I'll look around and see what we could use."

Barbara trying to be inconspicuous, continues to straighten up and reorient to the cabin. She stands at the doorway looking into the trees; *"Wow, things really changed around here in 30 years."*

Grandpa finally notices her and leans over to Cloud; "Who's that?"

Cloud slowly takes off his dress military jacket and throws it across the bed. With a peculiar grin; "Grandpa, it's Barbara. You remember, Barbara?"

Perplexed, Grandpa walks over and gently puts his hand on her shoulder. She turns to looks at him. Grandpa, amazed as Barbara exclaims; "Grandpa it's me, Barbara."

Joy and Jason watch, stunned, not understanding what is happening. Grandpa thrusts his arms around her and pulls her close with a bear hug; "Is this my...***Barbie Doll?***"

Joy, head shaking; "***Who..?***"

Grandpa turns with an enormous grin; "Barbie Doll! Joy honey... Barbara was your father's college girlfriend. Back in the day, you couldn't pry these two apart with a crowbar."

Joy and Jason sit open-mouthed, stunned; "Mom, you never told me you knew John or that you dated."

Joy is suddenly reconsidering her acceptance of Jason's

marriage proposal; *"Your mother once dated my father? Are you kidding me..? This is totally nuts, totally fucking nuts..."*

For years the cabin has sat at the base of a nearby 100-foot hill, Grandpas' Mountain. With all the lead content in the mountain it is a dead zone for the remote cell phone signals. However, on the mantle over the fireplace, Grandpa has his trusted UHF/VHF radio scanner. In the remote countryside, it is used to monitor all local wireless, emergency radio frequencies. It is a necessity in rural America to keep everyone informed of weather, police and fire department emergencies.

Suddenly a crackling Arabic voice is heard over the scanner on the mantle scanner; "Rafta, Rafta, are you there?" Moments later Rafta; "Use Arabic now, no one will understand you."

Serving in Iraq for seven years Cloud understands Arabic perfectly. Everyone in the room freezes as Cloud translates...

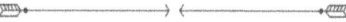

Pedro; "Where are you and where do you want us to go?"

Rafta; "They are close, get off Exit 214 and travel west. I'll give you the location in a few minutes. Stay silent until then. Use only these radios now. Cell phone coverage out here is very inconsistent, we must stay in touch."

Rafta gives Pedro directions to an abandoned farm a few miles from Cloud's cabin. Not long after, Rafta and his men are rejoined, parked a mile from the turn off, on a crushed stone farm road. All the men get out and rest under the shade trees. Rafta sees the intermittent GPS signal has stopped moving, at a location off the road.

He motions to Pedro; "Look, we will wait here through the heat of the day, then in late afternoon, we will go to that signal location to attack after dark. I will look at the aerial view of the area to prepare a plan of attack. Guns, maps, unrestricted access across the country; stupid Americans...giving us everything we need to do a well-planned attack."

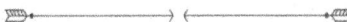

Cloud looks at Grandpa; "That is them, the guys you spotted in town." He is astonished that Rafta and his men are so close."

Grandpa shakes his head; "They are here, they have found us. How the hell did they do that so quickly?"

Cloud points to Jason; "Jason do you have your AR in your truck?"

Jason shakes his head discouragingly; "I only have my Glock with 15 in the clip and an extra mag on my belt."

Barb, do you have your phone? Joy your phone? Try to see if any of the new phones can get reception, you never know."

After quickly checking their phones, they both shake

their heads discouragingly; "No."

While running around his pickup to see if there is anything else that they may be able to use, Jason notices out of the corner of his eye a tiny device, magnetically attached to the side wall of the pickup. He cautiously pulls it off and brings it back to Cloud; "This is how they found us, a GPS tracker. They followed us up here all the way. Is there another way we can get out of here?" Jason slams his extra mag on the table, Cloud answers; "No."

"Jay, they probably stuck that tracker on your car and the limo. They did it right under the noses of the FBI. If they can do that, they can find us and follow us anywhere. No use running... We have to make our stand, here and now."

Cloud unloads Jason's extra magazine and reloads his own gun; "I'll load my Beretta, at least we'll have these." Cloud has been practicing with his pistol for the past several weeks and is confident that he could hit anyone at 50 yards.

Jason looks at Cloud dejectedly; "Sir, I hope I'm wrong. It is pure speculation, but I think these guys are heavily armed. The other day, AJ's Gun Shop just outside Oklahoma City was broken into and several AK's and even an RPG were stolen. Police and ATF attributed it to white supremacists, but it may have been these guys.

Grandpa stands by and listens attentively; "One of the guys at the minimart had an AK47. I don't think we should consider that a coincidence, we should consider them to be heavily armed."

Joy sits nervously rocking on the edge of the bed, listening; "Stop and think, should we try to get the fuck out of here and make a run for it. How many of them are there; eight, 10, 20, does **anybody know**?"

With the effects of the booze and meds wearing off, Cloud's military experience kicks in and he becomes unexpectedly lucid; "Joy honey, we would be taking a big chance. Some may be waiting just down the road. And, from what Grandpa has already seen there are at least eight of them and possibly even more. We are heavily outnumbered and outgunned."

Joy, skeptically shaking her head, unable to contain her emotions; "So why the **fuck** are we staying here?"

Grandpa is puffing his chest; "In the Art of War, Sun Tzu states: The clever general imposes his will on the enemy and does not allow the enemy to impose his will. We know this land, every god damn inch of it. Let's use that to our advantage. Let's ambush the motherfuckers. "

Though Grandpas comments are untimely and inartful, Cloud realizes; "... Wait a minute, Grandpa's absolutely right. I don't want us to get caught in the open, under any circumstances. They can stop us anytime, on the highway and wipe us out in a minute. They don't realize that we can hear them talking; let's use that to our advantage. "

Late in the day, the severe thunderstorm warnings are heard over the scanner. The deafening reverberation of treetop Cicadas blankets the area. Dark grey storm clouds obstruct the sun, creating a surreal orange glow on the horizon. One can now hear the muffled rumbling of thunder in the distance. Almost on cue, the cabin lights flicker then go out, a common occurrence with the storms. Joy jumps from the bed and anxiously paces the room, her fear of thunder and lightning rekindled.

John Cloud has few occasions to nurture and console Joy. As Joy elbows away from Jason, Cloud hesitantly walks with outstretched arms to the center of the room. Joy, with head down, inadvertently walks right into his embrace. Looking up and surprised, she does not recoil, but instinctively buries her head into his chest, sobbing hysterically; "Daddy."

"That's it, baby girl let it out, let it out... for all of us."

The two people who have been physically and emotionally detached for so very long, are now forged together. Cloud clutches onto her; "I'm sorry baby, sorry for not being there for you, for so many years. But I'm here now...I promise you that nothing, **nothing** will happen to you. I promise..."

"But daddy, there are so many of them coming to kill us...all of us."

Through his vacillating PTSD symptoms, Cloud is surprisingly lucid. He must now attempt to focus on the task at hand and refrain from conjuring images that could trigger his anxiety attacks.

Grandpa joins in a group hug; "Baby girl, it has been a long time, a very long time."

Joy leans her head into Grandpa's chest; "Yes Grandpa...too long."

After their long tight embrace Joy sits on the bed next to Jason, but still noticeably shaken.

Cloud, a veteran of several military actions, knows that panic is a soldier's worst enemy. Though not soldiers, he must calm everyone, instill confidence and hopefully in doing so, revive his own. He also recognizes that, with the exception of Grandpa, none of the people in the room have any combat experience. He must really come up with some unique strategy, and do it fast. He takes a deep breath; "Let's take stock of what we have and how we could use it. Come on people, think; we don't have a lot of time."

In an attempt involve everyone; "Okay we have all been here before, in the dark. We all played flashlight tag in these woods. Barb, Joy, Pop, *right?* "

Incredulously, Joy glances up; "Yah, but you wouldn't be murdered by a flashlight."

As Rafta sits with Pedro beneath a cottonwood tree, he is planning what he hopes will be his final attack on the Cloud family. He is finally able to plug his iPhone into a cigarette lighter jack to repower it; "Look, brother, this is the last location where we lost contact with the GPS tracker. If you look very closely at the aerial map you will see the roof of a small cabin there. Next to the cabin is a small creek. If you follow that Creek

North it goes under a bridge. Up there, do you see it? I want you and six men to drive to that small bridge. Park and hide your trucks, and walk along that dry creek bed. Make sure no one sees you when you pull off the road. See how the creek comes up beside the house. If we attack the house at night, I believe they will try to escape along that creek. All the other ground is high or has dense trees. I know because the American soldiers always like to use those creek beds for evasion. Also, no one will see you walking along that creek late afternoon and after dark. It is well hidden. Find that bridge and that creek, and wait there. I will radio you with my instructions."

As Pedro and six others load and check their weapons, they collect flashlights, extra ammunition and radios, then climb into two vans. Rafta and four others get into his van. Pedro does not read English very well. So, when it comes time for him to look at the paper road signs, he becomes confused and drives aimlessly through the surrounding countryside. All landscape and all farm road intersections look alike; plus, there are few if any distinguishing features. So, Pedro quickly gets lost amongst the dusty farm roads. Rafta can still be heard over their radio scanner; "Pedro, Pedro turnaround, turnaround. Pedro, go to the end of the road and tell me what you see, what does the road sign say?

Pedro hesitantly; "Linnncolnnn Road."

Rafta; "*What?* That's Lincoln Road, you idiot. You're going in the wrong direction. Turn around and go west. West into the sunset on Lincoln Road, another 5 miles. You will see a farmhouse, then a small red bridge over a creek. Drive off the road there. *Understand?*"

Pedro; "Understood, we will drive slowly and should get there in about an hour. I will bring all six of us. I will radio you when I see the house."

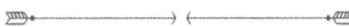

Cloud motions to Grandpa; "That's the Carter farm near the small bridge and Little Red Creek. It runs right past this cabin. It will take them some time to drive there then trudge through that overgrown creek-bed. By then, it will be dark. They intend to ambush us in the dark."

Grandpa with a sly look in his eyes leans to Cloud; "I have an idea. We don't know how many of them are in front of us but we know several will be coming up that muddy creek. They will be traveling in the dark right under our tree stand. I can set up an ambush there. Carlos and I can pick them off with our bows. In an hour or so it will be totally dark."

Shaking his head discouragingly; "Sorry pop, you will need a lot more than two skilled archers to hold off a half a dozen men with AK's."

Grandpa energetically paces the room, pauses, turns... then flings back the dusty rug and pulls open the trapdoor. He turns on his flashlight and quickly scurries down the basement ladder; "I'll get these bastards; I think I can prepare a big surprise for them." In a matter of seconds, Grandpa hurls up four cases of his special recipe moonshine. As he peeks up; "Jason is it? Come on son, give this old man a hand loading some crates into the back of my ATV."

No sooner than he scurries back up the ladder, he runs over to the bed, pulls off the sheet. Everyone watches in amazement as he moves with incredible speed. He grabs his camo outfit from off-the-wall and throws it under his arm; "I could use your strong back son." He tears the sheet, tucks half under his arm and runs out the door. Cloud watches in amazement, as Grandpa scurries out the door. Cloud waves at Jason, just follow Grandpa's instructions.

As Jason loads the four rattling crates to the ATV; "What are these for? Do you intend to drink them to death?"

Grandpa somewhat amused taps his nose; "Son, this is an old VC trick I learned in Vietnam, the hard way. Also, grab that rope over there and throw it in the back."

As they load up, he radios Carlos; "Carlos if you are willing my friend, I could use your help. Come quickly to the tree stand. Wear your hunting camo and bring your bow and all your hunting arrows. We're going to have some fun hunting tonight."

Carlos responds; "Okay Grandpa, I'll be right there."

Carlos quickly dons his full body camo, grabs his bow and runs out the door headed to the tree stand. He pauses for a second and gives Angelina a reassuring hug; "Stay here; do not move, no matter what.... Understand?"

Angelina stands obediently and hesitantly nods.

It is about an hour before sunset as they see the

approaching line of thunderstorms. So ominous, only the white billowing tops of the thunderheads illuminate the ground. Grandpa dons his camo-gear, turkey hunting hood, and hat.

Cloud trying to figure out what Grandpa is doing, stands in the doorway; "Grandpa, how is it they cannot hear you."

Grandpa, slyly; "Son, Daniel bought us four of these fancy whiz-bang, high tech radios. We can only hear each other but no one else can hear us; some kind of high-tech encryption shit. Kinda like what you used in the Army. Here, take a radio and try it out. Also, on the mantle next to the scanner are extra batteries, if you lose power. Listen to the scanner for Rafta. If there are any changes you can radio me. Okay."

Cloud, fiddling with the radio knobs; "Somehow, I think you have been planning for this moment."

Darting around energetically; "Son, I was born for this."

Grandpa and Jason drive off quietly in the battery-powered ATV. Jason sits beside him listening to the distant thunderstorms. It only takes a few minutes for them to stop beneath the tree stand. Grandpa jumps out and points; "Jay, take two of those crates over to the tree then climb up into the tree stand. I'll fill the buckets and you hoist and unload them. Come on boy, get up there.... Move... we don't have much time. "

After a few energetic grunts and moans by Jason, two dozen moonshine jars are stacked in the tree stand; "That's it, what's next?"

"Come on down, carry the other two cases to the other side of the creek, one over there and the other... over there, on those high banks. Tie a rope around each box then completely unscrew the lids. Let the long rope dangle. You got that? Hurry boy, **hurry**.!"

Confused, Jason lugs the boxes and looks back up at the tree stand; "Why?"

Grandpa, arms flailing wildly; "Just do it boy, do it! That's it, a little further over. That's it now, let the rope hang down, that's it, all the way. Now do the second crate over by that cottonwood tree over there. Yes, yes, that one. That's great... You're done, boy... now get the hell out of here. Son, when you get back to the cabin, there are plenty more cases down below. Cut some rags and place them in the jars and screw the lids back on. You know how to make a Molotov cocktail, **don't** you? Use them, use them all."

As Grandpa gets into this tree stand, he looks up at the sky and instinctively transitions to his stealth hunting mode, whispers; "Take the ATV back to the cabin and drive quietly, with the lights off too. I don't want those hombres to know that we are waiting. Quick... Good luck son. Now git!"

As Jason silently glides off, Carlos stumbles to the tree stand with bow in hand, breathing heavy. Carlos slowly lumbers up the tall ladder. Grandpa pulls their bows and dozens of hunting arrows up to the tall stand; "Put your harness on my friend. I wouldn't want you to fall and get hurt."

Leaning toward Carlos; "Do me a favor old friend, take

the lids off those jars, stick these cut up rags most of the way in and screw the lids back on, but not too tight.   Just leave one open for us, no use wasting them all."

The wind starts to swirl unexpectedly. The extremely humid 95° conditions are perfect for producing extreme thunderstorms. In the distance along the horizon, one can see rain falling beneath a crease in the clouds.   The slow trickle of water in the Creek begins to increase.

Jason drives back within seconds to the cabin, just as the wind begins to whip. Closing the door hard behind him; "Is it safe for Grandpa and Carlos to be in the tree stand in a thunderstorm?   Grandpa said something about using the remaining moonshine as Molotov cocktails. What would you like us to do sir?"

Cloud looking into the cellar stacked with dozens of moonshine cases ponders...; "Do you still have some juice in your quarterback arm?"

Jason eyebrows raised; "The last time I checked; it still worked pretty good."

Cloud pointing down; "Son, jump downstairs, and throw up a few more cases. Ladies, why don't you go downstairs where it will be a lot safer, I don't want anything to happen you."

Jason staring; "Yes, Joy that's a good idea. Why not get down below and take my Glock and a flashlight with you, just in case. I wouldn't want anything to happen to you or the baby."

Cloud immediately jerks his head around; *"**Baby, what baby**?"*

Joy walks up to her father and taps him on the chest; "It's a long story dad and we don't want anyone to worry. I can fill you in with all the details later. Don't worry it's okay."

Cloud shrugging his shoulders; "Worry, why would I worry?" Curiously looking at Jason; "Is it your baby?"

With an awkward grimace; "Well... no sir."

Shaking his head bewildered; "Not your baby, then whose baby is it?

Joy barks back; "It's Dawns..."

With all the commotion Cloud's anxiety is beginning to show.

Joy walks over to Cloud trying to calm him; "Dad, it's a long, complicated story we didn't think you could handle... just not yet. Just know I'm having a baby boy and he's your grandson. That's it.... Now let's focus, on the task at hand..."

Cloud knows that he cannot take any more psych meds as it will dull his senses further; *"I need all my wits about me."* With shaking hands, he gestures; "Quick, tear those bedsheets into foot long strip about three inches wide, about three dozen, quickly. Cloud throws some large firewood logs on the table at the window, overlooking the access road. He still keeps the old wood shutters closed and securely stacks the wood as a barrier against any bullets that may be fired through the window. "Jason, leave the jars to the ladies. Go down below, find some heavy planks and prop them against that door. We'll try to keep them from kicking the door in." Cloud looks around the room and notices his prescription bottles have been moved. Not wishing to arouse suspicion, he says nothing; *"I cannot think about drugs right now, I need my wits about me and a clear head. I will deal with my emotions later."*

The women proceed to tear up the bed sheets, inserting half into the unscrewed jars, then screwing on the lids. Jason sniffs, takes a sip from an opened jar then reflexively jerks his head back; "***Wow***, now I know why this stuff is illegal."

Cloud peering over his shoulder; "Yes I know, so be careful with any flame around those jars, they are highly volatile."

Rafta, following the GPS signal, finally finds what he believes to be the access road to the cabin, and Cloud's location. They pull off the road and park their van deep in the bushes. He radios to Pedro; "I believe I have found the cabin. I'm at a dirt road a few hundred yards from the cabin. Let me know when you get close to your position." Keeping their heads down, they quietly inch down the long access road. With the sun behind the dark clouds, they can barely see the outline of the cabin. Only the light from the towering thunderheads is reflected off its chimney. There are no lights inside the cabin, nonetheless Rafta knows they are there. He checks his iPhone GPS tracker again, and it has not moved. This was the place and the tracker hasn't moved for hours. Pointing; "There in the trees, there are the three vehicles we were following."

A few weeks earlier Cloud had the long access road cleared and leveled by a local farmer using a large D8 tractor. It leveled out the road, clearing old stumps, boulders, and saplings. An enormous pile of debris has been pushed about 40 yards from the house. Rafta kneels quietly along the side of the road in the undergrowth; *"This is nothing at all like our land in Iraq. Here it is, lush and thick where anything can grow. Why is it they need to come and invade our country? They have everything here."* While he sees a pile of stumps, logs, and debris, he will sit and wait for total darkness, awaiting Pedro's arrival.

Rafta points to his men; "Crawl up and spread out around these trees and stumps." On his radio he whispers; "Pedro, **Pedro!** How far have you traveled? Do you see the cabin yet? Keep your weapons on safe and do not attack until I give the signal."

Pedro; "Not yet, this creek is more difficult than what was shown on the map. It is tangled with branches boulders and sticky mud. Do you want us to move into the nearby field?"

Rafta tersely; *"No!* Just keep under cover, we have all night, you should be there soon. Let me know when you see the house."

Listening to the scanner, Cloud hears their exchange; "Pop. Pop, they are getting close. They will be coming down that creek right below you and will be there at any time. Keep your head down and cling to that old tree. I think the main guy, Rafta, is right down the main road just waiting for darkness, the right time to attack."

Almost giddy; "Not to worry son, we are in full camo. They couldn't spot us in broad daylight; in darkness, we'll be invisible. Carlos put on plenty of face paint... your hands too." A few minutes later Grandpa and Carlos sit silently.

As Pedro's men trudge noisily through the creek, they startle several deer drinking. The small deer herd burst across the food plot. Grandpa, being very familiar with the undergrowth, points; "Look my friend the deer have been startled from their bedding area. Dang it, there's that 150-buck, I was telling you about the other day. I told you he was in there. They are only a few hundred yards up the creek, should be along in about 15 minutes."

In the front doorway of the farmhouse sits Angelina, crunched into a ball, listening to the ominous rumble of the approaching storm. She flinches as she hears distinct thunderclaps. She has never seen such severe thunderstorms like this. Angelina worries now that her only family Uncle Carlos is in the darkness, awaiting her mother's murderer. She sits trembling, peering out to the darkening field. She doesn't want to be caught in the house alone with those animals. Another flash of lightning is seen high above, with accompanying thunder several seconds later. The enormous storm is almost overhead.

Since it is the Fourth of July, fireworks are commonplace in farm country. In the distance, you can hear the muffled sound of firecrackers and M80's. No storms will dissuade these heartland patriots from celebrating their holiday. Joy also hears the nearby thunder and jumps behind her father, grabbing his back. Cloud turns reassuringly; "It's only thunder baby girl...it's only thunder."

Despite the oppressive 95° heat, Angelina jumps up and dons Daniel's camo jacket. She removes the bow from the wall hook and grabs for her target arrows. She pauses for a moment, and cautiously attaches the razor-sharp hunting arrows and quiver to the bow. She does not hesitate, as she leaps off the porch toward the cut wheat field, on the way to the tree stand. As Angelina cautiously steps into the darkening field, she is attuned to every sound. She understands her precarious situation; *"Oh God... I'm out in the open, nothing to hide behind."* Clutching her side, she kneels to catch her breath; *"It was not this hot in the house."* As a deafening thunderclap explodes overhead, she falls forward to find refuge; *"St. Michael... St. Michael please give me strength."* The wind begins to violently thrash, the storm is almost overhead. She has learned from Uncle Carlos of the danger of these storms, sucking you up, never to be seen again. No sane person would be in an open field with the exploding lightning overhead; however, she must move on; *"I cannot stop now...I will not stop now."* As Angelina reaches the trees, encircling the food plot, she knows she is close, only a few hundred yards away. After feeling her way through the trees, she kneels to rest at the edge of the dense planted food plot. Across this field is Carlos and the tree stand. There she will wait and listen. She is shocked as several deer run around her; *"My God, look at the size of these beasts."*

With flashlights in hand, Pedro and his men slowly traverse the creek, only a hundred yards from the stand. Another call from Rafta; "Pedro, where are you? Where are you?" They struggle to zigzag past the large slippery boulders, squeezing beneath some fallen trees. As they get closer, Grandpa notices the scanning flashlights. Then, in the distance, Pedro is startled by the illumination of aerial fireworks, then seconds later loud explosions are heard. He doesn't understand the reason for the fireworks explosions; nonetheless, he must move on; *"I have no idea who is causing these explosions, but I must stay in this creek."*

Grandpa nods; "Carlos get your lighter ready, make sure it works." Grandpa and Carlos are used to sitting motionless for hours on end, a tactic honed from years of turkey hunting. High in this tall tree in the pitch dark, they are almost impossible to see. They wait for the men to enter the deep, half-moon trench below them. Grandpa grasps, then gently lifts one of the jars and whispers; "I will wait till they are all in between the two downed trees. They will be trapped there. Light the wick...."

Carlos flicks his lighter, immediately igniting the first wick, creating a ghostly blue flickering flame. Grandpa nervously tosses it into the ditch behind the last man, igniting the branches of the trees. There is a booming explosion dropping the men to their knees. The force of the explosion knocks the radio from Pedro's hand into the creek. They turn with weapons and flashlights scanning upward.

Energetically; "***Quickly***, keep them coming." He throws a second jar at the front of the group, producing another huge explosion. It is so loud that everyone in the cabin, along with

Angelina and Rafta, can hear it.

Screams echo, as the horrified men realize they are trapped. Angelina cowers in place, watching in awe as the fireballs rise, not understanding what is causing these explosions; *"Why is this happening?"*

Lit moonshine jars continue to be thrown right then left, then center. Trapped by the flames, the men scramble about, struggling to climb out of the trench. Frantically, they slip down slick clay embankments. They reach wildly for the overhanging tree roots. A few men huddle back, firing wildly into the embankment with their automatic weapons. One man spots a dangling rope and madly lunges for it to escape the blaze. Instinctively, he pulls the rope only to receive some slack. He aggressively tugs the rope and the box of opened mason jars crashes on and around him, causing an intense inferno. He runs around the creek screaming in pain as he burns.

Grandpa, recalling the agony his family has gone through; *"Burn you bastards, burn."*

The flaming alcohol spreads across the small stream producing unbearable heat. The frantic screams of the burning men are disturbing. Moments later the second rope is pulled and another dozen jars cascade into the blazing ditch. Two men frenziedly try to climb from the hellhole but slide back down into the flames.

Hearing the distant explosions Rafta imagines Pedro's men are coming under attack; "Open fire you fool's, open fire."

Automatic weapons pepper the darkened cabin. In the pitch-black room, bullets explode through the shutter and upper walls, but bounce off the lower stone foundation wall. The hundred-year-old cabin absorbs or repels most of the rifle fire. Nonetheless, everyone hugs the floor.

Both grandpa and Pedro can now hear the automatic weapons being fired at the cabin. Grandpa whispers to Carlos; "Okay my friend, grab your bow... it's time to hunt."

With only a dim flashlight illuminating their faces, all in the cabin lie cowering, grasping each other's hands for assurance. Cloud slides over to Joy to comfort his shivering daughter; "Come over here girl, get close." As the gunfire intensifies, Cloud's PTSD symptoms return with a vengeance. He begins to noticeably shake, sweating profusely from his face, as Joy looks on bewildered; *"What the hell is the matter with you, daddy?"*

Bullets shatter the wood window shutter, sending splinters flying in all directions. A large splinter hits Cloud's prescription bottles, sending it right in front of his face. An untimely reminder of his PTSD and his debilitating anxiety. Uncharacteristically, Cloud erupts into an aberrant outburst; *"Ahhhhh..!"* Everyone in the room is startled.

Rafta hearing the scream; "Stop your firing, listen."

Cloud yells out boldly; *"Rafta,* I know it is you out there, I recognize your stench."

"Col. Cloud, yes you recognize it, it is the stench of death.

Soon that stench will be on you and the rest of your family."

"You think this is some kind of game?"

"Yes, this is the adult game of chess. You came to my country years ago and took many pieces, now it is my turn to sweep away the pieces from your side of the board. But I will do everything I can to keep you alive, so you may watch as I butcher the rest of your family." Rafta motions for his men to open fire again.

Joy sees the unmistakable anguish on Cloud's face, realizing he may no longer be the hardened Army veteran that single-handedly neutralized the four bikers. Tightly grasping his hand, she screams; "**Daddy...** daddy, we need your help... N**ow!**"

Cloud quakes under the deafening gunfire then hearing his daughter's desperate plea, takes a deep breath... squeezing her hand reassuringly; "Don't worry baby I got this." Through his ordeal, he attempts to gain emotional control; *"If you don't want this to be the last day of the rest of your life, get off your ass... Take the initiative soldier."*

Grandpa hears the automatic weapons fire at the cabin, which gives him renewed impetus to kill as many as he can. While protected by the branches from the rifle fire, Grandpa and Carlos must shield their faces from the inferno below. Grandpa throws another jar at the top of the trench, close to an exit point. However, one of the men detects the movement above. He begins to spray his AK wildly in their direction; however, the tree absorbs all the damage. Soon, a few others spray the tree with automatic weapons, while others attempt to dance around the flames. With leaves and small branches falling all around, the sound of the automatic weapons is deafening.

From a distance, the sound of gunfire blends with the distant thunder and holiday fireworks. Grandpa continues flinging the flaming jars into the ditch. As one of the exhausted insurgents finally climbs from the creek, Grandpa grasps his bow with an arrow in place and in one fluid motion, aims and fires. From only 10 yards he cannot miss such a large target; *"Take that you piece of shit."* The razor-sharp hunting arrow punches into his upper chest and easily exits his lower back, generating a profusely bleeding wound. These hunting arrows are designed to easily penetrate the hide of a deer from over 50 yards. At this distance, it can easily enter and exit a man, leaving a gaping 2-inch bloody wound. As he falls back into the creek, he bleeds out quickly. From their concealed treetop perch both Grandpa and Carlos target and shoot at any man that moves. For experienced hunters, it is almost impossible to miss; any chest wound is certainly death. If they see no movement, they throw another lit jar. It becomes methodical. Grandpa realizing, they know his position boldly gives an Indian war cry; **"Ya... Ya...Ya..."** Looking curiously at Carlos with a shrug; "What the heck. Why not?"

Within a few minutes, all the men are dead from the flames or bleeding out from their wounds, except for Pedro. The shifty giant has been able to elude flames and the arrows; *"I must hide from this cagey enemy."* Pedro finally able to climb out, is cowering beneath the tree, camouflaged with creek mud. He stares straight up to locate his attackers; *"I know you are up there, where are you?"* He stands motionless, listening to the gasps of his dying companions. He finally spots a platform in the tree, takes aim and sprays the stand with his AK, hitting Carlos in the chest. He is immediately ejected from the stand.

Carlos falls almost all the way to the ground, however is caught by his safety harness and line. He dangles a few feet above the ground screaming and writhing in pain. He attempts to grasp his leg-knife and cut the safety line but is too weak to succeed. Angelina hearing her uncle's painful cries, lifts her eyes above the thick undergrowth. She cautiously inches closer on her hands and knees to identify the shadowy figure squirming on the line; *"I must see who this is, I must try to help."*

Grandpa is now alone in the tree stand. The rocking tree and thunder make it difficult for him to hear any movement below. He knows at least one man has survived the hellhole. He moves cautiously to light the three remaining wicked jars and drops them quickly below until there are no more screams; *"I know you fuckers are down there, I'm gonna fry every one of you sons of bitches."* He does not realize that Pedro has clawed his way out using his large knife and is fixed directly below him.

Pedro presses his muddied body against the tree, peering directly up into the obstructing branches. From that position, he can no longer see the stand but knows a stealthy enemy is above him. Frozen in place with wide eyes darting he seeks a target, weapon pointing straight up. He does not wish to divulge his position knowing; *"This man is crafty and very dangerous."*

Dressed in his camo, Grandpa is all but invisible

blending perfectly into the protective tree. His arrow drawn back aimed straight down ready to release. The wily hunter; *"Come on, show yourself... show yourself you bastard."*

In a heartbeat, their eyes meet, as they both fire. Grandpa gets hit in his thigh but not before releasing his arrow. He falls back onto his seat; *"God dammit... he nicked me."*

Pedro is also wounded, the arrow penetrating his right forearm, exiting his upper back. Grabbing his leg Grandpa does not see the badly injured Pedro hobbling away from the killing zone, seeking the safety of the dark field. As he staggers away; *"I don't think any organs were hit, I may have a chance."*

Grandpa, sitting back, looks down on the smoldering creek. He takes a white sheet fragment from the bucket and ties it tightly around his bleeding leg; *"Come on, you've been injured worse than this, you can handle it. Suck it up..."* Bright flames still radiate from the creek, obscuring his view of the darkened field. He loads another arrow, draws back seeking his next target. The rumbling storm and echoing gunshots from the cabin are the only sounds he can hear. Grandpa takes a deep breath and whispers into his radio; "Son... Son, we got all but one. I nailed him, but he still ran into the food plot."

Cloud anxiously grabs his radio; "Pop, are you all right?

Grandpa, looking down at his bleeding leg is irked; *"**Yes**, yes... I'm okay! Take care of yourself. I'll try to get to you in a few minutes."* He sits back, pressing his wound, and whispers; "Carlos... Carlos," but there is no answer. He cautiously peeks down and around the tree at his handiwork, and eagerly gulps from the opened jar; *"That'll teach those motherfuckers trying to kill my family."*

Angelina hearing Grandpa cry to Carlos, rises up and crawls further across the dense vegetation. The gusting winds lash the trees with the sound of the thunder reverberating. She plods slowly through the overgrown bean field. Tiring, she falls headfirst into the waste-high beans, her shining large silver crucifix flipping out of her jacket. In her left hand is Daniels bow with hunting arrow firmly in place.

While weakened from his wound and completely coated in mud Pedro is staggering directly toward Angelina. The 6'-4" hulk lurches cautiously, looking back at the fiery trench. He is uncertain of the number and location of his attackers. Bleeding and in pain, he angrily flings his AK rifle over his head, forming a sling across his chest. Grimacing, he wriggles his wounded arm through the sling; pressing his wrist tight to his chest; *"This should secure my arm in place until I get it mended. "*

Heat lightning flashes high above, Angelina sees a hunched-over silhouette staggering toward her. She whispers; "Carlos is that you?" Anxiously; "***Carlos***!" Her timid voice all but drowned by the wind and thunder. There is no response.

Pedro, bleeding from his forearm, stumbles through the field. He pauses a moment and notices a small indiscernible figure moving toward him. There is a brilliant lightning flash overhead with an immediate thunderclap. While Daniel's camo jacket cloaks her, Angelina's silvery crucifix pinpoints her position. Seeing a shiny object, Pedro hastily attempts to free his arm from the sling but his wrist is trapped by the silver turquoise bracelet; *"Come on... Come on...get off."*

They are only fifteen feet apart as he struggles frantically to free his arm. Instead, with his free hand, he angrily withdraws his large razor-sharp knife. Even at that distance, Pedro towers over Angelina. Terrified by the ponderous silhouette, Angelina realizes it cannot be Carlos or Grandpa and instinctively draws back her arrow to her chin; *"Who are you?"* Hysterically she screams; *"**Carlos!**"* As lightning bolt explodes overhead, she immediately recognizes one discernable object, the reflecting silver turquoise bracelet on Pedro's immobile wrist; *"I know the devil that wears this."* She releases the arrow at the silvery target, mystified at the illuminated red nock; *"Que Paso?"*

In a heartbeat, the arrow punches through the bracelet and wrist, and deep into Pedro's chest. Startled he feels surprisingly little pain from the razor arrowhead; *"What is this?"* He staggers back, dropping his knife attempting to unpin is wrist, then falls to his knees. He watches helplessly at the blood gushes profusely from his chest, spraying over the silver bracelet; *"How..?"*

Angelina inserts another arrow into her bow and steps boldly forward. As she draws it back again, she is standing almost eye-to-eye with the giant. In the darkness Pedro curiously searches for Angelina's face, then with another flash finally recognizes her; *"Do I know you?..... It is you...the little one...in Mexico? How...?"*

Knowing the fatal damage caused, Angelina angrily

lunges forward kicking him over backward; "You won't be having any more virgins in this life or the next, **Hombre Muerto.**" Without looking back, she slogs toward the flaming creek and sees Carlos' limp body dangling. She grabs his leg knife to cut him free. He falls to the ground, unresponsive.

Grandpa sees her and yells from above; "Is he breathing?"

Looking up sobbing; "Grandpa he is not moving."

He points to the darkness; "Child... run back to the trees, seek safety there. There may be more of these hombres out here. I will climb down to help Carlos. Go child...*go*."

Angelina listens to the gunfire coming from the cabin and remembers Carlos' words; "They are family, we must protect them." With an angry stare, she turns and without hesitation, strides along the darkened ATV path toward the cabin.

"Stay in the shadows child and do not come out, until you know it is safe."

Grandpa points his arrow along the smoldering creek then sits back; *"I'll take one more sip and save the rest for later..."* Seeing no movement, he cautiously climbs down the tree. He staggers to Carlos to check his breathing. Seeing that the bullet entered the center of his chest he places in hand over his heart; "Sorry my good friend." He picks up his bow and hobbles slowly back to the cabin in the darkness.

Bullets continued to intermittently pepper the cabin's stone wall. Rafta is very familiar with the marksmanship of US Army soldiers. Believing they might be well armed; he hesitates to charge the cabin.

The storm erupts overhead.

They only have one flashlight. John points; "Barbara, get the lighter off the mantle to light a torch for Jason." As the storm gusts through the porous cabin, Barbara tries to light the first moonshine jar wick. The wind blows out the tiny lighter.

Cloud; "Barb, do you have any paper? Pour some moonshine on it; fast, we need a bigger wick."

She looks around and remembers the papers in her purse. Instinctively she withdraws the three lavender colored DNA data sheets, recalling the disconcerting test results. Barbara, Joy, and Jason huddle shoulder to shoulder as she looks incredulously at Jason. Without hesitation, she rolls and dunks the sheets into the moonshine. In the dim light, Jason recognizes the lavender colored DNA result sheets and looks suspiciously at his mother as Barbara mouths; "No..."

Jason wondering; *"No...those are not the results or no, I don't want anyone to see the results."* Barbara vigorously shakes the lighter then flicks it again. A tiny fluttering blue flame emerges, enough to light the scrolled paper torch.

Through the intermittent gunfire, Jason withdraws his Glock and slyly squeezes through a back window. In a low voice; "Mom, carefully, hand me a few cases of moonshine." He first scans the darkness with his pistol for possible attackers, then places it on the woodpile.

Joy scurries across the floor to the window with the flaming torch. Jason lines up a few of the jars on the woodpile then ignites a few wicks. An eerie blue glow emerges. He now has an arsenal ready to launch. At first, he stumbles to find a stable place to stand. Ready to hurl he whispers; "John, I'm ready."

For years the area surrounding the cabin has been unkempt, overgrown with thick brier. Cloud thinks; "*They wouldn't try to come through that.*" Wiping away the sweat from his eyes, he raises his head up above the protective stone window ledge and through a bullet shattered shutter. Looking at the pattern of bullet holes, Cloud turns to Jason "Jay, the pattern of the gunfire through the cabin tells me they must be huddled fairly close together; probably behind the brush pile."

" How would you know this?"

"Informed speculation... We need to flush them out so I can get off a few shots. Understand...?"

"Just sight me in; how far and how much left or right." With a deep breath; "*I never threw a Mason Jar before. But it is about the same weight as a football. Shit... I hope this works.*"

With a brief lull in the gunfire, Cloud squats behind the table and peeks from behind the partially shattered shutter. With the pistol in hand; "Son, let it fly, straight over the roof as far as you can. Let's see what you got son." "*This better work or we are all dead..."*

Jason assumes his old quarterback throwing stance. With arm back and flaming wick dangling, he lets it go. The jar flies over the roof in a nice tight spiral about 55 yards and over Rafta's position.

The glass moonshine jar shatters and explodes brilliantly behind Rafta, startling everyone; *"What the hell was that?"* All the attackers hug the ground.

"They haven't moved yet. That was great, now do a 40 yard, right out pattern."

Jason grabs another blazing jar and flings it to the unseen position. This jar shatters and explodes into the tangled pile of brush and wood stumps. Rafta's head spins around; *"Where is this coming from?"*

Cloud; "Now do a 40-yard left out pattern."

With flames around him, obstructing his view of the cabin Rafta looks around not knowing where the firebombs are coming from; *"Where are they?"*

Another explosion erupts, igniting surrounding brush and nearby trees. Fearfully, two of Rafta's men jump up and try to escape the heat.

As Rafta yells; "Stay down you fools."

Cloud takes deliberate aim with the pistol through the

shattered shutter opening. With sweat dripping into his eyes he slowly exhales. **Pop... Pop...!** Two loud shots are heard as two insurgents hit the ground.

Angelina and Grandpa both see the explosions and hear the gunfire from a distance.

Rafta; "Move around and fire at the window." The intense flames are doing the job, as they keep their heads down and shoot haphazardly at the old cabin. Most bullets are absorbed by the stone foundation wall. A few penetrate hitting the stacked logs in front of Cloud.

Cloud pointing; "Ladies, I think it is time for you to go down into the mine. That's an order!"

As Barbara withdraws her compact, Walther PPK pistol from her purse; "No chance of that, I'm staying right here. I'll guard the door."

Cloud, flustered, knows not to argue; "At least stay low close to the basement hatchway."

Angelina, in her camo jacket, has just reached the tree line surrounding the house. From her position she watches as Jason hurls lit moonshine jars; *"Wow, that is amazing. How does he do that?"* She hides her head behind a large cedar and can see Rafta's fiery exchanges. Angelina wants to help any way she can, so she crawls beneath the underbrush, just as she did in Mexico. Still several hundred yards from the cabin Grandpa is still bleeding, and can only hobble; *"Come on old man get your ass in gear."*

Bullets begin to pierce the window where Cloud was firing. He must crouch down and get cover. Looking back; "Jay, keep throwing the same distance, just spray the area and don't stop. We have plenty of jars."

As the brush and wood pile inferno intensifies another two insurgents stand to escape the heat. With the intense gunfire exchange, Cloud has difficulty centering a target and controlling his pistol. Resolute, he sweeps the sweat from his eyes, steadies his hand and fires. Both men drop in their tracks. Cloud peaks out the window; *"Not bad...for this shaky old soldier."*

Rafta looks around and realizes that he may be the only one left; "Pedro, Pedro, are you there?" There is no answer. Realizing that he has not heard distant gunfire for some time; *"I started on this journey alone, and I will end it alone."* He scurries low, close to the ground to retrieve the RPG. The intense heat and smoke obscure his view of the cabin; *"This is not over..."*

Cloud checks his pistol and seeing there is only one round left, peeks up again to see Rafta aiming the RPG; **"Oh shit..!"** With sweat obscuring his target he gets off a shot, however, hitting a branch just missing Rafta.

Rafta flinches from the near miss and jerks the RPG trigger; **"Damm..."**

In an instant, the rocket is launched, but instead of hitting the cabin window, the shell hits the old stone chimney. All are stunned by the enormous explosion, as the chimney crashes down through the rickety wood roof. Flimsy interior walls crumble under its weight, as dense black soot billows up around them. A number of moonshine jars stacked on the floor are shattered and ignited, cascading flaming alcohol across the cabin floor.

Outside, Jason is thrown back by the blast. His stockpile of moonshine jars smash, igniting the woodpile. He searches for his pistol, but cannot retrieve it from the flames. He decides to find Joy; *"God dammit that's hot...I gotta get outta here."* and scurries back through the window. They now only have Barbara's compact pistol for protection. The old wood cabin is engulfed in flames, quickly becoming their private hell.

Through all the heat and smoke, it is impossible to see Rafta. Cloud scurries low across the floor amongst the burning debris and finds a stunned Joy and Barbara; "Come on Barb we have to get out of here." Jason, hearing Joy's screams, finds her beside the bed and clutches her arm. They have to make a choice; get burned alive in their inferno or attempt an escape out the front door. Cloud kicks the mangled front door open, yells: "Get out everybody... ***get out.***"

While Grandpa tries his best, the pain and his loss of blood make it difficult to move any quicker; *"Come on old man, pick up the pace."*

Angelina startled by the blast shifts around in the darkness. Just 10 yards away, she raises her bow and draws the arrow back, with Rafta's clearly silhouetted against the flames. She hears Joy's cries; *"Oh God, I hope they are all right."*

Through the smoke and flames, Rafta sees his stunned

targets staggering out of the burning cabin. From the ground, he quickly retrieves a nearby AK automatic rifle. As he confidently strides toward the cabin, he takes aim; *"I have you all... Now it is your turn to die."*

Angelina releases her arrow, which immediately pierces Rafta's side, the illuminated red nock protruding. In unbearable wincing pain, he spins around firing wildly into the bushes toward Angelina. While the arrow does not totally penetrate Rafta, he is nonetheless severely wounded, drops the rifle, and staggers into the dark underbrush.

It takes several seconds before they regain their senses. Jason walks over to Barbara and grasps the small gun from her hand; "Better let me take that, mom." From the shadows, Angelina sheepishly emerges; "I got him... just like Grandpa taught me. I really got him."

Walking up to the tiny young girl, Cloud clutches her close; "Yes you did little Angel, yes you did."

Angelina recalls Sr. Carolyn's cryptic prayer; *"Thou shall not be afraid of any terror by night; nor for the arrow that flieth by day. He will empower thee to deliver Satan back into his fiery pit."* Astonished at what just occurred, a smile comes across her face as she shakes her head.

Grandpa emerges slowly from the path toward the flames as Cloud walks up to him and checks his leg; "Pop, are you all right? Are you badly hurt?

Grandpa just shrugs his shoulders; "I think I can still

fight."

Cloud excitedly; "How is everyone... Joy, Jay? Barb, are you all right?"

Seeing some blood on Joy's face he instinctively embraces her; "Honey are you okay?"

"Yes, daddy I'm okay, *I'm okay.*" Points furiously; "Don't worry about me, *go find that son of a bitch*. He went that way."

Grandpa grimacing; "Let's track down this fucking animal and end this.... **Now!**"

Cloud picks up Rafta's discarded AK and checks it for bullets. The three men quietly stalk Rafta into the thick undergrowth; *"With an arrow wound in his side he loses blood quickly and cannot be very far off."* Rafta tries to hide in the dense vegetation behind a large tree.

"Give me that light." Grandpa snaps.

He slaps the flashlight to his side in a crude attempt to make it brighter. With the dimming light, Grandpa moves slowly; "I have tracked bleeding deer in the dark for 60 years. Son, watch to see if he sticks his head out."

As the ladies attempt to follow a few yards back; "Ladies go sit by the cars, he may still be armed." As usual, they don't listen.

Without anyone noticing, Angelina slowly slides back

into the undergrowth to hide.

While not hit through a lung or heart, Rafta is still losing life quickly. They slowly scan the trees and brush wandering through the bushes. Grandpa follows Rafta's intermittent blood trail like a bloodhound, whispering; "Quietly, over here."

Rafta, in his weakened state, attempts to break off the arrow but cannot. Instead, he tries to cover the illuminated arrow protruding from his side. The red nock is doing its job, exposing his position. Realizing his situation, he raises his bloody hand and peeks around the tree at Grandpa. As Grandpa moves cautiously to Rafta; "We got him, he's over here."

Hearing Grandpa's voice, the women move closer.

Joy grumbles; "I want to see this sonofabitch for myself."

Cloud points the AK at Rafta; "Hand up where I can see them, or I will blow you to hell." Finally seeing his face; "So was this all worth it you despicable human being?!"

Rafta peers up at Cloud; "Ah...it is you. Finally, we are face-to-face; no more oceans or armies between us." With a scornful smile; "Was it all worth it... You invaded my country... killed my entire family...and you are surprised that I seek vengeance." With labored breathing; "You... deliver death from the skies... and kill us by the hundreds but... when we kill one or two of you... you call us... terrorists. You are all weak...so very weak."

Cloud irate ; "You and I are very different. I did not kill

your wife and son. They were a tragedy of war."

"Whether... intentional or... unintentional... the end is the same. We all share the same ground in the end."

"The difference is in your intent. That is how *your* souls will be judged."

Hobbling unsteady, Grandpa tries to shine the dim flashlight closer to see Rafta's face; "**I want to look into this sonofabitch's eyes as he dies.**"

Unknown to all, Rafta still has his 38-caliber revolver in hand, hidden beneath his blood-soaked shirt; *"I only have one chance, and I have to make it count."*

Undaunted, Joy nudges her way up and angrily wrestles the pistol from Jason's hand. Hearing Rafta's voice, she elbows past Grandpa in front of Rafta; "**You sorry piece of shit**. You murdered my innocent family, **for what...?**

Rafta's life quickly ebbing, has difficulty speaking; "Ah.. it is you... his last child... his last remaining blood."

Cloud tries to restrain her as Joy gets inches from Rafta's face. "You know what, you know what you **fucking animal,** that arrow in you was shot by a little girl, **a little girl.** There will be no place in heaven for you now... **Die knowing that**..."

Rafta grimaces feigning his injury, leans to his side and fumbles from under his blood-soaked shirt for his pistol. Leering up into Joy's fiery eyes; "Such... are the tragedies of war...child. How does it feel... to be the receiving end of death... child?"

Cloud and Grandpa trying to pull Joy back; "I hope you burn in hell you **fucking butcher."**

Rafta clumsily burnishes his pistol, attempting to shoot Joy however Grandpa pushes her aside, placing himself in the line of fire. A shot is fired hitting Grandpa as he crumbles to the ground. Joy angrily thrusts the pistol at Rafta delivering three rounds to his chest. Rafta flinches with each round, scornfully smiling at Joy. He lays his head back gasping his last breath as he mumbles an indiscernible Arabic phrase...

As Cloud pulls the pistol from Rafta's bloodied hand, Joy drops her gun and falls onto Grandpa. He looks up at her; "Oh Joy, my Joy..."

From a distance, sirens can be heard. The first police cruiser arrives with flashing lights, then a few fire trucks. As the first officer scans the area, bodies are seen strewn around. He abruptly calls the dispatcher; "We are going to need a lot more units out here, a lot more. We have bodies everywhere."

Cloud and Jason emerge from the undergrowth carrying Grandpa into the light; "Jay we can sit him down over here."

The officer walks up to Cloud, seeing Grandpa, he radios in; "We'll need an EMT here immediately." He quickly runs back to his cruiser and pulls out his medical kit. They apply compression bandages to stop the bleeding.

"At first, your neighbors thought you guys were lighting off fireworks. Then, when they saw the cabin in flames, they put in a call." The Officer says.

Minutes later Grandpa is lifted into an ambulance by the EMT's. The EMT looks at Cloud discouragingly, whispers; "From the dark color of his blood, he was hit in the liver; it is not very promising."

Grandpa draws Joy close with Cloud behind her; "Joy honey stop this anger, family comes first; family is all we really have."

Clutching his bloody hand to her face; "Grandpa...I have news... **really good news**. I'm going to have a baby, a Cloud baby. A baby boy and we are naming him Daniel, Daniel Cloud."

Grandpa lays his head back smiling up to the sky; *"Thank you, Lord. Thank you for hearing my prayers and letting us keep our name."*

The EMT; "We gotta get the hell out of here. Let's move."

Once the ambulance drives off, Cloud leads several armed officers down the trail to the tree stand and smoldering creek. They scan the creek with their flashlights astonished by the number of heavily armed, dead attackers. So many men laden with automatic weapons, spent ammunition scattered everywhere. In the darkness, they see in the field an illuminated red nock. They find a huge man, precariously bent over backward, AK47 slung over his back, an arrow through his wrist and heart; "Whoever did this was one hell of a shot. Look at the size of this guy."

They attend to Carlos; however. he is dead.

An officer observing the scene with Cloud; "Jesus Christ.... Who the hell are these guys and what the hell happened here?"

Cloud casually shrugs his shoulders; "These guys.... They are all ISIS, coming for my family and me."

Officer astonished; "What... I thought the ISIS guys were hardened killers."

Cloud with an amused look; "I guess they never read about Custer's Last Stand."

After completing his statement, Cloud and a few officers walk back to the smoldering cabin, a fireman emerges from the rubble, arms cradling a few sooty moonshine jar. Fondly nods at Cloud; "...Evidence." As he is walking toward Cloud, he inadvertently trips over something.

Cloud looks down and sees a book; *"What the hell is this, it can't be that fucking book... no."* He bends down and to pick it up and immediately recognizes his ever-present Army notebook, and even more astonishing, it is opened to the page describing Rafta's son's killing. He examines it, hands shaking; *"I can't get rid of this Godforsaken book."* He leans back, is about to throw it into the smoldering cabin, then stops. Instead, pauses, and tucks it into the small of his back, and continues walking; *"I'll take care of this later."*

There are dozens of FBI and State Police now scouring the farm for more ISIS and collecting evidence. One of the FBI agents emerges from the thick brush brandishing a bow in one hand and gently holding Angelina's arm in the other; "It took us a while to catch this young girl scampering through the underbrush. Anyone know who she is?"

Joy kneels down and gently brushes back her tousled hair; "Are you all right honey?"

Angelina hesitantly just nods and in a shy voice; "Yes."

The trooper looks at Cloud; "Sir, do you know this girl? We found her hiding in the brush. She won't speak or answer any of my questions."

Cloud gently draws Angelina away from the officer, hugging her gently; "Officer, look at the name tag on her jacket, she is with me, she is a CLOUD."

The trooper looks at Cloud skeptically, then walks away. With the others surrounding Angelina, Cloud kneels down with hands on her shoulders; "We will be your family now, is that okay?"

Looking up and around at the smiling Cloud family, softly nods; "Yes."

Cloud looks up at Barbara; "Does that work for you?"

Barbara; "I lost you once, I will not let go of you again."

As Cloud looks over his shoulder and notices the EMTs carrying Rafta out of the brush in a body bag. Cloud, hands still shaking, has not taken any meds for several hours to abate his symptoms. He instinctively taps his leg for his mental crutch; the 50-caliber shell casing in his pocket. As they load Rafta's body onto the ambulance Cloud calls over; "Hold up a second, want to check something quick."

With trembling hands, he clumsily unzips the body bag and sees Rafta bloodied corpse; *"Well, you finally got what you wanted."* Pausing, he pulls out his old notebook and thumbs to the page referencing the death of Rafta's wife and son and is about to put it on Rafta's chest, then hesitates. He withdraws the 50-cal. casing from his pocket examines it for the last time, inserts it between the pages of the notebook, closes it; *"I pray to God that I won't need these again."* With shaky hands, places it on Rafta's chest.

EMT looking at Cloud; "Is that it, sir?"

"I guess so" *"I hope this will finally cast out my demons."*

The EMT zips back up the body bag and slides it in the ambulance. As the ambulance doors are closed and lights begin to flash, Joy comes up beside Cloud. Seeing her there shaking, he gently puts his arm around his shoulders and pulls her in close. They both watch as the ambulance drives off; "*I hope this is finally over.*"

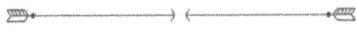

Standing out on the town road, watching as another flashing ambulance passes, she observes the smoldering flames through the trees. Elouise Lion's news crew is setting up, to produce another exclusive story; "This is Elouise Lion at the scene of what locals describe as a fierce gun battle. We understand from informed sources that this is where rival drug gangs had a shootout. As you can see from the emergency vehicles leaving, several gang members were killed. We will stay on the scene and provide you with more details as the story unfolds. This is Elouise Lion... reporting."

CHAPTER 13
July 2018 -- Leaving Their Mark

One year later Jason Moore and John Cloud are perched in that old tree stand donned in full-body camo. This is the first time since the killings that anyone has returned. With the rising morning sun peeking through the trees, no turkeys or keeper deer have emerged. The hunt is over. Both men sit back and remove their camo hunting jackets and hoods to stay cool. Now that many of Cloud's demons have been exorcised, he becomes more relaxed and conversant. Reminiscent of his Army days, he is clean shaved with the familiar military buzz haircut.

As Jason removes his hood; "Sir, I never asked, do you prefer John or Cloud?"

With a smirk, he hands an open jar of moonshine to Jason; "First, don't call me sir, just call me John."

Jason placing his bow on the overhead hook; "I really appreciate you bringing me up here. I know how important this place is to your family."

Gazing over the field; "Yah, with Pop and Daniel, now gone, coming here brings back a lot of memories, brings them closer to me." He pauses, takes a deep breath, exhales slowly and sips from the jar; "Thanks for joining me here today."

"By the way, I don't remember you bringing a jar of moonshine with you."

"I didn't, Grandpa left it here for us, the last time he was here."

Cloud, holding back his emotions, clears his throat; "So Jay… tell me, you went to school in Texas? Though your mom and grandparents were from Oklahoma, you never attended OU?"

"Well… John back then OU had a couple of good QB recruits and I just never got the offer from OU. I did get an offer from Texas and went there."

"So, you never went to OU and stayed in Texas until you relocated, OKC for your job?

"Pretty much stayed close to Dallas with my friends. Years ago, however… after I graduated from Texas, I did visit OU and went to a few frat parties with some Oklahoma high school buddies. Couldn't remember much though… Went to parties…got drunk…passed out… You know, that kind of stuff….. And oh ya, but promise not to tell… I never really told anybody but…I did have a few trips to their fertility clinic in OKC."

Amazed; "**Fertility clinic** visits. For what? You don't shoot blanks, do you?

With a peculiar grin; "No, quite the contrary. You know….. I'd rather not say, any more sir… I'd rather not say… It's kind of embarrassing… Kinda private stuff."

Changing the subject; "So, have you and Joy set a date yet for the wedding."

"Not yet, but I think it will be pretty soon, once she picks a date. Ya know how that goes?"

Smiling warmly; "It's really good to have you in our family. I know Grandpa was ecstatic that there is a baby Cloud to carry on the family name. I hope that's OK with you?"

"I don't have a problem at all with that, it's all about family."

Looking at him with a smile; "Ya know, it's like I've known you for a long time."

Jason nodding; "Yes, I know what you mean...for me too."

Cloud looks down placing the moonshine jar on the wood platform at his feet. In the early morning light, he notices the bloodstained planks beneath his feet; *"Damn that must be Grandpa's blood."* Disturbed he picks his feet up from the crimson traced wood.

Jason also immediately realizing what it is, picks up his feet; "Sorry sir, I didn't notice that earlier, no disrespect..."

"No need to apologize, son, it just gives a lot more significance to this place. Put your feet back down...it's okay. Grandpa wouldn't mind."

Cloud reaches down picks up the moonshine jar, unscrews the lid and with hands shaking, gently pours some over the blood stained planks. As he closes his eyes he begins to cry, then raises the jar to the sky; " **Fuck..!** I miss them, I miss them all. What a waste, what a fucking waste..." As he takes another sip; *"This kind of changes things pop, drinking this and sitting here, I guess I am now head of the clan and reluctantly accept my new role. Step up."* "Thanks, we love you all and miss you all. Don't want to waste too much though, he wouldn't like that... Plus, I have no idea when another batch is going to be made."

Jason, recognizing the loving gesture; "I guess that's all any of us can hope for, to be loved while we are here and missed when we are gone."

Looking at both men close from behind, we see the distinctive strawberry colored birthmark on the nape of Cloud's neck. As Jason brushes his head and the nape of the neck, we also see a strawberry colored birthmark; ***The Blood Mark.***

CLOUD; "I really enjoy this, how about you?"

"Yes sir, me too."

Cloud looking over the lush growing food plot; "So, what are the ladies up to today?"

"I think they are all getting together for some kind of a party."

Barbara is kneeling beside a bubbly bathroom tub. In

her typical mood setting fashion, she has her Pandora music playing in the background. As she dips her elbow; "Come on in the water is perfect."

Through the door emerges Joy, and almost slips and falls with her naked baby son Daniel Cloud; **"Oh shit...!** Sorry about that Barbara. I guess I will have to learn to control my language." Chubby legs dangling, Joy lowers him in and supports him into the tub.

Moments later, Angelina walks in with a daughter in her arms and is about to slip Carmella-San Miguel into the tub. However, the child grasps the silver Crucifix and will not let go. She laughs; "She always does that; I think it is to remind me of my mother. I use to play with my mother's Crucifix when I was a child." As the child releases it, she lowers her into the tub.

As the babies splash happily side-by-side Barbara asks; "May I bathe little Daniel?"

Curiously looking at Joy; "So, you never did tell me; when and where did you first meet Jason?"

A new song by ♪ Israel "IZ," Somewhere Over the Rainbow, begins to play. "Somewhere over the rainbow. Way up high. And the dreams that you dreamed of. Once in a lullaby. Somewhere over the rainbow. Bluebirds fly. And the dreams that you dreamed of, dreams really do come true...."
Joy, with a grin; "At the OKC women's clinic, more than a year ago."

"And, Daniel is your sister's baby... right?"

Joy casually, "Yup... By the way, I never asked, did you ever have a chance to run those DNA tests last year and get the results?"

Barbara, wide-eyed; "You know, I forgot about them entirely. Yes... Last year I did run the DNA tests and... no identities were discovered, no names came up, no one was identified."

"That's strange... None..?

Shaking her head nervously; "Nope... none."

As the music continues to play Barbara finishes bathing little Daniel, gently towels his head; we see the back of his neck revealing a strawberry colored mark, the distinctive Cloud family birthmark; *the Blood Mark.*

Barbara recalls a time when she was caressing the back of a young man's neck as he lay across her sun-bronzed thighs, stroking his strawberry colored birthmark; *"Somehow this looks oddly familiar to me."* Gently caressing the back by Daniel's head, she looks again to Joy; "So you never met Jason before that?"

Joy; "I don't recall... Why..?"

Barbara with a broad smile; "No reason...just curious..."

AquarianBooks.com

AquarianBooks.com

BOOK CLUB
DISCUSSION QUESTIONS

1. John Cloud is a complex, troubled character. Reflecting on his PTSD condition; what could he have done differently to address his illness? Was his notebook an aid or detriment to his condition?

2. Describe Grandpa Cloud's familial relationships. How important is Grandpa's influence on his family and the outcome of events?

3. When Sr. Carolyn gave Angelina the large silver crucifix, was she concerned with Angelina's spiritual or physical wellbeing? Was the crucifix important to Angelina?

4. Compare the multiple parent-child relationships in this book. How do they differ across families, generations and cultures?

5. Mohammad Rafta was also a soldier in his culture however, is very different from John Cloud. In what ways do the two men differ? How are the two men similar?

6. Consider all the women in John Cloud's life. How did those women relate to him and he to them?

7. John Cloud is emotionally ravaged by his military experiences and subsequent, horrific visions. Are you empathetic to his struggles?

8. How important is Angelina Ramirez to the Cloud family? Why?

9. How do the multiple characters demonstrate bravery and what motivated each of their actions?

10. Barbara Moore hid the results of three DNA tests. Whose name popped up as the match for all three DNA test results? What secrets is Barbara hiding? What could happen if she revealed her secrets? Is it appropriate for her to withhold that information?

11. Reflecting on the multiple references to blood in the book, why do you think the author chose "The Blood Mark" for the title?

AquarianBooks.com

ACKNOWLEDGMENTS

I wish to thank my many friends that gave their valuable time and offered great insights and suggestions. I appreciate the inputs from: Dave Moore, Barbara Racette, Helen Wong, Yianni Sinanis, Alketa Stroka, Marilyn Meo, Ruth Dornfeld, Idrian Resnick and Sarah Bradley.

A thanks to Athena Nomikos for her thoughtful review and to Geoff White for his thorough editing and my son Chris Uzzo, for his incredible marketing efforts.

With special thanks to Janice Samoeil, who made an incredible difference offering praise. Her literary perspectives and guidance that kept me on track.

Finally, to my beloved wife and life-long partner, Victoria (Vickie) Uzzo, who patiently listened and read the countless rewrites, offering encouragement. Without her reinforcement to my vision, The Blood Mark could not have been written.

AquarianBooks.com

ABOUT THE AUTHOR

 **Anthony Uzzo** was born and raised in The Bronx, New York. He is a Vietnam era veteran that proudly served in the U.S. Navy. He has lived in Connecticut, where he has worked as a Professional Engineer for over 42 years. He received an Engineering Degree from the University of Oklahoma, a Master of Engineering Degree from Manhattan College and a M.B.A. from University of New Haven. He is happily married for over 46 years to his wife Victoria, along with an incredible extended family.

While writing is his new passion, Anthony enjoys traveling with his wife, fishing, golf, stock trading, astrology and driving his Jaguar. Most of all he enjoys living on the shoreline year-round and spending time with family.

THE BLOOD MARK is his first published work. His strong interest in current events were the impetus for creating this riveting story. It took years to complete, because he focused on weaving complex, societal issues, with authentic, memorable characters.

The topics raised required graphic authenticity for them to be fully vetted. By addressing these sensitive, private questions in this way, it was hoped that the personal sacrifices made by the characters, can be fully appreciated.

www.ingramcontent.com/pod-product-compliance
Lightning Source LLC
Chambersburg PA
CBHW061935170626
46813CB00006B/2406